ANONYMOUS
SOURCES

ANONYMOUS
SOURCES

MARY LOUISE KELLY

G

GALLERY BOOKS

NEW YORK   LONDON   TORONTO   SYDNEY   NEW DELHI

G

Gallery Books
A Division of Simon & Schuster, Inc.
1230 Avenue of the Americas
New York, NY 10020

First Gallery Books hardcover edition June 2013

GALLERY BOOKS and colophon are registered trademarks of Simon & Schuster, Inc.

For information about special discounts for bulk purchases, please contact Simon & Schuster Special Sales at 1-866-506-1949 or business@simonandschuster.com.

The Simon & Schuster Speakers Bureau can bring authors to your live event. For more information or to book an event contact the Simon & Schuster Speakers Bureau at 1-866-248-3049 or visit our website at www.simonspeakers.com.

Designed by Davina Mock-Maniscalco

Manufactured in the United States of America

10   9   8   7   6   5   4   3   2   1

Library of Congress Cataloging-in-Publication Data

Kelly, Mary Louise.
   Anonymous sources / Mary Louise Kelly. — First Gallery Books hardcover edition.
       pages cm
   Summary: "A debut international thriller about a Pakistani terrorist's nuclear threat to blow up the White House"— Provided by publisher.
   1. Women journalists—Fiction. 2. College students—Crimes against—Fiction.
3. Terrorism—Prevention—Fiction. 4. Nuclear terrorism—Fiction. 5. Pakistanis—United States—Fiction. 6. White House (Washington, D.C.)—Fiction. 7. Washington (D.C.)—Fiction. I. Title.
   PS3611.E4433U56 2013
   813'.6—dc23
                                                                        2012042497

ISBN 978-1-4767-1554-4
ISBN 978-1-4767-1556-8 (ebook)

For Nick
Who has been there all along

Prologue

If, on an early summer's night, you wanted to kill a man, how would you do it? Would you lay a trap, sharpen a dagger, uncork a poison?

Personally, I've always leaned toward the dramatic. But looking back, I wonder now if the events of last summer didn't begin with a quieter sort of murder.

It was the first time he'd killed. He told me that himself. And while he didn't elaborate, I imagine he might have simply followed, simply walked, tracing the path behind his victim, taking care to keep his footsteps silent.

And then he would have stopped. Crouched. Listened. An assassin waiting for his moment. He would have been nervous. He would have watched until his mark turned, until he looked away, until the light on that lovely June evening slanted just so.

And then his blood must have roared and his muscles tensed and he must have known: *Now. It is time.*

1

Thomas Carlyle climbed the bell tower that night without quite planning to.

He'd arrived back in Cambridge two hours before, stiff and cranky after the long flight crammed in economy class. No one was home at the house on Brattle Street. Old pizza menus were gathering dust on the floor of the front hall, and nothing was in the fridge but a withered apple and several dozen cans of his mother's Diet Coke. So he'd dumped his bags and headed out. Fifteen minutes' walk to the local liquor store, and then—some old homing instinct kicking in here—another ten to Eliot House.

Eliot looked the same. Perhaps the most imposing of Harvard's dorms, it towered above the Charles River. Red brick, wide double doors, an overflowing bike rack out front. Students lounged outside the doors, smoking and giggling. Summer school must have started.

Thom caught the open door from one of them, nodded at the familiar-looking security guard, and turned right into the dining hall. It smelled of seafood—fish tacos, maybe—and frying onions. Dinner was in full swing.

Thom had eaten hundreds of dinners here, and fish tacos were among his favorites. But tonight he clutched his brown paper bag and headed straight for the far doors, through an archway, and toward the stairs marked H-ENTRY.

He took the stairs two or three at a time, up five flights. Then he cut down a hallway toward the door marked LEONARD BERNSTEIN '39, MUSIC ROOM AND TOWER.

He dug in his jeans pocket for the key. It turned. So the lock hadn't changed either. Two more flights, darker and narrower now. The linoleum was worn thin and stained.

When he reached the seventh floor, a small metal plaque informed him that Bernstein used to practice here in 1936. Yes, and it didn't look like they'd bothered to redecorate it since, Thom thought to himself. He smiled. He was in decent spirits, actually, considering the jet lag, and the girl. At the top, one last door. He jiggled the lock and it swung open.

The tower room was small. Dusty. Low ceilings. Surprising, really, given the grandeur of the Eliot tower and dome from the street. In the fading light Thom took in the grand piano hulking in the middle of the room. He'd always wondered how the hell they'd hauled it up here.

But the reason he'd come was for the windows. Two huge and perfectly circular windows, each maybe six feet across, one framing each end of the room. The right one was long since painted shut, if it had ever opened. But the left one bore two ancient-looking brass latches. Thom unhooked them and then remembered to kick at the bottom panes, where the paint always stuck a bit. And there it was. The whole window spun open on creaky hinges. He wedged his paper bag into the crack to keep the breeze from slamming it shut again, then hooked a leg over, lowered himself onto the sill, and peered down across the steep slate roof.

Senior year, he and his roommate, Joe, sometimes crawled right out across the roof, inching along until they could straddle the dormer windows. They would knock back a few beers and watch the girls crossing the courtyard, their laughter and teasing voices floating up from far below.

Now he looked down at the Charles River, curving toward Boston and glowing golden at this hour. On the far bank rose the dome of Harvard Business School. Thom's destiny, the way things were going. He shook the thought from his head and cracked open one of the bottles he'd purchased, walking here through Harvard Square. A thick, syrupy oatmeal stout. Not exactly the thing for this summer weather. But studying in England this past year, he'd lost his taste for the watery American lager that had been the staple of his weekends here in Eliot House.

Thom took another sip and watched the boats gliding along the Charles. Lord knew how many hours he himself had logged on this river. By the time he made varsity crew, the boathouse had felt more central to his college experience than any library, and the blisters across his hands had hardened like tiny stones. A sculler flitted past, then an eight-man crew. Was that Boston University? But why would they be practicing so late, and on summer break at that?

He squinted and craned forward, trying to make out what colors were painted on the oars. It was at that moment that hands reached from the shadows behind him. The blow landed at the bottom of his skull. A crack of wood against bone. There was a moment of perfect silence, before Thom swung his strong arms, clawing behind him. But the foot was already on his back. One kick, but hard enough to launch him off the sill and onto the roof ten feet down.

He crashed into the pointed tip of a dormer window and rolled, grabbing for a gutter, a ledge, anything. There was nothing, and he fell, wide-eyed, into the gathering twilight below.

2

For me this story begins in a tiny, greasy wine bar in Harvard Square. I was waiting, as usual, for Jess. I checked my watch. Scanned the sidewalk again. Sighed.

Still, there are worse places to be stuck waiting than the patio of Shays. The service is terrible, old beer rings stain the tables, and you're not ten feet from the buses crawling up and down JFK Street. But they're generous with their pours. Any place that gets three glasses from a bottle of wine deserves the benefit of the doubt. And Shays is one of the few places in Cambridge where you can order a drink and sit outside. It was a glorious evening for that: one of the first really warm nights of the year, warm enough to believe the New England winter might finally be over, warm enough to leave your sweater at home.

I stretched out an ankle and admired my new Louboutin sandals. They'd cost nearly a week's pay from the *Chronicle*. Shoes are a weakness of mine. I eyed my empty glass and conceded—not my only one. I inherited a tendency to drink from my mother. That's not an excuse, just a fact. My mother can knock back the better part of a bottle of single-malt Scotch in a night. I generally stick to gin. Clear, simple. They say that people drink to forget. To numb the pain. But I drink because it tastes good. Because it feels good. I find that nothing numbs the pain. We'll get to that.

For the moment, I was focused on looking around for a waiter and a refill. That's when my phone buzzed. It was the newsroom, an all-staff e-mail. The police scanner had picked up some sort of incident under way on the Harvard campus: 101 Dunster Street. Cops were on the scene, an ambulance dispatched. The *Crimson*, the college newspaper, had already slapped a "Breaking News" banner across its website and was citing eyewitness accounts of a body. We had a late-shift general-assignment reporter en route, but it could take a while in traffic. Was anybody close? Who could perhaps file a quote or two for the website?

I felt a prickle of annoyance. I'd been at work early this morning to finish up a series for the weekend magazine. And it was such a beautiful night. But I had a feeling Dunster Street was the one right around the corner. I looked around. Still no Jess in sight. So I slid a $20 bill on the table, tapped *I'm on it* into my phone, and grabbed my bag.

BY THE TIME I ROUNDED the corner from JFK onto South Street, I could already hear sirens. I turned another corner. Followed the flashing lights down to where Dunster Street ended in a neat cul-de-sac and a number of imposing redbrick dorms. *Houses*, as I knew Harvard modestly called them.

I could see police already cordoning off the area. I would have to work fast. I strode toward the officer who appeared to be in charge. He was bunched in a group with two other cops in front of a large, white doorway. ELIOT HOUSE, read the neatly painted letters above the arch.

"Hi, wondering if I could ask you a couple questions. About what's going on in there? We're hearing reports of a body . . ."

The officer raised an eyebrow. "And you are?"

"Alexandra James, with the *Chronicle*. Can you confirm what kind of call you're responding to?"

The officer shook his head and motioned to another cop.

"No reporters. Frank, can you please help this young lady back behind the tape?"

"Yes, sir, but any guidance at all? Is this an accident or a crime scene?"

But he was already turning his back. The one named Frank was steering me none too gently back onto Dunster Street.

I scowled, stepped beneath a tree, and pulled out my phone. No new messages. The other *Chronicle* reporter must not be here yet. I watched a second ambulance pull up. But its sirens were silent, and the paramedics took their time getting out. No sense of urgency. Clearly whatever had happened here was over. Some poor person had died, and that was that. I hated this kind of reporting. I've never been a subscriber to the "if it bleeds, it leads" school of journalism.

Still, I was here. Worse, the newsroom knew I was here. No point in completely embarrassing myself with the editors. I surveyed the scene again. The police commander and his buddies were still blocking the door marked ELIOT HOUSE. That's where the action was. And no one who could tell me anything was being allowed to leave. Then I noticed a long, low-slung extension that seemed to connect Eliot House to the next dorm.

I tracked back. KIRKLAND HOUSE, read a brass plaque on the wall. A guard was posted here too, but he seemed to be letting people inside. I watched them flash cards at him: Harvard IDs, presumably.

So this might be a way in. I glanced down: I would never pass for a student in these heels. I groped inside my bag and dug out the flip-flops that I wore to ride the subway to and from the office. Then I peeled off my suit jacket. I had on a plain white T-shirt underneath. That was better. I tucked my phone and reporter's notebook under my arm and stashed my bag under a bush.

My timing was good. Three girls were just turning up the granite steps toward the guard. Backpacks, jean shorts, long hair. I walked up and touched the closest one's arm, then began chattering as if we were old friends. The girl started. Stared at me. And then began to chatter back. It was getting dark by now; I could have passed for someone she knew. One of the many advantages I've found to being a female reporter is people find you less threatening. They assume you're friendly, that you won't hurt them. Sometimes an inaccurate assumption in my case, but useful nonetheless.

I bunched closer to the girls, ducked my head, and kept talking. They waved their IDs. The guard waved us past. I waited until we were well away from him before I looked up. We had stepped through a black iron gate and under several arches, into a square courtyard.

"And apparently he just fell, like, dropped right in front of the windows while she was eating," the girl now clutching my arm was saying. She looked stricken.

I nodded, only half-listening and eager now to get away. Where was that passageway I'd spotted from outside? Of the doorways on the far side of the courtyard, the one that looked most promising was marked DINING HALL. I waited until a few others joined our circle and then slipped away. Inside, the hall was dimly lit and cool. A few scattered students sat hunched over their dinner trays. I kept moving. The kitchens must be back here. I have a pretty good sense of direction and this felt right.

I kept expecting to run into another cop, a kitchen supervisor, some sort of official who would demand to know who I was and what I was doing here. But the kitchens were deserted. Whether dinner would normally be over or the meal service had been cut prematurely short by whatever was happening in Eliot House, I wasn't sure. Steam was still rising from enormous pans of rice and what looked like tacos. I lurched around a wall of cereal dispensers and headed down a short stairway toward a vending machine. This might be right. Another turn. No. Dead end. I was spinning around to retrace my steps when I nearly bumped into a short, droopy-looking man. His name—PEDRO—was embroidered on his gray shirt and he was jangling keys. A janitor. I was caught. But I ventured a question.

"Sorry, I'm lost. I'm trying to get into Eliot House. Back upstairs?"

He stared at me. A moment passed. Was he weighing whether to call security? Did he not speak English? To my surprise, he finally nodded. "Yes, back upstairs. This way."

He stepped in front of me and led me back up, past a grill area and along a tiled hallway, crammed with serving carts and stacks of cutlery. The floors were slick, dishwater and juice spills. We walked through several rooms, past another set of cereal dispensers, trays of steaming shrimp. How vast could this kitchen be?

And then the janitor nodded toward a corner and I saw it: a whiteboard, half-smudged, announcing *Eliot Intramural Playoffs—Soccer 9pm v. Mather.*

Eliot playoffs. Eliot House. I was in.

THE ELIOT HOUSE DINING HALL was entirely predictable. High ceilings, massive carved chandeliers, an oil painting of a man I presumed to be Mr. Eliot himself dominating one wall. I went to Columbia, so I'm no stranger to the Ivy League's self-important splendor. But Harvard really does take it to another level. A copy editor once slapped the headline "The Patina of Privilege" on a story I'd written about renovations in one of the Harvard libraries. I had winced; it seemed too cutesy. But inside Eliot, taking in the gleaming floors, the mahogany-paneled walls, I had to admit he had a point.

This elegance—or pretension, depending on your point of view—does not extend to undergraduate fashion. The dress code tonight seemed to range from cutoffs to sweatpants. I glanced down in relief at my own flip-flops and T-shirt and crossed the room.

Half-eaten trays of food sat abandoned on tables. The action was at the windows. Students were pressed up against eight enormous windows that ran the length of the room. It was strangely quiet, considering there had to be a hundred or so people in here. They were all listening to whatever was happening outside.

I squeezed into the thickest throng. I couldn't see a thing.

"I just got here. What happened?" I whispered to a tall boy who seemed to have a better view.

"They're zipping him up."

"Who?"

"Him. The guy who jumped."

I wiggled my shoulders and jostled sideways a bit, until the crowd shifted just enough for me to see.

There it was: A blue plastic body bag. A wheeled gurney. Police and paramedics milling about on a wide terrace. And beyond heavy stone railings, another grassy courtyard.

"When did he jump? Did you see it?"

"No. I—I don't know. Half past six maybe? My roommate's up there." The tall boy pointed across the courtyard to a second- or third-floor window. "He keeps texting me. He says he heard it. A big thud. I guess he landed faceup. You know, like, you could see his eyes were open."

"Oh. Poor guy."

"Yeah. But they covered him up. One of the dining-hall ladies. She ran right out. She had a yellow cardigan and she put it over his face."

I shook my head. Then I pulled out my phone and started typing. It had been an hour since the newsroom first sent out an alert. The editors would be going crazy.

LATER THAT NIGHT, THE UNIVERSITY released a statement.

It was with great sadness that they reported the death of Thomas Abbott Carlyle, twenty-three, of Cambridge, Massachusetts. Mr. Carlyle was a magna cum laude graduate of the college and had recently completed a postgraduate year as the Lionel de Jersey Harvard Scholar at Emmanuel College, Cambridge University, in England.

He was remembered as a gifted student, a talented rower, a generous friend, and a beloved son and brother.

The family had been contacted and did not wish to comment. The media was asked to respect the family's privacy at this difficult time.

I STUCK AROUND UNTIL NEARLY eleven o'clock.

By then the police had rolled in spotlights to illuminate the courtyard. They combed the grass for anything that might have fallen along with the body. Police tape and a dark stain marked the spot where Thomas Carlyle had fallen.

I asked around and no one seemed to know Carlyle. Then again, these were summer-school students. They'd only just moved in themselves.

At one point, the commander who'd tried to throw me off the premises appeared. He cleared his throat and delivered a terse update. There was no cause for alarm. Police officers would be posted outside tonight and at least through tomorrow. They would be interviewing eyewitnesses to piece together exactly what had happened to Thomas Carlyle. Anyone with relevant information was asked to leave his or her name and phone number. The university would release more details as appropriate about this tragic incident. For now, students should return to their rooms.

I listened to this advice from a back corner, my hair pulled low across my face. I didn't think he would recognize me from earlier in the evening, but I do tend to stand out, and there was no point in risking it.

On my phone I tapped out one last advisory, relaying everything I knew back to the newsroom editors. They seemed to like the yellow cardigan quote. That got posted to the website right away.

It had been a slow news day, and a death and police investigation at Harvard would likely make tomorrow's front page. But frankly, I didn't see much of a story here. It was terrible, of course. A promising young man's life cut tragically short, and all that. I figured the police and the autopsy report would reveal soon enough whether this was a suicide or an unfortunate—maybe drunken—accident. Neither was exactly unheard of on a college campus.

I shoved my phone in my pocket and stood up. It was late. I had what I needed. The crowd had thinned out, and there seemed no point incurring the wrath of that Cambridge police commander if he wandered in again. I decided to call it a night.

3

I don't consider myself superstitious. But I do follow something of a ritual every time I land a story on the front page.

On these mornings—and there have been many of them now—I lock my little apartment and walk the fifteen minutes across Harvard Square to the T-stop. Out of Town News still stacks up neat piles of the *Chronicle*, alongside the *New York Times* and the *Wall Street Journal*. I shell out the exact change and carry it onto the train with me, savoring the feel of newsprint on my fingers and the thrill—yes, it's still a thrill—of seeing my name above the fold on page one.

Today, if I may say so, my story read pretty damn well. The headline wasn't wildly creative but it was accurate enough: "Harvard Student Falls to His Death; Police Promise Full Investigation." The critical thing was the dateline: "Inside Eliot House, Harvard College."

Most of the competition had stories datelined, at best, "Cambridge, Mass." The other papers had been forced to quote heavily from either the *Crimson* or, I noted with satisfaction, my own reporting. No one else had gotten inside.

Getting inside is my specialty.

I've never loved the stories that are the bread and butter of a big-city newspaper: violent crimes, contentious city-council meetings, natural disasters, and subway strikes. They make good copy. But they're a little obvious. I love the stories no one knows are there.

I like to think I'm good at getting people to talk. Sometimes all you have to do is ask. The simple questions work best. Pick one, ask it over and over, don't let them dodge it, and you'd be amazed at what people will tell you. With more sophisticated sources, you have to earn their trust. Call them on a routine story, get it right, call them back the next day for feedback. Pay your dues. The best stories grow out of a tiny detail someone lets drop, a crumb that doesn't initially seem significant. But then you consider it alongside another crumb that a different source might have dropped weeks back. I gather these morsels patiently, hoard them, until I begin to make out a path that I can follow.

All this crumb-gathering has earned me one of the *New England Chronicle*'s most prestigious beats, higher education. I can't say higher ed makes my pulse race. But my beat offers one critical quality: it is relentless. Boston is home to more colleges and universities than any city in the world. There are more ivory towers than you can count. That means there is always, always something to write about.

This is good on the nights when the ache begins in my chest. I don't give in to it more than a couple of times a year. I can go for days now when I barely think about what happened. But when it starts, I can feel the ache move up from my chest to my throat to knock me behind the eyes. I used to vomit with the guilt. The regret. *Regret*—the word does not begin to capture what I feel.

You wouldn't expect it, but on these nights I do not drink. I think because if I did, I would never find it in me to get up again. Some scrap of self-preservation tells me I have to just lie there and ride it out. Eventually, the newsroom will call. And I'll get up and go to work again.

4

"Morning, Ginger!"

My friend Elias Thottrup, the paper's national security reporter. He's based in the DC bureau; I hadn't realized he was around. I narrowed my eyes and pretended to scowl at him.

"Why, good morning, Shorty," I purred. "You know how I love it when you call me Ginger."

He chuckled and kept moving across the newsroom. "All right then. Carrot Top, if you insist. Coffee later?"

I nodded. Patted my hair self-consciously. Another trait I inherited from my Scottish mother. Salon highlights tame it to a shade I like to think of as strawberry blond. But I was overdue for the salon, and I had to admit my hair was looking particularly fiery this morning.

Well, nothing to be done about it right now. I threw my bag under my desk, swapped my flip-flops—the same ones that had served me so well last night—for a pair of ridiculously high heels, and flipped on my computer. The *Chronicle* newsroom was still quiet at this hour. I was starting to scribble down the three voice mails flashing on my phone when Hyde Rawlins rounded the corner.

Hyde is managing editor of the *Chronicle*. He looked harassed. At eight thirty in the morning. Not a good sign.

"Ah, Ms. James. The celebrated correspondent returns triumphant. A tip of the old chapeau and all that. Nicely done. However. You'll need to get right back over to Harvard. Now."

"Why? What's happened?"

"It's not what. It's who. Thomas Carlyle's father is what's happened. Last night we seem to have missed the minor detail that this kid was the son of Lowell Carlyle."

I looked at Hyde blankly.

He rolled his eyes. "As in the White House counsel? As in the president's lawyer? As in one of the most influential men in Washington?"

"Oh."

"Indeed. Quite. Mr. Carlyle is understandably grief-stricken and furious and on the warpath to find out exactly why his son fell out of a fifth-floor window last night. Apparently he is not overly impressed so far by the exertions of the Cambridge cops. The Washington bureau has it from his office that he was on the seven a.m. shuttle up today. Mrs. Carlyle too. So if you would please get yourself back over there and see what you can dig up?"

"Sure." It was starting to come back. Lowell Carlyle was a bigwig at Harvard Law School. He had taught constitutional law. And then the president asked him to come to Washington. When had that been, a couple of years ago? I don't follow Washington politics closely, but my vague impression was that Carlyle was well regarded. Which meant that if he was on the warpath, as Hyde had indelicately put it, he would have the support of powerful allies not just at Harvard, but at the White House.

THE COP POSTED OUTSIDE ELIOT House this morning was considerably friendlier than his colleagues the night before. But he still wouldn't let me in.

He'd kept his eyes trained on me as I made my way down Dunster Street from the T-stop in the square.

"Let me guess," he called, as I approached his post outside the front doors. "Fox News? *USA Today*? I know you're not CNN. They're already here." He gestured toward several television trucks, satellite dishes stretched toward the sky, parked around the cul-de-sac.

I grinned. "Looks like they beat me to it this morning. I'm with the *Chronicle*, actually."

"The *Chronicle*? You don't say. You wouldn't know anything about this reporter who's got the chief all worked up? The one who sneaked in last night and heard the briefing meant for students only and ran all the quotes in today's paper?"

I rearranged my features into a picture of innocence. "No. Really? Shocking, honestly, the things some people will do for a story. But listen, Officer . . . ?"

"Galloni."

"Officer Galloni. Great. Have Thomas Carlyle's parents been here yet this morning?"

"Afraid I couldn't tell you that."

"Did you guys find anything when you searched the grass last night?"

"Couldn't say."

"Any further insight into whether this was an accident or a suicide or what?"

"Afraid I really, definitely couldn't tell you that. Even if I knew." He winked as he said it. Looked like he was enjoying himself.

"Right. I guess I'll just take a quick look inside then and be on my way." I made to step around him.

He burst out laughing. "Nice try. I think you'd better be going before I have to arrest you. Miss—er—Miss James, you said it was?"

"I hadn't, actually." I studied him. Maybe a few years older than me and not bad looking.

My own looks are not subtle. It's hard to be subtle with screaming red hair. I'm taller than average, five feet seven inches, and not conventionally beautiful. Or at least I never thought so: too many freckles, too strong a jaw. But I have long, lean legs and I'm curvy in the right places. I dress well. And now that I've hit my late twenties, I seem to have grown into my looks. Jess says I'm "striking." Judging by the wolf whistles I get on the street, I'd say I pull off "sexy" on my good days.

So now I decided to test whether Galloni was immune. I tilted my head, pulled back my shoulders, and stepped close.

"You know," I whispered, "if you were just to lean down and tie your shoe for a second, you would never even notice me walking past. And then I could do my job, and you could get on with doing yours, and everyone would be happy."

"Can't do it."

"Ten minutes. I won't touch anything."

"I really can't. Sorry." And he actually looked it.

Hmm. So he wasn't immune. But he wasn't budging either. I stepped back.

"Well, then, it was nice to meet you. I should get going. Sorry to trouble you, Officer Galloni."

"It's Lieutenant Galloni, actually. And no trouble at all, Miss James."

I could feel his eyes on me as I walked away. I was glad I'd kept the heels on.

DUNSTER STREET CURVES JUST ENOUGH that the front steps to Kirkland House weren't visible from where Galloni stood. I paused when I reached them. I was pretty sure it wouldn't be illegal, technically, to sneak into Eliot House again. But Galloni, however charming, had delivered a warning: they knew I'd trespassed once. I wasn't sure I'd get off so lightly if the police caught me trespassing a second time around the scene of an investigation.

Still, it was tempting. I glanced around. There was no guard this time at Kirkland House. I decided to see how far I could get before someone stopped me. I crossed the courtyard. Glided back through the Kirkland dining hall, back toward the enormous kitchens, behind the grill, past the food trolleys. It turned out to be easy. A few cooks and dishwashers glanced my way, but no one made to stop me. I marveled, not for the first time, at what you can get away with if you look as if you know what you're doing.

Within five minutes I was standing in the middle of the Eliot dining hall. I would have to be careful. Breakfast appeared to be long finished, lunch was not yet served, and the dining hall was nearly empty. I headed to the far end, away from the main entrance where Galloni was stationed. A pair of swinging doors gave way into a stone foyer.

I knew from a couple of stories I'd done on undergraduate life that Harvard houses are organized around stairwells known as entries. A-Entry, B-Entry, etc. A few dozen students live in each one.

Where I found myself now was apparently the bottom of H-Entry. Some sort of student common room was at the far end of the foyer. Stairs rose up to the right. I wasn't exactly sure what I was looking for, but I thought it might be useful to get a closer look at where Carlyle had fallen. I was heading for the glass doors that led out into the central courtyard when they swung open. A cop walked in. Navy uniform, gold badge, talking on a handheld radio. I froze.

"Miss, you mind? We're trying to keep this area closed off a bit longer." He brushed past me and moved toward the stairs.

"Sure. Sorry." I nodded. As I backed toward the doors, I watched him duck. Police tape was stretched across the banister and running up the stairs. His radio crackled and another cop appeared on the half landing.

Outside in the sunlight I stood blinking for a minute and trying to get my bearings. Across the courtyard I could see more police tape, still ringing the spot where Thomas Carlyle's body had fallen last night. It didn't look like the bloodstain had been cleaned up yet, but then again it was hard to tell, I was so far away. H-Entry was at the opposite end of the dining hall, almost a hundred yards from where the body had fallen. I could see other neatly labeled entryways now, ringing the courtyard. No cops or police tape at any of the other doors. This didn't make sense. Why would police have cordoned off just one entryway? And one so far from where Carlyle had landed?

I was pondering this when a tall figure emerged from the main entrance. Galloni. He was talking to yet another cop. I looked behind me. The police were there too. I was trapped.

5

Lowell Carlyle sat on the edge of his bed and stared out the window. He had shared this bedroom with Anna for forty years. Forty good years. Their three children had all been conceived in this room. Two daughters, and then a son.

The boy had been born too early and sickly. Over the years, his sisters sometimes teased him about it. About how the runt of the family had grown into a giant. Six feet tall before he turned fifteen, and then he'd kept on growing. A varsity athlete, stroke of the Harvard crew. It was hard to imagine how small he had once been.

But Lowell remembered. Those first days, when no one could say whether Thom would make it, he had lain in the incubator, hooked up to wires and monitors. The nurses had judged him too weak even to breast-feed, and instead they fed him sugar through a tiny tube. Lowell and Anna were not allowed to pick him up or to hold him. But they were allowed, after carefully scrubbing with soap, to reach inside and lay a hand on their son's chest. It had moved Lowell beyond words to realize that when he did this, his son's heartbeat would slow, as if he sensed his father's presence and it helped to calm him.

Lowell was not a religious man; he viewed the world with the ordered mind of a lawyer. But he was a man of faith—faith in his own and his family's place in the world, faith that hard work would get you somewhere, faith that good would prevail over evil. Over those terrifying days in the neonatal intensive care unit, Lowell had sat for hours with his son. He sat and watched and promised: I will love you and you will know it and that will be enough. That will be all that matters. Just live. Just please live.

When had he lost sight of that? Lately he had pushed Thom so hard about law school. Hounded him about it, as if Lowell's approval—as if his love—depended on it. Who cared? What did it matter what Thom grew up to be?

And now . . . Lowell forced air into his lungs. He was in shock, he knew that. The call last night had seemed unreal. It still seemed unreal, even now that he had been to Eliot House, had seen the police tape and the red stain for himself.

Anna had not come with him to Eliot. She was downstairs now. She would want to talk about the funeral arrangements. She would be pushing him to take time off and focus on the family. On healing. But he couldn't bear that. He didn't want to heal.

He picked up the phone from his bedside table and called his secretary at the White House. She answered tearily, babbling sympathies.

He thanked her. Said the family thanked her. And then he asked what he had missed in the office so far. He insisted on scheduling a conference call for later in the day. Pack my schedule as full as you can, he told her. Fourteen-hour days.

Anything to avoid remembering.

6

I t took Marco Galloni a second or two to spot her and do a double take. But even from this far away, the hair was unmistakable. Shit.

He motioned to his colleague to head back and guard the front entrance. Then he jogged over.

"What the hell? Really, what the hell?"

Alexandra James winced. "I'm sorry. I haven't touched anything, and I'm leaving now."

"You got that right."

He puffed his chest out and glowered at her. "You know, I could book you right now. For trespassing. Interfering with an ongoing investigation. Maybe even obstruction of justice. What are you thinking?"

"Well, to be honest, I'm thinking something strange is going on here. He fell from those windows up there, right?" She leaned back and took in the full scale of the building. Five floors of dorm rooms and then the dome of a bell tower rising another hundred feet above. "So why have you got cops and police tape all over the stairs at that end of the house down there? The H-Entry end?"

"No reason. Now let's go."

"It doesn't make sense. Did something happen there?"

"Maybe. Maybe not."

"Maybe? Maybe, meaning yes? Come on. Give me something."

"Miss James. That'll be enough. Let's move it, please." He took her arm.

"Lieutenant." She put her hand over his. "I gather you're in charge here today?"

"Er—yes."

"I would really love if we could find a way to work together. I mean, it would be such a shame if they found out back at the station that I managed to evade the stringent security perimeter set up by the Cambridge PD not once, but twice. That would look so terrible, wouldn't it?"

He stared at her. "Is that a threat?"

"No. Merely a statement of fact. But let's not get ugly." She smiled up at him. "I know you have to throw me out now. But while we're walking, what about it? What happened down at H-Entry?"

"Unbelievable." He shook his head. Today was only Wednesday, and already it was shaping up to be a bad week. Monday had kicked off with a reprimand for arriving ten minutes late for work. Then the shift supervisor had gotten on his case for failing to report a smashed taillight on his cruiser. And now this business with the Carlyle kid. He'd been stuck at his desk well past midnight last night, playing referee as the Harvard police, Cambridge cops, and the Feds gleefully worked at cross-purposes, each jockeying for a piece of the action. The chief had gone ballistic this morning, waving the *Chronicle* around the break room and demanding to know what kind of clowns had let a reporter sneak past the perimeter and into Eliot House.

Galloni had been sent to ensure it didn't happen again. And now, despite the chief's typically subtle promise to break Galloni's balls if there were any problems, here she was again. Galloni was seen as something of a rising star within the Cambridge PD. But he could not afford another mistake this week. The promotion to lieutenant was recent. If word of this got out, the chief would stick him on night shift from now until Christmas.

Galloni sighed. He couldn't decide if it made the situation more or less annoying that the reporter in question was extremely attractive. He'd watched her walk away this morning. Great legs. She looked like she knew it too.

She was still smiling at him. "Please. Tell me what happened. I have to file a story either way. Help me get the facts right."

He hesitated. Goddamn it. Finally he blew the air out of his cheeks and met her gaze. "You are extremely pesky, you know that? I suppose it's not a fireable offense to tell you it doesn't look like Carlyle fell from the fifth floor."

"Why not?"

"Well, we talked to the students in all those rooms up there. They didn't know him, never saw him. Now, though, see how there's a big, round window way up there, another twenty feet up from the fifth floor?"

She nodded.

"So there's a little room up there. Inside the bell tower. Some sort of piano room. You get to it from that H-Entry stairwell. That window was propped open, and the janitor says it shouldn't have been. So we're thinking maybe he jumped from there. Or fell. Whatever. Okay, Miss Snoop? Are we done?"

She stood still for a moment. "Why would he have been up there? He'd already graduated, right? He wasn't a student here anymore."

"Got me on that one. But there were a couple of beer bottles on the floor up there, and the cleaning staff swear that they just cleaned a couple days ago. Nobody's signed out the key since. Who knows. Maybe this Carlyle kid had a key from when he used to go here. Maybe he was looking for somewhere quiet to hang out and get drunk. The thing that . . ." Galloni stopped and looked away.

"The thing that what?"

He shifted and looked uncomfortable. "Nothing. Doesn't matter."

"Come on."

"It—you did not hear this from me."

"Of course not."

"They will hang my ass out to dry if anyone knows you were back here."

She touched her hand to her heart and nodded. *You have my word.*

He hesitated again, then lowered his voice. "So the guys bagged up the beer bottles, you know, tagged them for evidence, just in case. Might as well, right? And here's the thing. They dusted for fingerprints, just to be certain this Carlyle kid was up there, that he'd opened the window."

"And?"

"And nothing. Nothing. Not one print. The window, the doorknobs, the banisters all the way down the whole damn seven flights. The whole place was wiped clean."

7

From several hundred feet away, another man was watching.

He'd watched all morning as people came and went through the great swinging doors of Eliot House. He'd watched the television crews jostle for a shot, and the cops try to shoo them away.

He clenched and unclenched his fingers and then wrapped them tight around the paper cup of tea he'd bought, now cold. His hands would not stop shaking.

It was done, wasn't it? Not a perfect plan, admittedly. Such a scramble. But it was done. The boy was dead. He felt reasonably sure that

Thomas Carlyle had not had time to tell anyone what he'd heard, not even had time to suspect much.

But the man couldn't have taken the risk, could he? Not after all the planning, the years of training and patience and work. One stupid mistake, and it could have unraveled everything.

Two nights ago the man had tossed and turned in his bed, realizing the gravity of his error. By dawn he had decided: Carlyle must be silenced. And there was only one way to make absolutely certain of that. The man had never killed before. That was not his role in the network. But he could not see a way around it, and there had been no time. He tried to make it look like an accident. Perhaps he had succeeded; it would be some days yet before the autopsy report was finished.

The turn of events had shaken him. He had committed murder. The man looked down and made another effort to steady his hands. He should not be here, he knew. But he wanted to know what the people investigating the scene looked like. In case they found something. In case they came after him. As, in fact, one of them did.

But it took her a while.

He wouldn't meet her face-to-face until nine days later.

8

The third and final time I sneaked into Eliot House was that evening. I'd wasted a couple of hours on an awkward and not particularly fruitful attempt to speak to the Carlyle family. They own one of those mansions set back off Brattle Street. Glossy white paint, wide front steps, gas lanterns framing the door. I'd walked the twenty-five minutes from Eliot House and then cringed as I rang the doorbell. I'm not known for timidity when chasing a story, but it seemed in unspeakably poor taste to impose on a grieving family the day after their son had died, to ask . . . What? What could I possibly ask?

How do you feel?

Or:

Why might he have been drinking alone on the roof of his old college dorm last night?

Or, worse still:

Do you know of any reason why your son might have wanted to kill himself?

Awful. Hideous. They didn't pay me enough to do this.

I was rehearsing an opening along the lines of *How would you like people to remember your son?* when the door opened. To my relief, it was not Mr. or Mrs. Carlyle, but a younger man. Perhaps a friend of Thomas's. Or a family friend. He stepped onto the porch, half-closed the door behind him, and politely informed me that the Carlyles had no comment, no statement, would not be speaking to the press.

I nodded, tried again. "I understand. I would rather not be troubling you, really. And I'm so sorry for the family's loss. But I have to do my job, which is to write a story on what happened, and I want to get it right."

I was talking fast, hoping he wouldn't shut the door in my face. "The statement the university put out said he'd just finished a year abroad in England. Was he back living here, at home?"

The man stood still for a moment, then shook his head. "No. I mean, he hadn't had time yet. He'd only just landed. He'd been back in the States for all of three hours, we think. His bags are all just . . ." The man gestured vaguely toward the inside of the house.

"It was a fellowship year he was doing, is that right? Do you know what he was studying?"

"Economics, I think. Or history. To tell you the truth, I don't think Thom was doing all that much studying this past year." The man smiled sadly. "He'd met a girl. English. She was going to come over this summer. To meet everybody. He told Anna all about her."

I noted the name. Anna. That must be Mrs. Carlyle.

"Thom and Anna are—were—they're very close. He called her, you know. On the way from the airport, when he landed. To tell her he was home safe. And that was yesterday and then a few hours later she gets a call that he—that it—about what happened." The man paused, cleared his throat, and turned to go back inside.

"Thank you. I'm so very sorry." I heard the bolt slide into place. I started back down the driveway.

I knew I should head back to the newsroom. Start writing up what I had so far. It was late afternoon and Hyde Rawlins would be stalking the cubicles, chasing down what was on offer for tomorrow's front page.

But right now what I had was pretty thin. I didn't have a sense of what kind of guy Thom Carlyle had been. I didn't know why he'd fallen from the top of Eliot House. I wanted to be able to picture it, to see what he had seen in the moments before he fell.

And so I went back.

THIS TIME NO GUARD WAS posted outside. The television trucks were gone too. Students were coming and going from the main doors, and I walked right in. The cops must have figured they'd collected whatever evidence they could find, and now dorm life was getting back to normal.

I checked the courtyard first. By this point I knew where I was going. The dark stain had been scrubbed away, but the ring of police tape was still there. People had left bouquets of flowers. I turned toward H-Entry.

Here the police tape was gone. I walked up a flight. Another one. No one stopped me. I could hear music from behind one of the doors. Students were home. There was no sign of cops. I kept climbing, but on the fifth floor I hit a dead end. At the end of the corridor was a door marked LEONARD BERNSTEIN '39, MUSIC ROOM AND TOWER. It was sealed with the POLICE— DO NOT CROSS tape. I jiggled the knob. Locked tight.

I slumped down against the wall and tried to imagine what had happened here last night. There were three possible explanations. The most likely, surely, was suicide. Thom might have climbed up the bell tower to throw himself from the top. Maybe the tower had some symbolic significance from his undergraduate days here. Or maybe it was just a really tall tower—tall enough to guarantee you wouldn't survive a fall—for which he happened to have the key. The major problem with this theory was that so far I'd found no reason to believe he'd been depressed. I'd had the *Chronicle* reference librarians scour his record, his Facebook page, old *Crimson* cuttings. They'd found no trace of trouble, no hint of anything other than a nice kid with good grades and a lot of rowing trophies. You never know what's going on in someone's head. But from a practical standpoint, why would someone bent on killing himself have taken the time to wipe the railings free of fingerprints?

So maybe it was an accident. He might have been drunk. Leaned out too far, slipped. The autopsy would presumably turn up whatever drugs or alcohol were in his system. Galloni did say they found beer bottles up here. But he'd said a couple of bottles. I found it hard to believe a twenty-three-year-old athlete could have gotten drunk enough off two beers to fall off a roof. And there was still the issue with the fingerprints.

Which left the most sinister possibility. What if someone else was up here last night? Carlyle had been a big guy. He would not have gone without a struggle. I knew—the yellow cardigan story—that he had landed faceup, eyes open. But what if his skull was already shattered when he hit the ground?

9

BY NINE THE NEXT MORNING, I was back at my desk. My byline was front page again in the morning paper. I had the details about Thom Carlyle falling from the bell tower instead of a fifth-floor bedroom. And I'd been the only one to report the fingerprints, or lack thereof.

I picked up the phone and dialed Lieutenant Galloni. I'd already bugged him twice yesterday to check facts, and I knew he would soon stop taking my calls.

But the Carlyles weren't talking. There was nothing more to see at Eliot House. The funeral wasn't scheduled yet, and the autopsy report might still be a day or two from completion. Meanwhile another

Chronicle deadline was looming tonight, and right now I had no leads.

"Galloni," he answered.

"Hi. Alex James here again. Just a quick question."

"Look, I really can't—"

"I know. I don't want to get you in trouble. But I thought of something. The key. Didn't you say nobody had checked it out? From the janitor's office? I'm still trying to figure out what he was doing up there. You know, how he got up there."

"Yeah. Make that two of us," Galloni said wearily. "But there's no story with the key. We've got it."

"You do?"

"We do. And if you promise to stop calling me, I'll tell you that it was in Carlyle's jeans pocket the whole time. Okay? Like I said, he must have had a copy from when he was a student there. Maybe he liked to play piano or something. There's a big old grand piano up there. Anyway, there's no mystery about how he got up there. He let himself in. Just wish I knew why."

I absorbed this. "And the autopsy report? Any news?"

"Nope. I told you, it takes a while. They have to do toxicology, tissue testing, all that stuff."

"Right. When you get it, will you please let me know?"

"Absolutely not," he replied, but it sounded like he was smiling. "Somehow I have a feeling you'll find out about it just the same."

I sighed and hung up. I had the itchy feeling I get when I'm onto something but I don't know yet what it is. I had to admit I was intrigued. It didn't hurt that Thom Carlyle turned out to have a famous dad. That guaranteed the story would enjoy front-page prominence for at least a couple more news cycles. The latest rumor from the Washington bureau was that the president himself was clearing his schedule to attend the funeral.

It didn't hurt either that one possibility was murder. Terrible for Carlyle, of course, but at this point he was dead either way. And murder would be a much more interesting story to chase than an accident or suicide. Still, the pieces of the puzzle didn't fit together yet. An apparently talented and popular young man had been alive and chatting with his mother thirty-six hours ago. Now he wasn't. So far I couldn't find a good explanation for why.

IT WAS AN HOUR LATER, after a walk around the block to buy the espresso now cooling on my desk, that it finally came to me what to do next. Or rather, where to go next: England. Carlyle had stepped off a plane from London just three hours before his death. The people he'd spent the last year with would be there. Perhaps some answers were there. I could try to find the English girlfriend, take a look around his room, track down his professors. Maybe Thom had said something to someone. At the very least I ought to be able to pull together some sort of a profile, a bit of color about what his last days had been like.

I rifled through the papers on my desk. Where was that statement Harvard had issued the night he died? Finally I found it:

Mr. Carlyle was a magna cum laude graduate of the College and had recently completed a postgraduate year as the Lionel de Jersey Harvard Scholar at Emmanuel College, Cambridge University, in England.

I smiled. I'd been so preoccupied with trying to make deadline that I hadn't really absorbed the details. Cambridge University. Emmanuel College. This was a place I knew.

Cambridge had represented a compromise between my father and my mother. My dad is American. More precisely, he's a New Yorker, born and bred. Take him beyond the five boroughs and it's like watching a crack addict deprived of his fix: he just doesn't function. It remains a mystery to me that he fell for my very Scottish mother. They have lived happily together in Brooklyn for three decades now, but she clings to her Scottishness with the zeal of an expat. I am told I spoke with a broad Glaswegian accent when I started nursery school, despite having never lived outside New York. I do remember being teased for calling pants *trousers*, and cookies *biscuits*, and so on, and for expressing astonishment at the notion that potatoes could be eaten in nonfried forms.

My mother taught me to roll my *R*'s. Also to cry during *Braveheart*, to describe raw, rainy days as *dreich*, and to never buy my underwear anywhere other than Marks & Spencer. But she gave up on convincing me to consider Scotland for university. I was too like my father on that front. We both had our hopes pinned on Columbia. I got in early, didn't even apply anywhere else. Then, midway through college, the English department nominated me for a fellowship. Junior year abroad at Cambridge University, all expenses paid. My mother leapt. It wasn't Scotland, but at least it was Britain. Maybe I would meet a nice boy from Edinburgh.

So I went. I didn't meet a boy, at least not one that lasted. But I loved it. And now, eight years later, I could picture the streets that Thomas Carlyle had walked, in the weeks before he died.

THE EDITORS LOOKED SKEPTICAL. THREE of them were gathered in Hyde Rawlins's office: the foreign editor, the national editor, and Hyde. The Washington bureau chief, Jill Hernandez, was supposedly listening in by speakerphone, but so far she hadn't said a word.

"I mean, obviously I'm all in favor of staying out front on this story," the national editor was saying. "But isn't whatever happens next going to happen here? The investigation is here. The family is here. The funeral will be here. Shouldn't you be here?"

I shook my head. I had anticipated this argument. "The family isn't talking. We've tried. And my police sources"—no need to mention there was only one—"my police sources I can work by phone. I don't need to see them. The point is, the people Carlyle knew—the people he was hanging out with this past year—they're all in England. They would know how things were going, what he was thinking. We should be talking to them. And they'll tell us more in person than if I cold-call them on the phone."

"We do have a reporter in London already, you know," the foreign editor cut in. "Why don't we have Charlie scoot up to Cambridge and sniff around?"

The room fell silent at that. Charlie Swift, the *Chronicle*'s London correspondent, had filed maybe half a dozen stories in the past year. I wasn't even sure he still worked full-time. Charlie was ancient. He'd secured the London gig decades ago, and subsequent generations of management had failed to dislodge him. I suspected Hyde would have fired him and closed the bureau years ago except that it gave Hyde an excuse to visit London every so often to check up on things. The idea of Charlie Swift's hoofing it to King's Cross station, jumping on a train to Cambridge, and producing a front-page scoop within the next forty-eight hours was ludicrous. But the foreign editor persisted. "Also, as I think we all know, the overseas travel budget is not what it used to be. I've already had to cut back the Africa famine series. I don't think we can just be assigning random jaunts without a formal story proposal and paperwork."

I saw Hyde stiffen. He was well aware of the budget constraints his newsroom operated under; he'd just never seen them as applying to him personally. Or to his favorite reporters. I would wager quite a lot of money that he had never bothered with formal proposals and paperwork before jetting off overseas.

Now he leaned back in his overstuffed, leather desk chair. He plumped a silk pillow behind his back and kicked his loafers up onto the matching ottoman. The *Chronicle* newsroom was a warren of bland cubicles and scuffed taupe carpets. Hyde's office, on the other hand, looked like a cross between an English gentlemen's club and a Turkish harem.

He was old-school. He dated from the days when the *Chronicle* maintained foreign correspondents all over the world. Not just in Moscow and London, but in Caracas, Nairobi, Phnom Penh, Beirut. Hyde had filed from all of them. Eventually he'd found himself back at headquarters, overseeing the foreign coverage. But it was a dwindling empire. One by one, he'd been forced to shut down the bureaus he'd once run.

Hyde got promoted when the old managing editor quit a few years back. He ran a good paper: The *Chronicle* won a Pulitzer last year for stories on corruption in the mayor's office. But anyone could see Hyde's heart wasn't in local news. The relics in his office were testament to more exotic datelines. A silk rug from Tehran that smothered the taupe wall-to-wall, framed flags from countries that no longer existed, a handwritten thank-you note from Boris Yeltsin. Twenty years ago, he would have been the one clamoring to fly to England to chase a story.

He cleared his throat. "If I'm not mistaken, a trifling pot of money does still exist for investigative projects. And Ms. James is already acquainted with Cambridge University, no?"

Hyde's habit of addressing reporters by their last names was both endearing and a bit affected. It was also useful for gauging where you stood. He was the opposite of a parent: you knew you were in trouble when he used your first name.

"I did my junior year there," I agreed. "I still know people. I've still got my university ID." This sounded feeble even to me. Hyde raised his eyebrows. I tried again. Rattled off a list of all the people I was planning to talk to. Half the names were made up, but it sounded impressive and I would substitute real names once I got there and started reporting.

"And you could file something for, say, the Sunday paper, I presume?"

I nodded. Surely I'd figure out something to file by then.

"Well then. We're agreed." He began shuffling through a pile of papers on his desk.

I saw the foreign and national editors exchange sour looks. I thought I heard a snort down the line from Washington.

Hyde ignored them. "You'd best hurry then, my dear. Get yourself on a flight over tonight."

FOR ONCE, THE *CHRONICLE'S* IN-HOUSE travel agent was helpful. A last-minute, Boston-to-London, round-trip ticket didn't run cheap, but there were plenty of seats. She booked me on a flight leaving Logan in five hours. Just enough time to race home, pack a case, and taxi to the airport. I swept my notebook and a camera from my desk into my bag. What else? Batteries. A phone charger. Both my passports—British and American—from the top drawer. I looked around for Elias to tell him I'd have to take a rain check on coffee, but he was nowhere to be found.

On my way out, I stuck my head around Hyde's door. He was barking down the phone at someone. I waited a minute until he turned, then held my hand up and gave a little wave. *Thank you*, I mouthed.

"Hold on." Hyde put his unlucky caller on hold. "Bon voyage. Don't make me regret this," he ordered.

"Do my best."

"Find his bedder. They always know the gossip."

I smiled. Typical of him to have already thought of the bedders. They were an institution at Cambridge—the housekeepers who knocked on students' doors each morning to make their beds, wipe their basins, empty their trash. Bedders did indeed know all the gossip, and some were less discreet than others.

"Also, let's do be careful. Carlyle's father—his connections—make this a bigger story than it might have been. No mistakes on this one. Double-source everything. And try to keep people on the record."

I nodded.

"Oh, and Ms. James?" He was already turning back to his call. "What airline are you flying?"

"Um . . . let's see . . . British Airways."

He brightened. "Delightful. I couldn't trouble you to bring me back a Burberry then?"

I must have looked bewildered.

"The spring version, preferably, without the belt. Size forty-two long."

"Sorry . . . a Burberry coat?"

"Yes, yes, it's British Airways for God's sake. They've got hundreds of them in the lost and found. Sitting there going to waste, you know. Marvelous resource. Just ask the first-class attendant before you get off."

I had to bite my lip to keep from laughing. It was sometimes hard to tell whether Hyde was kidding. He didn't look it. Still, he'd backed me going on this trip. If I managed to pull it off, bringing him back a Burberry seemed like the least I could do.

10

FRIDAY, JUNE 25

I RUBBED MY BLEARY EYES and stared out the bus window. Twenty more minutes to Cambridge.

The flight over had been uneventful. At Heathrow I'd grabbed my bag and steered for the bus terminal. It's the cheapest way to get up to Cambridge. Probably the fastest too. I toyed briefly with renting a car, given the *Chronicle* was paying. But the thought of fighting London traffic on my own was discouraging. Not to mention that I hadn't driven on the left side of the road in years.

So here I was on the National Express coach. It was just past eight in the morning. Just past three in the morning back in Boston. No point dwelling on that, or I'd be tempted to head for a nap. And today was going to be busy.

I ticked again through my plan. Taxi from the bus terminal to the hotel. Drop my bags in my room, splash some water on my face, and get going. I was pretty sure I remembered how to get to Emmanuel College. I had lived just a short walk away in Corpus Christi College during my time at Cambridge. And I'd had friends in Emmanuel. I'd eaten dinner there a few times, met for pints of warm lager in the Emmanuel student bar. I vaguely remembered ducks, some sort of pond.

But the main thing I remembered about Emmanuel was that it was full of Americans. Specifically, Harvard students. Dozens of them rotating in and out on various exchanges and fellowships. I'd done some research on my laptop as I waited at the gate for my flight to be called. The Emmanuel website bragged happily about its most famous alum: John Harvard, who of course went on to lend his name to the world's most famous university. He'd spent his own student years in England, at Emmanuel, back in the 1620s and '30s. The two universities had nurtured the relationship in the intervening four centuries. And at some point, they established the most coveted fellowship of all: the official Harvard Scholar.

I say most coveted because apparently Harvard Scholars enjoy three key privileges. First, they're forbidden to take exams or pursue a degree during their year at Cambridge. In other words, they're forbidden to actually study much. This is because of privilege number two: they are required to throw as many parties as possible. Seriously. The scholarship, I read with interest, comes with a five-figure entertaining budget. The idea is to serve as a kind of resident Harvard ambassador to the university. Of course, this is Cambridge, so the partying probably leans more toward black-tie banquets and sherry tastings than all-night kegfests. Still, not bad work if you can get it.

This was how Thom Carlyle had spent the past year. He would also have enjoyed the third perk: the Harvard room. Make that rooms. Two bedrooms, a tiny kitchen, and a huge sitting room in the most imposing old dorm in the college, reserved each year for the new Harvard Scholar. Thom had presumably been living there until three days ago.

If I could find the Harvard room, I might find his bedder. And then I might be onto something.

BY MIDMORNING, I WAS STANDING outside the front gate of Emmanuel College. I brushed my hair behind my ears and checked my earrings. I hadn't wanted to take the time to change, so I was still wearing what I'd worn on the plane: cotton summer dress, Chanel ballet flats, a cream cashmere cardigan. It wasn't the most businesslike attire, but then that wasn't the point. Today my task was getting women to talk to me. Thom's bedder. His girlfriend. I needed to appear nonthreatening, nice.

From the street, Emmanuel looked grubby. Passing cars had blackened the stone façade. Soot stained the windowpanes. Emmanuel wasn't as imposing as some of Cambridge University's thirty other colleges. Today it didn't look particularly welcoming either. The heavy iron front gate was locked tight and a sign outside read COLLEGE CLOSED TO VISITORS. I ignored this. The sign was meant for tourists; I considered myself exempt.

I stepped through a narrow side door and into the porters' lodge. From behind a counter, two porters looked up. It's the same system in every college: A handful of usually plump, usually gruff old men are charged with guarding the college gates. They also deliver the mail, prowl the grounds, and chase tourists and drunken students from the pristine lawns.

"Hi, just dropping this in the pigeonholes," I said. I waved a piece of paper from my bag and kept moving. Did students still have mail pigeonholes? Or did everyone just text each other these days?

"Hallo there. Can we help you, miss?" The porter acted as though he hadn't heard me.

"Oh, I'm fine. Just dropping this." I waved the piece of paper again.

"Ah, an American, is it? Visiting today?"

I did not have time to get into a lengthy conversation. And I suspected that the truth—that I was a reporter trying to sneak into the private quarters of a recently deceased student—would not go down so well.

Instead I pretended to pout. "Why, don't you remember me? Alexandra James, from a few years ago? I was in Corpus Christi. But I used to eat lunch here after lectures. I'm just back for a visit. I need to say hello to some people."

Then I batted my lashes at him. I am constantly amazed that men actually fall for this. But they do. The porter looked entranced.

"Well, then. Welcome back, love. Know where you're going?"

"Absolutely." I smiled prettily and turned through the far door, into Front Court.

FRONT COURT WAS LOVELY, I remembered now. A perfect square. Cloisters framed an ancient clock rising above a Sir Christopher Wren chapel. The pale stone here glowed, unsullied by the cars crawling past outside.

I didn't have any idea where I was going, but I didn't want to let on in case the porters were watching. So I strode across the cobbles, under archways, until the court opened into a wide meadow. Here were the ducks I remembered. The pond. I looked around, then walked up to a girl sprawled on the grass—apparently not taboo in this particular part of the college.

"Hi, sorry to bother you, but I'm trying to find the room where John Harvard used to live. Isn't it somewhere right around here?"

She looked up, registered my American accent, nodded. They must get tourists in here all the time. And I'm sure the Americans all ask where John Harvard lived. "That building there." She pointed. "Old Court. Don't think he really lived there, though."

I thanked her and walked over. It was a graceful old brick façade. I counted three entrances, and I headed toward the one she had indicated. Inside a bike leaned against the wall. Music blared from behind a door. The dorm was clearly occupied, even over the summer. I started to climb. Steep, battered stairs. There was nothing to indicate I was in the right place. But on the second-floor landing I caught my breath. T. A. CARLYLE, read small letters painted neatly above a doorway.

I tried the door. Locked. I knocked. No answer, of course. Now what?

I scampered back down the stairs and into the sunlight. Presumably the same bedder would clean all three stairwells. Morning was the logical time to clean. So maybe she was around, busy in one of the other entrances just now. I checked the second entry. Nothing. But sure enough, the door to the third entry was propped open by a vacuum cleaner. I walked up the stairs until I spied an open bedroom door. Someone inside was whistling.

I peeked my head around the door and rapped softly. A woman glanced up. Fiftysomething, baggy flowered skirt, permed hair going gray, a sponge in her hand. Bingo.

I asked the obvious question. "Are you the bedder here?"

"Yes." She looked wary. Probably pegged me for a tourist and was getting ready to shoo me out.

"Great. So I—I wonder if you can help me. My name is Alexandra James. You must have known Thomas Carlyle?"

I could see that caught her by surprise. She was staring, trying to size me up. Finally she nodded.

"I'm so sorry about the news. I . . . ." I paused. It would be easy to pass myself off as a friend, a sister even. But I do have some scruples. It's one thing to bend the rules to get into a place, another thing to lie to a source. So now I needed to tell the truth. But I would probably only get one chance, and this woman might slam the door on a reporter.

I went with this: "I'm from Boston. Where Thomas was from. I'm trying to figure out what happened. How he died, I mean. I was hoping—I didn't know if it might be possible to look in his room? To see if he left anything? Or just to see what it looked like?"

She shook her head. "No, you'd have to ask the porters about that. But he didn't leave anything. I mean, mind you—he left a right mess, but it's tidy now. I've tidied it. Bless him. Poor lad."

"I see. I've come all the way over, though—could I just stick my head inside? Just in case?"

She shook her head again, more firmly this time. "Are you family?"

"No." It was time to come clean. "I'm a reporter, actually. With a big newspaper in Boston. But I don't want to disturb anything or get anyone in trouble. I have to write a story about what happened to him. So I wanted to see what his life here was like. Can you—could you help me?"

"No, you'll have to talk to the porters, love. Or the master. You shouldn't be here." As predicted, the woman was shooing me out, trying to close the door.

I took a breath and changed tactics. "Sure. Sorry to trouble you. I guess I need to find someone who might know who he was friendly with. Or, you know, whether anything might have been troubling him. Someone who knows what was going on behind the scenes around here."

I stood back and watched her twitch. She would be struggling with herself. It was a point of pride among bedders to know precisely what was going on behind the scenes. But after a few seconds, she pursed her lips tight and shook her head.

"Well, thank you anyway." I sighed. "You couldn't possibly point me toward a cup of tea on the way out? I'm just off the plane and parched for a good cup. They don't know how to make tea properly in America, you know."

She seemed to relax slightly. A young lady in need of tea was something she could handle. And quite right that Americans didn't brew it correctly. "They'll have tea in the dining hall. Should be opening for mealtime shortly."

"Could you show me which way that is? I'm a bit turned around."

She nodded curtly. Led me out of the room, pulled the door closed, and locked it behind her. We climbed down the stairs and out into the courtyard.

She waited until we were outside before she spoke again. "That's the Harvard room." She tilted her head up toward a pair of windows on the second floor.

I followed her gaze. "And he just moved out earlier this week?"

"Yes. Left his room in a right state. Always so many people in and out."

I waited for more, but she was silent.

"He had a girlfriend here. Was she—does she live here in college?"

"Petronella." The woman nodded again. More silence.

"Petronella?" Where did the English come up with these names? "Would you know if she's still around? I mean, I suppose she'll be flying over to the States. For the funeral."

Silence.

We kept walking.

"I'd love to speak to her. If she wants to, of course. I'm sure she's heartbroken. This must have been awful for her."

Silence.

We walked on.

"A right tart, that one," the bedder suddenly spat. "None of my business, mind you. But I wouldn't think she's exactly dying of heartbreak."

I raised my eyebrows. Waited.

"Lives over there, in North Court." She pointed. "And the dining hall's just there. They'll fix you up with some tea."

"Thank you." I hadn't gotten this woman's name. But the moment seemed to have passed. "Thanks very much."

"Petronella Black," she was muttering as she turned around. "A right piece of work, that one."

11

The Emmanuel dining hall was painted robin's-egg blue.

Breakfast smells of fried tomatoes and bacon were still wafting from the kitchens. I was half-tempted to ask for some. There is nothing better for a hangover than a proper British cooked breakfast. Trust me. I would know.

But I was not hungover today. Just jet-lagged. And I was actually quite enjoying myself. It was a sparkling morning. Normally at this time I'd be stuck listening to an endless faculty debate or plowing through the fine print of some graduate-school budget.

Truth be told, I was growing a bit weary of the education beat.

Not weary enough to move on. Not yet. But the day was coming when I would be ready to jump to a bigger pond. Washington, or back home to New York, or perhaps overseas. That is, if any foreign bureaus were left. Not a given considering the current state of the newspaper business.

The first time I set foot in a newsroom, I was twenty-one. It had dawned on me, belatedly, that college graduation was looming and I had no inkling what to do next. Inertia led me to contemplate just sticking around. Doing my PhD at Columbia. And then, I don't know—teach or write books or whatever people with PhDs in English did with their lives. Thankfully, my father intervened. Perhaps it was horror at the prospect of footing the bill for yet more years of Ivy League tuition. He ordered me to at least go through the motions of applying for a job.

So one afternoon I found myself interviewing in the newsroom of the *Wall Street Journal*. A story was breaking—it had been an exceptionally bad day for the markets—and you could feel the place hum. Editors were shouting for copy, damn it, not in an hour, not in a few minutes, but *right now*. I barely understood what they were talking about—the FTSE and Hang Seng elude me still—but I got the urgency of it. That the editors weren't looking for poetry, just your best effort at that moment. God, what a relief.

Some journalists will tell you they're drawn to the profession because it allows them to give voice to the voiceless. The Nick Kristof types who want to save the world. I'm afraid I'm not that noble. I just need deadlines. I find them liberating. What a gift, to have a job that requires you to file nearly every day, no matter how dreadful a day it's been. You are forced to just get on with it.

The *Journal* did not offer me a position that day. I hardly left them a choice: my ignorance of all things financial must have been glaring, and I didn't have a single sample of published work to my name. But I was hooked. Two months later I talked myself into an internship at the *Chronicle*. And here I still am, grateful every day to have escaped the luxury of reflection afforded by academia. For me, it would have proved paralyzing.

Still. I looked around now at my surroundings. This particular corner of academia was beautiful. The high windows and polished floors of the dining room of Emmanuel College—Emma, as it's known here—were serene in the morning quiet.

I leaned back against a long wooden bench and sipped my tea. The request for tea had not been a ploy, or at least not entirely. Whenever I cross the Atlantic, an internal switch seems to trigger. Back in Boston, I crave coffee. Preferably of the strong, black variety. But in Britain, I drink endless cups of milky tea. I find the ritual calming. That's my Scottish blood. It is a fiercely held belief in Scotland that a cup of tea can sort out most problems. The really tough ones might require a stiff gin and tonic. Or three.

But that would come later. First I had to get my story. I stood up, straightened my dress, and prepared to meet Petronella Black.

I PAUSED OUTSIDE THE DOOR. From behind it came shrieks, then a giggle, then a crash.

I checked the wall again. P. P. BLACK, it read. This did seem to be the correct room.

From inside came another shriek, more laughter. I pressed my ear against the door. Two voices. One deeper.

Then the door swung open and a tall boy in jeans backed right into me. Nearly knocked me off my feet.

"Christ!" he shouted. "What the hell?"

"God. Excuse me." I do not blush easily, but I could feel my face turning as red as my hair. There was no way to deny I'd been eavesdropping. "I was about to knock—I wasn't sure I had the right room."

He stepped back and looked me up and down. He lingered a bit longer on my legs than seemed strictly necessary. Then he raised his eyebrows. "So you thought you'd lurk outside for a while to make sure?" His accent was English, upper-class. "I do hope we were entertaining. I mean, crikey, if you've been out there for the last twenty minutes—"

"Oh, shush, you." A female voice from inside the room cut him off. "You were looking for me, I presume? May I help you?"

"I hope so. Are you Petronella Black?"

"Yes. And you are?"

I stepped halfway into the room. "Alexandra James. I'm from Boston. I wondered if I might ask you about Thomas Carlyle."

"Oh." Petronella went very still.

The boy—actually more of a man, now that I looked at him—shifted his weight. "Righty-o. Just on my way out. Later?" He shot a glance at Petronella.

She nodded. Frowned. Once the door clicked shut, she looked up. "Did you know Thom?"

"No." I studied her. Petronella Black appeared to be in her early twenties. She possessed that peculiar English beauty that would fade, and soon. But today she was stunning. White-blond hair like silk brushed her shoulders. Her eyes were very blue. She was sitting on the edge of the bed, slim legs folded beneath her. The sheets were crumpled, and she radiated a glow that in my experience comes only from either a very recent workout or very recent sex.

"No, I didn't know him." No point beating around the bush. "I'm a journalist. I work for the *New England Chronicle*. I've written a few stories about Thom. But I can't figure out what happened to him—why he died. So I wanted to talk to you."

I watched for a spark of recognition. If my boyfriend had just died in a different city, I'd be reading the local paper to see what people were saying.

But Petronella gave no indication she'd ever heard of the *Chronicle*.

Instead she narrowed her eyes. "I've spoken to Thom's parents. And to the police. I don't believe I have anything more to say."

"Sure." I nodded. "But there are things you can't say to a guy's mother, I imagine. Was anything wrong when Thom left here to go home? Was there anything—I don't know—anything that might have been bothering him? Or anyone who might have been bothering him?"

"I don't see how that's any of your business."

"The thing is, I've got to write a story, whether or not you talk to me. You and Thom were—very close, as I understand. This must all have been horrible for you."

Petronella reached for a cigarette. She lit it and glared at me. "That is most certainly not any of your business." Her voice was surprisingly deep for such a small person. You could hear the breeding in it. Petronella Black came from money.

"Okay. Fair enough. Let me start over. Do you know what happened his last day or two here? Who he might have been with?"

She shrugged. "He had a party. He was always having parties. He loved a crowd, the drink, the chat. That's what I liked about him. But it was never . . . He thought . . . Well. It hardly matters now."

"He thought what?"

"Nothing. You'd best leave now."

This had not gone well. Then again, it was amazing she was speaking to me at all. "Just one more thing. Any friends I should speak to? People who were at the party, or rowing buddies, maybe? Anyone Thom might have confided in?"

"You've talked to Joe, I assume."

"Joe?"

"Thom's best friend."

"Joe. What's his last name?"

"I don't know," she snapped. "He's American. They were roommates at Harvard. Why don't you do your job and find out his name yourself?"

"I'll do that." I stood up. "Thank you. I'm sorry for your loss."

On the landing outside, I stood for a moment to collect my thoughts. I was trying not to leap to conclusions, but was there any explanation aside from the obvious one for what I'd just witnessed? The giggling. The tousled sheets. The bedder's comments. What kind of a girl jumped into bed with another man three days after her boyfriend had died?

"PETRONELLA ALWAYS SOUNDED LIKE KIND of a bitch to me," Joe Chang was saying down the phone line from Los Angeles. "I mean, I never met her, but just the way Thom talked about her. He sounded both totally hot for her and totally miserable, you know? Anyway, what kind of a name is Petronella?"

I smiled. "I think it's a London society thing. All the girls from Sloane Square seem to be named things like Jemima or Nigella or Petronella."

"Bizarre."

"Yeah." Joe was the first person I'd found who actually seemed to want to talk about Thom. It was refreshing not to have to drag information out of a source. On the contrary, I couldn't shut him up.

"I figured he'd be a prick, you know? I mean"—Joe lowered his voice and attempted an aristocratic accent—"'*Thomas Abbott Carlyle.*' I couldn't believe it when I saw the roommate assignments our freshman year. I'm this full-scholarship kid from LA. My Chinese was better than my English back then. My Spanish too, I'm not kidding, from all the guys at school. And I get stuck sharing bunk beds with Mr. Boston Brahmin. They do that on purpose, to mix it up in the freshman dorms. But Thom was cool. He really was. We had different crowds, but we always roomed together. He was my best friend. I think I was probably his." Now Joe sounded as if he might cry.

"You still talked, when he was over here in England?"

"Sure. Every week or so."

"I need to figure out what happened on Tuesday. Why Thom was up in that bell tower, and why he fell."

"Well, the first one's easy."

I sat up. "I'm listening."

"We went up there all the time. Senior year especially. I used to do dorm crew. You know, clean the showers and vacuum the floors so you can satisfy the work requirement for financial aid? So I had the master key for all the doors in Eliot House. I found that bell-tower room one day cleaning over in H-Entry. I was supposed to be dusting. Didn't seem like anyone ever used it. So I made Thom and me copies of the key. Please don't print that in the paper. I mean, I don't know what they'd do to me now, but still."

"You two—what'd you do up there?"

"Hang out. Drink a few beers. Talk about stuff. You know."

"You don't find it weird that Thom went up there by himself?"

"No. I guess he hung on to his key. It was a cool place to go sit, just to think about things."

"Joe"—I paused—"do you think, then, that Thom went up there, had a beer or two, and just—slipped?"

"No way. I thought about that, after . . . after what happened. No way."

"Why not?"

"We used to do that—crawl out across the roof, to get a better view. We'd get, like, twenty feet out from the big window. Wedge our feet up against the top of the tiles. But I nearly fell once. All the way down, I mean. Lost my grip and skidded. Scared the shit out of Thom. After that, we never crawled down. Just sat in the window, on the ledge. He wouldn't even lean forward much."

"So you're saying, you don't buy that he slipped, that this was an accident?"

"I do not buy that he slipped."

We were both silent for a moment.

"You said it was a cool place to go, to think about things. Do you know if Thom had anything in particular on his mind?"

Joe sighed. "I don't guess that this matters anymore. But, yeah, he was really worked up about the LSAT. The test for law school. You know Thom's dad is the president's lawyer?"

"Yes."

"He wants—wanted—Thom to be a lawyer too. That was the expectation. Lowell Carlyle can be very persuasive in conveying his expectations. I don't think Thom ever questioned him. He wanted to please his dad. And it was a good fit for Thom, anyway. So he took the LSAT this spring, studied for it and everything. And then he just got his score a couple weeks ago. It was a 151."

"What's that mean?" I had no idea how the LSAT worked.

"That's, like, terrible. For a guy from Harvard. I don't know what happened, because Thom is smart. But I guess he had a bad day. Thom thought with a 151 he might not get into law school anywhere. And forget Ivy League."

"Couldn't he just retake it?"

"Yeah, that's what I asked him, but I guess they average the scores. So even if Thom rocked it the next time, he'd still score pretty low. Thom said—I mean, he realized there are worse problems in the world. But law school was . . ." Joe struggled to find the right words. "The whole time I've known him, Thom never talked about doing anything else. It was a very big deal to his family. A very big deal to Thom. When he told me about his LSAT score, he sounded just lost. He hadn't figured out yet how to tell his dad."

"What about Petronella Black? He must have talked about it with her."

"No idea. I guess so. He was crazy about her. He was talking about marrying her, did you know that? But then every time I talked to him, they were fighting or not speaking to each other or something."

"And you never met her yourself, you said."

"No. Maybe I will on Tuesday."

"Tuesday?"

"The funeral. Memorial Church, at Harvard. They just announced it."

THAT NIGHT, IN THE ENORMOUS, claw-footed tub of my hotel bathroom, I leaned back and scowled at my drink. Didn't the bloody English invent gin and tonics? Why, then, when you ordered one from room service—at a hotel in the heart of sodding England—why did they deliver it without a trace of a lime or lemon? And God forbid they include an ice cube or two. I sipped. The drink was tepid. The tonic was flat.

Then again: at least it was large. At least it was gin.

I sank lower into the scalding water. I was exhausted. The overnight flight, the time change, the not particularly productive day of reporting. I didn't have much of a story yet. But I was beginning to see the outlines of a feature I could cobble together for the Sunday paper. A ticktock account of Thomas Carlyle's last days. It would not exactly be Pulitzer material, but it would advance the story a little. I could make it a pretty piece of writing to help set up the funeral on Tuesday. I still needed to track down a professor and ideally a rowing friend or coach. Then there was Petronella Black. I wasn't sure how to convince her to talk. But I would need to go back and interview her on the record.

For tonight, though, I was done thinking about her. I wanted more gin and then I wanted to get to bed.

I gulped at the drink and ran my fingers through my hair and over the soft, saggy skin of my stomach. Over the silvery stretch marks. Try explaining those on a third date. The marks are the only physical evidence that I have given birth. I was so young when it happened that the rest of my body snapped back into place.

For a long time I rarely thought of her. Now, as I've said, some nights it hits me so hard I can't stand up. But losing my daughter has also made me strong. It has made me a better reporter. Because it has made me fearless. It is easy to be fearless when you have nothing to lose. And what do you have to lose, when you've already lost the thing that matters most?

12

The next morning I needed the cooked breakfast.

Sausages, two eggs, beans, oily mushrooms and tomatoes, fried bread, the works. A big pot of tea that I was allowing to steep too long to boost the caffeine content.

Luckily room service had shut last night at eleven, cutting me off after four drinks. Otherwise I might not have made it down for breakfast at all. As it was, I was feeling ravenous. I ordered an extra basket of toast and marmalade and gobbled it down.

My plan, such as it was, was to get back to Petronella's room early enough that she would still be in bed. If I could catch her off guard, before she'd dressed and done her makeup, I might be able to coax something out of her.

So I swigged down the tea and was back outside Petronella's door by eight o'clock. Practically the middle of the night by grad-student standards.

This time it was quiet.

I knocked lightly. No answer. I knocked harder. This time I thought I heard a groan.

I had to knock a third time before I heard footsteps padding across the room. The door opened a crack.

Petronella squinted at me. "You."

"Good morning. I brought you some coffee. Here we are." I handed her the latte I'd bought on the way over. "It's skim. Hope that's okay."

I smiled brightly, as though this were all perfectly normal and the only question was whether I'd gotten her coffee order right. Before she could react, I pushed the door open a little wider and stepped inside.

"No. No, no, no, no, no, no, no. You can't be here."

"Well, now, here's the thing. I need to interview you and I'm not leaving until we've talked. It'll only take about fifteen minutes. So I suppose we might as well get started."

I glanced over at her desk. "I'll just sit here, shall I? Let me get out my notebook."

She shook her head. "You have to go. Now."

She looked annoyingly gorgeous. I need a shower and a good ten minutes' wrestling with the blow-dryer before you would want to cross my path in the morning. Petronella, on the other hand, already looked radiant, all tousled blond hair and long, tan legs.

She also looked terrified.

A moment later I found out why.

"Nella," called a deep voice from across the room. "You might as well get it over with."

"Jesus!" I jumped. Turned toward the bed. A head popped up from under a pile of pillows and covers. The same man I'd seen here yesterday.

Now this was an interesting development.

I caught my breath. Then I squared my shoulders and walked over. Held out my hand. "I didn't realize. And I don't believe we were properly introduced yesterday. I'm Alexandra James."

"Lucien Sly." He grinned. Shook my hand. He appeared to be enjoying himself.

"Lucien, for the love of God!" snarled Petronella.

"Darling, she's just doing her job. It can't be helped. Why don't you make up a few quotes and then see her out?"

Petronella went scarlet with fury. "Lucien, enough. Please. And as for you"—she turned on me—"as for you, leave now or I will ring the police."

But I was starting to see a way in. "You know, I suppose it would be a cheap shot to point out how my story will read in tomorrow's paper if you throw me out now. Yes, definitely a cheap shot. But let's see . . ." I flicked through a few pages in my notebook. "So then, it's Miss Petronella Black, beloved girlfriend of Thomas Carlyle, found curled up in bed with a Mr. Lucien Sly—"

He interrupted, "Lord Lucien Sly, actually."

"I beg your pardon?"

"It's just a title, old family thing, you know, but we might as well get it right. If it's for the newspaper and everything." He grinned again, wolfishly.

Despite myself, I grinned back.

Petronella seemed to snap. "Get out," she hissed.

Remarkably, this seemed intended for Lucien and not me. I turned my back modestly as he pulled on jeans and shoes. The two of them whispered together for a moment and then he crossed the room.

"Nice to meet you, Alexandra." Then he lowered his voice. "Oh, and I liked the skirt better. They're worth looking at, you know."

Confused, I followed his gaze. He was staring at my legs. They were hidden today beneath white linen trousers.

"I'll bear that in mind, your lordship."

"Do." He winked at me, blew a kiss over to Petronella, and shut the door.

OVER THE NEXT HOUR PETRONELLA shared quite a lot of useful information.

That Thom had wanted to get serious, that he'd asked her to come to the States with him, that he'd asked her to marry him.

He'd gotten down on one knee, she told me, in the same tone of disgust one might use to relate that Thom had decided to let his toenails grow out.

Petronella's response to Thom's gallantry had been to dump him. The night before he flew home. The night before he died.

She declined to be specific about when she had started up with Lucien Sly. It seemed obvious there had been some overlap with Thom Carlyle. But whether Petronella Black was a slut wasn't any of my business. The interesting thing was that she and Thom had argued the night of his last party here. Argued so bitterly that they'd broken up. He'd flown home alone.

I ventured that it was a reasonable conclusion that Thom was depressed when he arrived back in the States. That he might have had something drastic in mind when he climbed the Eliot House bell tower.

But she shook her head. She was sure Thom hadn't killed himself. She couldn't say why, just that he wouldn't have done that. She swore she had no idea what had happened up in the bell tower. None of the possibilities—that he jumped, that he fell, that he'd been pushed—none of them made sense to her.

Finally I leaned back. Petronella struck me as shallow and immature. But she also struck me as someone telling the truth.

"Will you be flying over for the funeral Tuesday?" I asked by way of wrapping things up.

"I suppose so. They'll be expecting me."

I raised an eyebrow. "Really? I don't think the Carlyles will be thrilled to see you. I mean, no offense, but you did just dump their son and you're already with another guy."

"They don't know any of that."

"Maybe not yet, but they will once my story comes out."

She jerked her shoulders back. "You can't actually use any of this. Not in the paper. I want this all to be off the record."

"What? No. Sorry. We've been on the record this whole time. I told you up front that I'm a reporter. I told you who I work for. You've been watching me take notes the entire time we've been talking. Of course I'm going to use all this."

"But I will look ridiculous!"

"Possibly. Though I'm not sure you can blame my reporting for that."

She shot me a withering look. "I'm going to call my father. And my lawyer. You'll be hearing from them."

"Fine. Tell them to call my editors."

"I mean it. I don't want my name in the paper."

"Petronella. With all due respect, grow up."

Instead, she stood up. Walked right over and gave me a little shove.

"I am warning you, don't print a single word of this. Don't you dare. Or I will make you very sorry."

She was trying to intimidate me. I'm afraid she had the opposite effect.

Try me, sister, I was thinking as I walked out. Try me.

13

Later that morning I wandered down to the Emmanuel boathouse and found a few rowers who said they'd known Thom. They all were polite and gave me a few passable quotes about what a great guy he'd been.

Then I walked back to the café where I'd bought the latte earlier, found a table, and called Marco Galloni.

He had wisely avoided giving me his cell number, but it was easy enough to get it from the desk manager on the night shift. I told her he was expecting my call.

Which he clearly was not.

"Hello?" he answered groggily. "Who? Miss James? Don't you know it's Saturday morning?"

"I know. That's why I waited till seven your time. And call me Alex," I said sweetly.

I could hear mumbled swearing on his end. "Seven *my* time? Where are you?"

"Sorry to wake you. But I'm in England and it's already noon over here. I thought you might want to hear some of what Thom Carlyle's girlfriend has been telling me."

"Hang on." I could hear him shuffling around. Pots clanging. Water being poured. Galloni must be brewing coffee.

"Right. Okay. Miss James. Alex. Fill me in on your adventures over there in jolly old England."

So I told him about my conversations with Petronella, Joe, the bedder. About the terrible law school exam results and about Thom getting dumped. About all the reasons, in short, why Thom might have been awfully depressed on Tuesday night.

"Hmm" was all he said.

"Your turn. What about the autopsy? What did it find?"

"I think the chief's going to do some sort of press availability this afternoon. You guys should send somebody."

"I'm sure we will. But since I'm on a different continent right now, what about just giving me the headline?"

"Can't. I don't want to get out ahead of the chief."

"What about we talk now, and whatever you tell me, I promise to sit on it until after the press conference."

I waited.

Galloni was quiet. Finally he said, "I want to be off the record. We're just talking. Anything you want to quote, you get it from the chief later."

"Deal." I doubted Galloni would give me much anyway. Junior guys are usually less willing to leak to reporters than their bosses. Not because they know less, but because they're more likely to get fired if they get caught.

But Galloni surprised me. "His blood alcohol level was .06. Guy his size, probably means he drank two or three beers. No other drugs in his system."

"Two or three beers wouldn't be enough for him to fall out of a window."

"I wouldn't have thought so, no."

"So this wasn't an accident."

"Can't rule it out. But I wouldn't have thought so."

"Well, what about suicide? I've got his best friend and his girlfriend laying out some pretty compelling reasons for why he might have been thinking along that line."

"We didn't know about all that. We'll have to interview them. But you met her, right? What's she like? Worth killing yourself over?"

Hardly, I thought. But Thom had apparently seen a different side of Petronella Black.

I considered how to put it. "Somebody here described her to me as a *piece of work*."

"And?"

"I'd say they have a point."

We were silent for a moment.

Then I asked, "Cause of death?"

"His skull was shattered. As you know. And his neck was broken."

"Could the coroner tell if those injuries were necessarily caused by the fall? I mean, could he have already been hurt before he fell?"

I could feel Galloni weighing how much to say. "The injuries are consistent with a fall from that height."

"But you can't rule out that maybe somebody brained him at the top of the tower and then threw him down?"

"I wouldn't have put it quite like that, Alex, but, no. We can't rule that out."

"Just one more thing. Would you steer me away from focusing on the fingerprints? It seems like that's the most interesting piece of evidence you've got. That the doorknobs and banisters were wiped down. No prints. Seven floors. Somebody wiped them clean."

"The janitors say they wipe down the stairwells regularly."

"Do you buy that?"

He paused. "No."

I took a deep breath. "So you think Thom Carlyle was murdered."

"I didn't say that."

"Would you steer me away from it?"

He didn't say anything.

"I understand I can't run with this in the paper yet. But here's what I think. You guys are convinced that Thom was murdered. But you don't have a suspect. Or a weapon. Or a motive."

I could hear Galloni sipping his coffee.

"Well?"

"I gotta go," he said.

The line went dead.

PETRONELLA NEEDN'T HAVE WORRIED.

The story I filed for Sunday's *Chronicle* was nicely written, full of colorful details, and devoid of any actual news.

Here's my lede:

CAMBRIDGE, England—The name "T. A. Carlyle" is still neatly painted in curling white letters above his door here.

But the rooms that Thomas Abbott Carlyle called home until this past Monday now sit empty. And throughout this ancient college, friends are mourning the loss of a young man whom they recall as a graceful athlete, an ambitious scholar, and a generous host.

I threw in the quotes from his crew buddies at the boathouse.

And I included the details I'd dragged out of Petronella about Thom's last party:

> One of Carlyle's key duties as Harvard Scholar was to entertain fellow Harvard alums studying at Cambridge University. His last night here was no different. According to Petronella P. Black, Carlyle's girlfriend and a candidate for a graduate degree in physics at Cambridge, Carlyle invited about two dozen people to his suite last Monday night.
>
> "People from his course, people from my lab, some rowers," Black said. A crowd of friends and acquaintances mingled and danced until around 2:00 a.m. They sipped sherry, sparkling wine and beer and sent out for Middle Eastern food sometime after midnight, Black said.
>
> "He was always having parties," Black added. "He loved the crowds, the drink, the chat. That's what I liked about him."

I left out the bit about Thom's proposing and Petronella's breaking up with him in the wee hours after the party.

Hyde and I had gone back and forth about it, with me arguing that it spoke to his state of mind on the day he died, and Hyde ruling it gossipy and gratuitous.

He also deleted all my wicked references to Petronella. I'd had great fun back in my hotel room, dreaming up ways to make her look rotten and sprinkling them throughout the story:

> Black, who shooed her new boyfriend from her bed in order to continue the interview . . .

Another version read:

> Ms. Black said she is "devastated" by Carlyle's death and that her "heart goes out to his mum and dad." Her current lover, Lord

Lucien Sly, declined comment, and Black threatened legal action if
we mentioned him in this article.

Hyde excised these without comment. I knew he would. It's a kind
of game we play.

He left untouched the section I included near the bottom with the
official autopsy results. The press briefing had been pretty dry, at least
as far as I could make out from the transcript. And my conversation with
Galloni had been off the record, so I couldn't quote him at all.

It was frustrating.

I'd now been reporting this story for close to a week. And I'd reached
the same conclusion as the Cambridge, Massachusetts, police department.

Meaning, I was increasingly sure that someone had killed Thom
Carlyle on Tuesday night. But I didn't know who—or how—or why.

14

Panic.

He could feel the sweat crawling down his neck, behind his knees, clammy under his arms. He searched his pockets again. Then his suitcase: every pouch, every pocket. He unzipped the lining. Ran his hand beneath the cheap satin. Lifted his possessions onto the floor, one by one, until the case sat indisputably, accusingly empty.

Then he swore and kicked it. It was impossible. He had been meticulous. Brilliant, even. He had made no more mistakes.

And yet. The phone was not here.

The cell phone. The third one. He searched his memory. It was the one he had used to reconfirm the shipment. Six days ago. And then where had he put it? Had he seen it since then?

The man leaned back on his heels. Rocked back and forth, thinking. It must have fallen out somewhere. He still had a few hours before his train. He could retrace his steps, search for it. It was an inexpensive phone; no one would look twice at it. He was supposed to go quiet now anyway. No more calls.

He was flying tomorrow. He had paid for the ticket with a shiny new credit card. He would check the one suitcase, to avert suspicion. This was his last day in England. In his new passport picture he was smiling. Friendly, wholesome looking.

He must not lose his nerve now. There was only one way to proceed: follow the plan. They had worked so hard. And now they were waiting for him.

15

Sunday morning I slept late.

I decided I'd earned it, after three front-page stories this week. I dozed until midmorning and then I took a long jog.

Cambridge looked the same as when I'd studied here eight years ago. Not surprising. Eight-hundred-year-old institutions aren't prone to sudden change. I ran along the river, down the Backs, the prettiest part of the university. Then out across Jesus Green and a few loops around Midsummer Common. I must have done five or six miles, farther than I'd run in months. But it was such perfect weather and it felt so good to be moving that I kept going, past the boathouses, back across Parker's Piece.

My adrenaline finally gave out near the front gates of Emmanuel. I slowed from a jog to a walk to a limp. A blister was flowering on my right heel. By the time I turned the corner outside my hotel, my face was tomato red and I was soaked in sweat.

That's when I bumped into Lucien Sly.

He was coming down the sidewalk straight toward me, balancing two coffees on a little cardboard tray, when I almost collided with him.

"Aha. Hello again. We seem to be making a habit of this, don't we?"

"Hi. Hi there." I backed up a step. Then I ran my hand over my damp ponytail, tried to unstick my running shorts from my thighs, and wondered whether I'd brushed my teeth this morning.

"Enjoyed your story today. I pulled it up online. Pity you couldn't work me in."

"Yes. That was indeed quite a loss for the readers of America."

He threw his head back and laughed. He was big. Maybe six feet two, six feet three. About the same height Thom Carlyle had been. Petronella liked her men tall.

He was wearing what looked like expensive Italian loafers with old jeans and a frayed white polo shirt. His dark curly hair flopped over his eyes. Lucien had full red lips, olive skin, hooded eyes. For a British aristocrat, he didn't look particularly British. I wondered if the Sly family tree had some Italian blood. The only giveaway was his crooked teeth. What is it the British have against orthodontists? A Cartier Tank watch gleamed on his wrist. He looked like a total toff. I liked him.

"How much longer are you staying?" he asked.

"Flying home tomorrow."

"Well, if you get bored tonight, a few of us are heading out to the Eagle." Cambridge's most famous pub. "You should come."

"Umm. Not really my scene. And I'm sure Petronella would be just delighted to see me."

"She's driving down to London tonight. Then heading over to Boston for a few days, as I'm sure you know. Anyway, tonight will be fun. And I would so hate for you to be lonely on your last night in England."

I stared at him. Unbelievable. He was blatantly hitting on me. This from a man whom I'd only ever met because he constantly turned up in bed with Petronella Black.

I was still staring, trying to think of a suitably chilling response, when he touched my shoulder and started walking away. "Do come. It'll be good fun. Oh, and, Alex? Great shorts."

I smiled. I couldn't help it. Lucien Sly might be an upper-class arse, but he was charming.

Mind you, there was no way I was going tonight.

BACK IN MY ROOM I stood under the shower for a while. Then I toweled dry, ordered tea and tomato soup from room service, and called Hyde.

He was mildly complimentary about my story. Said it was getting some play on the Boston NPR station. Then he asked when I was coming home.

"Tomorrow, hopefully. If I can get on an afternoon flight. It was too tight to get it organized for today."

Hyde said that sounded fine, that the funeral was definitely set for Tuesday, and that he would have the news admin desk work on getting me access to cover it. Security was going to be crazy. The president was flying up. "Just for the morning. He's got those trade talks in the afternoon. Then he's going . . . Bastard!"

"Excuse me?"

"Bastard cork. Sodding, stupid, son of a . . . Hang on." Hyde put the phone down. More cursing. Then a pop.

"Hyde?" I checked my watch, did the mental calculation. "Isn't it nine in the morning there?"

"Yes, Ms. James. Nine in the morning on Sunday. You are familiar, I presume, with the concept of Sunday brunch? At which one might serve such frivolities as a Bloody Mary or a mimosa?"

"You're hosting a brunch today?"

"I never said that. Don't leap to conclusions, James. Stick to the facts."

"You're making yourself a mimosa."

"That is one possibility."

"Or you just woke up in the mood for some bubbly?"

"I can neither confirm nor deny."

It occurred to me that I wasn't exactly in a position to judge someone else's drinking habits. If Hyde wanted to pop a bottle of champagne at 9:00 a.m., that was his business.

I pictured him sitting there. An elegant man, still wiry in his sixties. Sharp eyes. But his defining physical characteristic is a mane of thick, gleaming silver hair. It is never mussed. Behind his back reporters call him the Silver Fox. I wondered what he would be wearing at home on a Sunday morning. I couldn't see Hyde lounging around in a sweatshirt and jeans. A smoking jacket? Some elaborate kimono he'd picked up years ago during a stint in the Tokyo bureau? I couldn't actually imagine him in anything besides the dark suit he wore to the office every day. That may be because I've never seen him outside the office. I have no idea what his house looks like, or his wife.

But in our way Hyde and I have quite an intimate relationship. This is because he knows my secret. Or most of it, anyway. He's the only one besides my parents, and he's known for years, since my early days at the *Chronicle*.

I was hired as a summer intern right out of Columbia. After the summer they offered me a trainee reporter slot. I was assigned to the night cops shift, where I was supposed to listen to the scanner and call around the police precincts every few hours to check what was going on. I was terrible at it. I couldn't make sense of the codes the dispatchers used, and the big busts always seemed to unfold when I got up to use the bathroom or to make another pot of coffee.

After a while I lost interest. Started calling in sick. And I was sick, in a way. I had started the crying jags earlier that year. Crying, and scratching myself. I would take my fingernails and rake the soft, white skin inside my elbows, down toward my wrists. Scratch and scratch until red welts opened and the blood came. I was too chicken to do it with a knife. One particularly bad week I lay on the kitchen floor for two straight days. Didn't bother to call in sick. Didn't call in at all. I just couldn't move.

On the third day I slunk into the newsroom.

I had prepared an elaborate lie about food poisoning from dodgy sushi. *The salmon nigiri,* I was going to tell them, *I'm pretty sure it was the salmon.* But I was unlucky, or so it seemed to me at the time: Barry, the regular metro editor, was out that week. Hyde Rawlins was filling in. He was still foreign editor then, and I barely knew him. He had a reputation as a hard-ass. He liked to fire people. Our Johannesburg correspondent had lost his job recently for missing deadline. So had an assistant foreign editor. She had confused Mubarak and Mugabe in a headline and then misspelled Hamid Karzai on the front page.

Hyde had spotted me not long after I walked in and summoned me to his office.

"How kind of you to join us today, Ms. James. I hope you're rested. But might I ask where you've been?"

I clutched at my stomach and launched into the sushi story.

I hadn't gotten far when he cut me off. "Save it, Alex. Let me ask again: Where have you been?"

I stared at my feet. Couldn't think of what to say. Then the truth popped out. "I've been lying on my kitchen floor. For two days. I couldn't move."

He looked interested. "Go on."

"I—I hadn't really planned to get into this."

He waited.

"It's because—I—because—of my daughter."

"Oh. I hadn't realized you have children."

"No. I mean, I don't."

Hyde looked confused.

Once I'd started I couldn't stop. It was almost a relief to tell someone. I told him how I'd gotten pregnant at seventeen. The father was a guy I barely knew. Stupid, so stupid. My mother had cried. Said I was ruining my life. Said there would be plenty of time to have babies when I was ready, when I was older, when I wasn't a child myself. I was too far along by then to consider an abortion, and so I'd gone away until it was time.

But I'd lost the baby, I told Hyde Rawlins. She had died at birth. I never even gave her a name. And then I went back to school and tried to forget about her.

For a long time it had worked. And then, suddenly, it didn't anymore. It seemed crazy to mourn a daughter I had never intended to keep; the plan had been to give her up for adoption. But here I was, I told him. Going through the motions of my first grown-up job. And then going home after my shift and sobbing on the floor of my apartment.

When I finished, we had sat in silence for a while.

"I'm sorry," he said finally.

"Thank you." I sniffled. "I bet you're wishing you'd let me stick with the sushi story."

He frowned and shook his head. Then he swiveled around in his leather chair, pecked at his keyboard for a minute, and printed out several sheets of paper. He handed them to me. "This came up at the futures meeting this morning. It's the metro desk's notes so far on the city's new contract for trash collection. Something shady about it. They can't follow where the money's going. I want you to look into it. You can update me directly until Barry gets back."

I don't know what reaction I'd been expecting, but this was not it. "You're assigning me a story?"

"That would appear to be my job around here."

"I thought you were going to try to console me. Or else fire me."

"Still an option, Ms. James. Definitely still an option. But I think right now the best thing all round might be for you to work."

"Oh."

"I want you to go get me this story. Knock it out of the park. And when you've nailed this one, you're going to go get the next one. And then the next. See? I need stories. And you, my dear, you need to work."

So I did.

The trash contract story had taken me months. I learned all kinds of things about racketeering and the cartels that control the garbage-collection industry. The kickbacks flowed in all directions; our graphic-design team had a field day producing flashy charts and diagrams. In the end we ran a four-part series. It won a prize and cost the chief of the Department of Public Works his job. But most important, from my point of view, it kept me off my kitchen floor for a while.

That was five years ago. I am now twenty-eight years old. Hyde has never spoken of my daughter again. Neither have I. He just keeps assigning me stories, and I keep trying to knock them out of the park.

16

That night I lay sprawled across the green-and-yellow-flowered duvet of my hotel bed, leafing through the new issue of *Tatler*. It's a guilty pleasure of mine whenever I'm in the UK. *Tatler* is a British society mag, written for and about girls like Petronella Black. If you absolutely must know which West End bar Prince Harry is frequenting, or which caterer can whip up champagne cocktails for a soiree on your Notting Hill roof terrace, or how to score a ticket for the Stewards' Enclosure at the Henley Royal Regatta, then *Tatler* is the magazine for you. Sadly, these are not the concerns that dominate my waking hours. But who can resist living vicariously once in a while?

The July issue featured a cover spread on an Irish starlet I'd never heard of, and a fashion column by someone named Isabella Sterling. Ms. Sterling pronounced that high heels were now officially out, especially stilettos. This autumn, she predicted, fashionistas would be sporting square toes and sensible wedges.

Riiiight. Isabella Sterling obviously knew nothing about shoes.

I tossed the magazine onto the floor and was just wondering what to do next when my cell phone rang.

I looked at my watch. It was nine at night. I looked at the phone. A London number I didn't recognize.

"Hello?"

"Alexandra James?"

"Yes, who's this?"

"This is Petronella Black."

Spooky. Almost as if my *Tatler* reading had channeled her.

"I need to speak with you quite urgently," she said in her posh little accent.

I sat up straight.

"Petronella, if this is to threaten me with your lawyers, I'm really not in the mood. And if you bothered to read my story today, you'd know there wasn't much about you anyway."

"What? Oh. Good. But this is about something else."

Something else? "Okay. I'm listening."

"It's—it's perhaps nothing, but I would prefer not to discuss it over the phone. It's just very strange."

"Well, feel free to come over. I'm at the Crowne Plaza."

"No, no, that won't do. I'm down in London, you see. I fly to Boston tomorrow. For the funeral. Why don't we meet for breakfast. Let's say at my club. The Groucho, on Dean Street, in Soho. If you could be there at eight."

Good grief. The girl was too much. Her private club. And the last bit had been issued not as a request, but as an order.

"Let's say eight thirty," I said, just to be petty.

Truth be told, I was a little curious what was on her mind. And I was going to London tomorrow anyway, to fly home myself.

Then there was the fact that if I wanted to annoy Petronella Black, there were more enjoyable ways to do so than turning up half an hour late for breakfast.

THERE ARE BAD IDEAS, AND then there are really bad ideas, and this one probably ranked as one of the worst. But the prospect of flirting, knocking back a few drinks, and irritating Petronella all in one go was too alluring to resist.

By nine thirty that night I was penciling in my lips with a deep-plum color and digging through my suitcase for the highest pair of heels I'd brought. Take that, Isabella Sterling. By ten minutes to ten I was outside the Eagle pub.

Above the main door a blue plaque informed me that Watson and Crick had come here in 1953 to celebrate mapping the structure of DNA. Cambridge is like that. No matter where you go, someone more brilliant than you has already been there and done something far more interesting than whatever it is you're about to do.

I stepped inside.

He was easy to spot. Lucien Sly and two other guys were at a table in the far corner. Lucien had his head tipped back and was howling with laughter again. I stood there watching him. This was what made him attractive, I realized. You wouldn't trust him for a moment. But he radiated happiness. There was a vitality about him, a sense of someone completely comfortable in his own skin. It was foreign to me, but I admired it.

I walked over.

When he saw me, he stood and pulled out a chair. Wiped tears of mirth from his eyes. Introduced me around. "Alex, meet Peter and Nigel.

Peter and Nigel, meet Alex. Pete, you wouldn't be so good as to go buy the next round?"

Pete had the glazed look of a man who's already consumed one too many. But he staggered off obediently. He returned with four pints of warm beer. They slopped across the wooden table. Then he shook a pack of cigarettes at Nigel, raised his eyebrows in a questioning look, and the two of them stepped outside for a smoke.

Lucien smiled at me. His eyes were warm. He didn't seem particularly surprised that I had come.

"Well then. How was the rest of your day?"

"Fine. Interesting. Petronella called me."

"Did she? Splendid." He didn't ask why.

"She asked me to meet her tomorrow."

"Smashing."

"Not to pry, but may I ask how long you two have been seeing each other?"

"You may. A few weeks, I suppose. Maybe longer. Off and on. Nella and I aren't exactly exclusive, as you may have gathered."

"Mm-hmm. What about Thom Carlyle then—did you know him?"

"No. That is, not well. In passing, as it were." He looked not the least bit embarrassed. "Wretched luck, what happened. Poor chap. Have you figured it all out yet?"

I shook my head. "No. Still trying. There are bits that don't make sense."

"Like what?"

"Too many to count."

"Mmm. And must you still fly home tomorrow?"

"Yes. I've got to get back for Tuesday. For the funeral."

"Rotten business."

"Yes."

"So."

"So." I kept my eyes on the table and traced my finger along the slippery rim of my glass.

He smiled again. "Allow me to change the subject. Would you think me a terrible scoundrel if I suggested we leave right now so I could take you home and take you to bed?"

"Lucien!"

"Just asking."

"I'm afraid you'll have to work a bit harder than that."

"The lady's wish is my command." He grinned. Pretended to give a little bow. "But you do know where this is going, don't you?"

I did. I'd known it from the moment I'd walked in the door. Perhaps from the moment I'd bumped into him that morning. The anticipation was delicious.

"Another drink then?" he asked.

"Yes. Gin and tonic this time. Hendrick's if they've got it."

Another two rounds later we left the Eagle. Pete and Nigel had never reappeared. Perhaps they too could tell where things were going.

Outside it was starting to drizzle. The cobbled street was slick and quiet. I pulled my sweater tight around me and started to walk. It was a moment or so before I realized Lucien was no longer at my side. I turned around.

He was still standing outside the pub. Watching me.

"Bloody hell, woman," he groaned. "Those legs. I could stand here all night, just watching you walk."

And then he jogged over and picked me up and kissed me. My head was spinning. This was wrong in all kinds of ways. But at that moment—Lord, did it feel good.

AFTERWARD IN BED I LAY awake.

Dawn would soon come. This time of year in England, true darkness lasts a few hours at most. I tried to figure out what time I had to get up. Breakfast in Soho at eight thirty, so I'd need to arrive at King's Cross station in London by eight. That meant catching a 7:00 a.m. train from Cambridge. Assuming they left on the hour. I needed to pack. Shower. Check out. None of that would take long. If I was up by five, I should have more than enough time.

I glanced over at Lucien. He was out cold on the other side of the bed. In the moonlight his heavy features—the full lips, the slightly hooked nose—looked softer, graceful even, like a statue, or the profile on an ancient Roman coin. Luscious man. He had been very good. Pure pleasure. Of course, it helped that we would never see each other again. Soon I would be tucked back home in my flat in Cambridge, Mass.

My legs were aching. From the sex or the jog or both, it was hard to say. I let my thoughts wander. My best friend, Jess. I needed to call her and grovel. We'd traded messages, but I still hadn't properly apologized for standing her up outside Shays on Tuesday. My hairdresser. Must call and get my highlights done. Hyde. He'd be wanting another installment on Thom Carlyle. My parents, still living in the house in Brooklyn where I grew up. I should go see them. My daughter. My baby. I still thought of her that way, although it would have been her tenth birthday this year.

I shook my head. Mustn't go down that path.

Mustn't try to make sense of it tonight.

I closed my eyes. I should try to sleep for an hour or two. Tomorrow I could tackle putting my life in order. Yes. That seemed like a reasonable plan. But that was before I knew quite how crazy my life was about to get.

17

In Harvard Square, Jess Mitchell turned her key in the lock and let herself into Alex James's apartment.

She had come for the shoes, and it only occurred to her now that she should have brought along orange juice and bagels, so her friend wouldn't return home to an empty fridge. Not that Alex deserved any special kindnesses. What she deserved was a good kick up the backside. Jess was still seething about being stood up, *again*.

But that was Alex. Sometimes she just disappeared, as if she had fallen off the face of the earth. She could go weeks at a time. You learned not to ask.

Jess turned and walked into the kitchen. It was a pretty flat, wide windows looking out over stout birch trees and the Charles River. She checked the fridge. Empty. Alex was a decent cook, actually, but she appeared to survive on a diet of coffee and take-out spicy tuna rolls. And gin. Jess checked the freezer. No bottles. Probably the same strategy as Jess adopted for chocolate: best not to keep it around, or it would just get consumed.

The bedroom was a total state. Alex must have been in a hurry when she packed for England. Dresses, apparently considered and discarded, were strewn across the bed. Lipsticks littered the top of the dresser. Books were pulled off the shelves and dropped in piles on the floor. It looked as if a tornado had blown through. Appropriate.

"How *is* the Force of Nature?" Jess's father would ask when his daughter's best friend came up in conversation. You knew what he meant. She had a ferocity that was either reassuring or quite frightening, depending on whether it was directed at you.

Take the night a man broke into their student flat. It had happened their sophomore year at Columbia; the two girls had just moved in together. Around four in the morning they had been woken by a crash. In the shadows of the hallway they found a man. Big, mean looking. Jess remembered the jolt of terror she had felt, the instinct to flee back into the bedroom, bolt the lock, call the police. But Alex had charged him. Just run at him, pounding him with her fists. Insane. He had kicked her off but she kept attacking, until he must have decided it wasn't worth it, and he ran, back out the door and into the night. Alex had stood there, sweat and adrenaline steaming off her skin. And Jess had understood that her friend had a side to which Jess did not have access.

That said, the girl had great shoes. Jess rummaged around the closet until she found what she had come for: a slinky pair of Bruno Maglis with thick, gold heels. Fabulous. They would go perfectly with the outfit she had planned for tonight.

She left her friend a note on the kitchen counter:

Welcome home, Stranger.

    I am holding your gold Brunos hostage. Part of your punishment for ditching me at Shays. You can make it up to me over dinner when you get back. Your treat. The Indian place?

Grumpily yours,

J

ACROSS THE RIVER IN BOSTON, Hyde Rawlins tightened the belt on his silk kimono and poured himself another glass.

The champagne was an indulgence he permitted himself on the weekend. During the week he tried to stick to dry white wine. He kept a bottle chilled at all times, in a small refrigerator tucked behind the sofa in his office. Another flagrant violation of newsroom regulations. Personal fridges were banned, both because they gobbled up electricity and because their stashes attracted mice. But Hyde doubted the mice were interested in sauvignon. And he liked to pour himself a generous glass every evening, just to take the edge off the workday.

Reporters were sometimes invited to join the ritual. They could tell—based on whether he used their first or last names when calling them into his sanctum—whether they would be sharing his wine, or one of the less attractive offerings from the private fridge. Over the years that Hyde ran the foreign desk, it had become something of a competition among the reporters to bring him back a bottle of the most revolting local tipple they could find. A long-fermenting bottle of guava brandy from Namibia was considered the unofficial winner. The collection also included a terrifyingly yellow Italian limoncello, a vile Danish liquor called Gammel Dansk, and a home-brewed Mongolian spirit that smelled like paint thinner. After a trip to see her relatives last year, Alex had proudly contributed a bottle of Buckfast, the fortified wine favored by Glasgow soccer hooligans.

Hyde relished summoning reporters who hadn't managed a byline in a couple of weeks. He would watch them squirm as he poured himself a glass of good wine, smiled pleasantly, and then pointedly replaced the bottle in the fridge. They knew what was coming: a healthy measure of the guava brandy. The routine was obnoxious, but effective. The reporters nearly always found a way to file a story the next day.

Hyde enjoyed running a newsroom, for the most part. His heart wasn't in local news, it was true. But through creative accounting and the grim determination of Hyde and few of the other old guard, the paper managed to cling to its Washington office and to six foreign bureaus: Beijing, Jerusalem, Cairo, Mexico City, Berlin, and London. If you could count old Charlie Swift in London as a bureau. Really, Hyde should shut down Berlin and open Islamabad. It was where the story was now. But he couldn't stomach the idea of not having a single reporter on the Continent. It was bad enough he'd had to shut Paris and Rome. It killed Hyde to run wire copy from the great cities of Europe. But at least he was still in the game. Well into his sixties, he retained a boyish amazement that he'd found a profession where you actually got paid to travel the world, interview interesting people, and write about it.

He missed being out in the field. Hyde was unlike other star reporters of his generation in that he'd never hankered for the life of a war correspondent. As a young man, he had watched his contemporaries break news from Vietnam and did not envy them. Danger and bloodshed did not appeal. Instead, he preferred to install himself in elegant flats in cosmopolitan cities. Then he would set out to meet the people who made them tick. He was a beautiful and a fast writer. He saw that while one could keep busy covering the never-ending cycles of coups and floods and currency devaluations, the way to really capture a place was to write about its people. The foods they ate, the sports they played, the gods they worshipped. His eight-thousand-word Sunday-magazine article on the renaissance of Chianti—filed after three weeks of "research" in Tuscany and accompanied by an expense report staggering enough to earn him his own cost code in the paper's accounting office—remained a standard to which the interns aspired.

Perhaps the happiest years were his stint in Istanbul. Having persuaded the then foreign editor that Turkey was a key listening post for the Arab world, he befriended the local CIA station chief. Together the two men spent their evenings on the spy's balcony. Hours slipped by as they smoked, topped up each other's whisky, and watched oil tankers motoring up the Bosporus Strait. The station chief claimed to have radar that could track covert Soviet subs gliding down from the Black Sea. He claimed the Agency could intercept and listen to every word the Russians said. Hyde never quite knew whether to believe his friend on this count. But he did pick up all kinds of gossip about the Russian mob, narcotics trafficking, and other areas the CIA had deemed of interest.

One of Hyde's early editors had once warned him that the glory days of a newsroom were always ten years before you got there. Alas, he had now reached an age where he believed it. He had no idea how the young journalists who worked for him could stand the demands that were placed on them. Web build-outs. Podcasts. Live blogs and reader Q&A's. Always another news *platform* hungry for you to file. Worst of all, editors who insisted your phone remain always on, always with you, the better to reach you around the clock. He supposed this was true across all industries, in this era of efficiencies and multitasking. Yet it pained him that reporters could no longer disappear for weeks on a boondoggle like his legendary Chianti quest.

And yet, they kept coming. Take Alexandra James. Smart girl. She could have gone to law school like nearly every other Ivy League grad of her generation. Or off to earn a fortune on Wall Street. Six years she'd worked in his newsroom, and he was still trying to figure her out. She was clearly driven. Clearly talented. But she was also young and inexperienced. And there was the thing with her child. It had left her . . . somehow . . . damaged. As if something critical in her had broken and was still deciding whether to heal.

Hyde sipped the last of his champagne and wondered what Alex would come up with on the Thomas Carlyle story. She was testing him. One of Hyde's vanities was a conviction that he knew exactly how much leash to give his reporters, and when it was time to rein them in. Five decades of journalism had also led him to believe that the world was crazy, and most people were nuts. He had an inside joke with his wife: *everyone outside our bed is insane.* People did crazy things all the time. That was good for journalists. It meant if you dug deep enough, for long enough, there was always a story.

He hoped Alex James was the type of reporter who would find it.

He also hoped she would remember to bring him back a Burberry coat.

18

By 9:02 a.m. I was both ravenous and ready to throttle Petronella Black.

I had walked through the front door of the Groucho half an hour before, right on time. No, there was no table booked for Miss Black, the girl at the reception desk told me. Yes, they knew Miss Black, and if I was her guest, I was welcome to wait for her in the brasserie. Just turn right at the main bar and keep heading toward the back of the club.

I took a table in the corner and practically inhaled a cup of tea. I looked around. I'd never been inside the Groucho before. It's a private club for media types: screenwriters, journalists, actors. Also It girls, which I guess was the category Petronella loosely slotted into. The London newspapers are always reporting rock-star sightings at the Groucho; Mick Jagger has been known to turn up, and Bono was spotted dancing on the bar at Stella McCartney's last birthday party. A few years back an incident involving a member of parliament, two television starlets, and a Ziploc Baggie of cocaine in the ladies' room made headlines.

But on a Monday morning the Groucho was disappointingly subdued. Most of the other tables were occupied by men in gray suits, reading the *Financial Times*. I drummed my fingers on the table and waited. And waited.

I had just lifted my hand to order scrambled eggs and a croissant—I was past caring whether Petronella showed—when she appeared in the doorway. She was luminous. All legs and big blue eyes and that pale-gold hair sheeting down her back. I watched as just about every man in the room stopped eating and pretended not to stare. Would it be exciting or bothersome to possess that kind of beauty?

She pretended not to notice, or maybe she was so used to men's staring that she really didn't. She crossed the room and plopped into the chair across from me. A waiter rushed over to spread her napkin across her lap and pour her coffee. She was wearing a white, zippered catsuit with an Hermès scarf knotted around her waist. Just the thing, obviously, for a seven-hour transatlantic flight to your boyfriend's funeral. I glanced down. Strappy gold Jimmy Choos with four-inch heels. They were great shoes, I had to hand it to her.

"Did you find the place all right? I was worried you'd gotten lost," I said acidly.

She ignored me. She didn't apologize for being late, didn't even say hello. She took her time stirring milk into her coffee and then looked up. "I don't know if this is important or means anything or not. But yesterday before I left Cambridge, I went to Thom's room. I hadn't been there since—since what happened—and I kind of wanted to say good-bye, you know?"

I nodded.

"And I also wondered if there was anything of mine there that perhaps I should collect. I mean, he had packed up to move home and everything, but just in case. Everything between us ended rather abruptly, as you know."

I nodded again.

"I still have the key Thom gave me, so I could let myself in." She fished around in her handbag for a moment and pulled out an ordinary-looking brass key. "I mean, the point is, the door was locked." She looked at me significantly. "And I went in, and everything looked all right. Quite neat and tidy, actually, nothing like when Thom lived there. And I was just looking around in the drawers and things when I heard a noise. From the second bedroom—the one Thom used mostly for stowing his skis and luggage and things. And then the door opened—I nearly fainted—and out walks Nadeem. He nearly frightened me to death."

"Who's Nadeem?"

She frowned. "Nadeem is—I think he's Indian or Pakistani or something. Nadeem Siddiqui. He works with me at Cavendish. Or not really with me. He's guest-lecturing for a term, or something like that. But he's tied somehow to Cavendish. Quite an odd chap, really. Though I did try to be nice to him."

"And what's Cavendish?"

"Cavendish Laboratory. It's the physics department, basically. My department. I told you I do research there with high-energy particle accelerators."

I didn't bother to hide my smile. Petronella was starting to remind me of a Bond-girl villain. A blond bombshell in a white catsuit with an advanced degree in some incomprehensible branch of physics. You couldn't make this stuff up.

"No, you hadn't mentioned that," I said. "But anyway, why was this Nadeem person in Thom's room?"

"Well, that's just it. He was quite strange about it. He'd been at the party, you see. The party on Thom's last night. I'm the one who'd invited him. He was in the common room at the lab the other day when a few of us were talking about it, so I invited him along. I didn't actually expect him to come, of course, but never mind. He did. It turns out he and Thom already knew each other. They'd met at a lunch or something, I don't know. Anyway. I think he left before we ordered the takeaway."

"But what's that got to do—"

She raised her hand to shush me. "I'm getting to it. So when I saw him yesterday, he said he'd lost something. He thought he might have left it at the party. So he'd come back to look, but he couldn't find it. But, Alex, here's the thing."

"Yes?"

"The room—the second bedroom, where he was looking. I can't think why he would ever have been in that room at the party. Thom used it as a storage room, you see? And when I looked past him—past Nadeem—it was a total state. Like a bomb had gone off. The mattress thrown off the bed to the floor, the shelves pulled out from the walls. It looked . . . ransacked. Even Thom wouldn't have left it like that. And as I said, the rest of the suite looked as if it had been cleaned."

"Right." I remembered Thom's bedder saying she had straightened up.

"So I asked Nadeem what he'd lost and could I help him look. He said it was nothing important, and he closed the bedroom door behind him, and that was that. He walked me out and we said good-bye. And it wasn't until last night as I was driving down to London that the other thing occurred to me. Which is, how did he get in? I told you I had to use my key. The door was locked. So how did he get in? And what was he doing in there, with the main door all locked up behind him?"

"I don't know." I thought for a moment. Pressed my finger onto my bread plate to collect the last few croissant crumbs. "What do you think he was looking for?"

"Oh, I've no idea. I'm sure none of this has anything to do with anything. It didn't seem worth bothering the porters with it. But it does seem—quite strange, doesn't it? It felt like I should tell . . . someone. So I thought of you."

I took out my notebook and scribbled down the name—Nadeem Siddiqui—and the details of the room as Petronella had described them. "I have to say I don't know if there's anything sinister about it or not. And I'm not actually going back to Cambridge. I'm flying to Boston myself today, to write the story about the funeral. But if I've got a few minutes before my flight, perhaps I'll try to track him down and ask a few questions. Lord knows I don't have any other leads at the moment." I slapped my notebook shut.

Petronella nodded, lifted her arms over her head, and stretched. The catsuit stretched with her. It was quite a sight. "I'm sure it'll turn out to be nothing. You'll let me know if you find anything out? Now, if you'll excuse me, I do need to run to get to Heathrow on time." She picked her phone up off the table. "I've just got to ring Lucien quickly."

I blushed at the name. Lucien Sly might well still be asleep in my bed at the hotel back in Cambridge. I'd managed to sneak out without waking him.

I stood up. "I'll be in touch. See you at the funeral, maybe. Have a safe flight. Oh, and give his lordship a kiss for me."

Petronella looked up, startled.

I walked out.

I TURNED LEFT OUT OF the Groucho and then left again onto Old Compton Street. Sex shops, wine shops, pubs. I wheeled my Samsonite behind me. I was looking for a café or a hotel lobby or even a park bench where I could make a phone call or two.

I wasn't sure what to make of my meeting with Petronella. I couldn't think of how this slightly strange lab colleague of hers could possibly be connected to Thomas Carlyle's falling out of the Eliot House bell tower. Still, it did seem odd that he'd been caught rummaging around Thom's room. Thom's *locked* room. There would probably be an innocent explanation. But it seemed worth calling and asking Nadeem Siddiqui what it was.

Finally I found a café. I ordered yet another pot of tea and called Galloni's desk at the police station. No answer. I left a voice mail explaining that someone might have broken into Thom's rooms at Emmanuel, and that Thom's girlfriend had seen him, and that she was landing in Boston later today if they wanted to send somebody over to talk to her. I don't usually consider it my business to pass tips along to law enforcement. But Galloni was proving a useful source, and it never hurts to return the favor once in a while.

Next I fired off an e-mail to renew my interview request for Thom's parents. Lowell Carlyle's secretary at the White House had been polite, but discouraging. No chance until after the funeral, if ever, she'd said. Still, it couldn't hurt to keep trying.

Then I looked up the number for Cavendish Laboratory. A receptionist answered on the second ring. I got passed around and hung up on a few times until eventually a woman with a heavy German accent told me Nadeem Siddiqui no longer worked there.

"Are you sure?" I pressed her. "I think he was there just last week."

"Yes. He was here for the one term. Do you need his forwarding address?"

She read out a street name and house number in Cambridge. I copied them down and thanked her. Within a couple of minutes, I had the phone number and was dialing.

"Hello?" The voice sounded English, older, female. Not promising.

"Hello, I wonder if I might speak with Nadeem Siddiqui?"

"Nadeem?" The woman sounded bewildered.

"Yes, is this the correct number for Nadeem Siddiqui?"

"Well, isn't he the popular one now."

"Oh, good, you know him?" I said with relief.

"Course I know him. My lodger for the past four months, isn't he? Mind you, nobody ever bothered to ring him when he actually lived here."

Now it was my turn to sound bewildered. "So—you mean he doesn't live there anymore?"

"No, dearie. You've missed him. Moved out, he has. Just this week. Left everything neat as a pin. Nice lad, that one."

My heart sank. "Do you have any idea how to reach him?"

"That's what the other one asked. No, I've no idea. He paid his rent in cash and I don't expect I'll be hearing from him again."

"The other one, did you say? What other one? Was someone else looking for Nadeem?"

"Just that gentleman showed up yesterday. Handsome, but an odd bird. Wanted to see the room. I asked, was he wanting it for himself? It's got new carpeting and its own private bath, you know. But, no, he didn't want to take it, he just wanted to look around. Very odd bird."

I thanked her and hung up.

Then I sat for a moment and thought things over.

Nadeem Siddiqui had left town because the academic term was over. Maybe he'd forgotten to pack something—something utterly pedestrian, such as his tennis racket or a pair of glasses. And he'd asked a friend still in Cambridge to go back to his room and look for them. There were perfectly logical explanations for everything I'd just heard.

Still.

I checked my watch. I would need to leave for Heathrow soon to make my flight back to Boston. I didn't move. On the sidewalk outside the café, the morning routine of the city was unfolding. Tourists wandered past, maps in hand. Sanitation workers wheeled trash bins to the curb. A bicycle messenger whizzed by.

Hyde wanted me on that plane so I could get back to cover the funeral. That was obviously the responsible thing to do. But Hyde was the first to tell his reporters, *Always trust your gut*. I hesitated one more minute. Then I got up and took the train back to Cambridge.

19

I was at Cavendish Laboratory by lunchtime, and for the next several hours I was exceedingly efficient.

Cavendish was mostly a dead end. The German woman I'd spoken to on the phone was summoned to the front reception to help me. She was tall, with grayish-blond hair scraped back into a bun. She looked visibly irritated at having now been disturbed twice. But I did manage to learn that her name was Gitta Juette and that she was deputy director of the lab's nuclear-physics research group. She said Siddiqui had been working for her, just for this past term, part of a pilot exchange program with Pakistani scientists. He'd given a few lectures and helped with research here. He finished up a little over a week ago.

"Can you be more specific about what his research here focused on?"

Now she looked at me suspiciously. "I'm sorry, tell me again what exactly this is regarding?" I had told her my name and that I needed to speak to Siddiqui on a professional matter.

"I'm with an American company and I'm doing research." Which was true, if not exactly the entire truth.

"Well, I'm not sure I can help any further. I didn't know him well, to be honest. He kept to himself and he wasn't here for long. Although sometimes we chatted a bit in German. He speaks German beautifully, did you know that?"

"No, I didn't." Then I pressed her: "I know you gave me his address here, and thank you for that. But his landlady says he's moved out and she doesn't have a way to contact him. Would you have any other information? Perhaps an e-mail address?"

"I can't give that out. But I tell you what. I'll get you the number for the coordinator who helped arrange the exchange. Okay? And if he wants to put you in touch, he can."

She turned and started to walk toward a set of double doors. I followed her.

"No. Just wait here, please."

A few minutes went by and then the phone on the receptionist's desk rang. The receptionist answered and scribbled down a message. She tore the paper off her pad and waved it at me. "Dr. Juette said to give you this. I'm afraid she's going to be tied up for the rest of the day."

Smart woman. I looked at the paper. It had a name and a number starting with 00 92. An international dialing code. Pakistan, presumably.

* * *

AT MY NEXT STOP I got a much warmer reception.

Mrs. George Forsyth laid out tea and cakes, insisted on making fresh cucumber-and-butter sandwiches, and generally fussed about as if she'd been expecting me for weeks.

"How kind of you to call," she said, beaming at me. "Nadeem is such a nice boy. Very polite. He's a Muslim, you know, but one mustn't judge."

I tried not to choke on my tea. "Right. Yes. Mrs. Forsyth, how long did he live here with you?"

"Let's see. He must have come in March. Yes. So just a short while. Since Mr. Forsyth passed away—God rest his soul—I've let out the two top rooms. It brings in a bit of pocket money, and it's nice to have the company. I try to pick quiet ones, but sometimes it's hard to tell what they'll be like. Do you know Nadeem well?"

I decided to risk the truth. "No. I've never met him, actually. I'm a reporter and I want to interview him for a story."

"That's nice, dear." She didn't seem fazed. "Is it a fitness story?"

"A—a fitness story? Um, no. Not precisely. Why do you ask that?"

"Just that he was so sporty. Dearie me, always getting up early to go exercise. Weight-lifting nonsense." She raised a plump arm and pretended to make a muscle. "And then of course all that fruit he liked to eat. I baked this cake with the last of his bananas." She pointed enthusiastically at my plate.

"Oh." I looked down. It was excellent banana bread.

"Mind you, I've baked enough banana cakes to last a lifetime," she chattered on. "I'll have gained two stone before they're all gone. And the freezer's still stuffed with them."

I tried to steer the conversation back to Siddiqui. "You said he liked to get up early. Did he have friends he exercised with? Anyone you remember coming round?"

"No, no, I told you. No one ever visited when he actually lived here." She giggled. "I suppose you'll be wanting to see his room, too?"

I followed her up the stairs. It was an ordinary room. Single bed, a desk and chair, a small sink in the corner. No books on the shelves. Everything wiped clean. I sighed. This had been a dead end too.

Mrs. Forsyth was staring out the window. "I do wish they would hurry up and collect that crate," she tutted. "It's been there nearly two weeks this time."

I followed her gaze. Near the back of the forlorn-looking garden sat a huge wooden packing crate. It was nearly the size of a car.

"Furniture delivery?"

"No, bless him, that's the bananas."

"The bananas?"

"The delivery crate for the bananas. He got them every few weeks. I told you. I don't know how he ate as many as he did."

"But—you don't mean—that entire crate was full of bananas?" I stared. "But that must hold hundreds of them. Thousands, even. Where were they from?"

"Pakistan, of course. He said bananas in the shops here don't taste the same. He likes the Pakistani ones he grew up with. And they won't ship just a few bunches at a time." She smiled fondly, as if recalling a wayward child. "They are really splendid bananas, I must say. I just wish he'd chucked out that box before he went."

On my way out I peeked over the garden wall at the crate. It must have been five feet high and eight feet long. On the top it was stamped KARACHI, PAKISTAN. On the side was this logo:

Habibi Farms—Pakistan's Finest Produce. No one can beat the taste of our fruits!

20

There are two ways to make Hyde Rawlins happy, so far as I can tell.

The first is a very good, very cold bottle of sauvignon blanc. The second is a very good, very well-reported story that he can run on the front page of his newspaper.

Unfortunately I was not in a position to produce either today.

By four o'clock I forced myself to stop procrastinating and call him.

"Hyde Rawlins," he answered.

"Hi, Hyde."

"Ms. James. Is that you? How are you? Where are you? Except . . .

that can't possibly be you. Because you're on a plane right now flying back here to Boston. Aren't you?"

"Actually, I couldn't make that flight. I had to go see Petronella this morning, and then I got some leads to chase here."

"You had to go see Petronella?"

"You remember, Thom's girlfriend. Except I'm not sure we can really call her that. Since she dumped him, or so she says. But she's flying over for the funeral anyway."

"Is she now? What a novel idea. Flying over for the funeral, I mean. I seem to remember giving someone a direct order to do exactly that. A reporter, as I recall. Does that ring any bells?"

"Yes. And I'm sorry. But couldn't someone on the national desk do it? I mean, is anyone there actually likely to say much? We won't be able to get close to the family. And I wanted to chase down these leads over here."

Hyde sighed long-sufferingly. I could picture him removing his reading glasses, running his fingers through his silver hair. "I see," he said finally. "Tell me about these wonderful leads."

"Well. I'm trying to find out about a man named Nadeem Siddiqui. He was at the party Thom hosted last Monday night. He seems to be an unusual character. I met his landlady. He ordered enormous—I mean really, really huge—crates of bananas delivered from Pakistan. Someplace called Habibi Farms."

"Mmm-hmm."

"He's a nuclear physicist. Also, and I'm not sure if this is relevant, but Petronella ran into him in Thom's room yesterday. He wasn't supposed to be in there. Somehow he'd gotten in without a key and was nosing around."

I carried on for several more minutes, trying to explain.

Eventually Hyde interrupted, "So, let's summarize. You have discovered a Pakistani scientist with a prodigious appetite for fruit who may or may not have any connection whatsoever to the death of Thomas Carlyle?"

"Well, yes, but . . ."

"And meanwhile the wretched Miss Black has bumped into our Pakistani friend, which is newsworthy . . . Why was it again?"

"The room was locked, Hyde," I said sullenly.

"Alex."

I winced. My first name. Bad sign.

"Allow me to follow up," he said. "What does the fruit company—what was it? Hamdaani Fruit? Husseini Foods?"

"Habibi Farms."

"Right. What do they say about the deliveries? Can they give you a number for Siddiqui?"

"I haven't checked them out yet."

"And this 'exchange coordinator' for the scientists, would he give you Siddiqui's number?"

"I haven't had a chance to call him yet."

"What about the porters at Emmanuel? Did they say they'd let anyone into Carlyle's room or lent out a key?"

"I need to go over there and ask."

"*Alex!*" exploded Hyde. "If you're going to go on a wild-goose chase, at least chase the goddamn goose!"

I let this hang there for a minute. Then I repeated slowly: "Chase . . . the goddamn goose?"

"Chase the goddamn bastard goose, Alex. Don't feed me these half-baked conspiracies about a Pakistani banana fiend and an airhead ex-girlfriend—"

"Petronella's not an airhead. A bitch, maybe, but not an airhead."

"Whatever. This all sounds like total rubbish to me. But if you think there's something there, report it out. Make the calls. Ask your questions. Do your homework. And then write me a goddamn story."

"Okay. Thank you. I'm on it."

"Good." Hyde let out a deep breath. "And, Alex, contrary to your apparent impression, my patience is not infinite. You've got one day."

* * *

BACK AT THE CROWNE PLAZA hotel, the front-desk attendant gave me a knowing wink. I took it to mean Lucien Sly's presence this morning had not gone unnoticed.

I ignored him and checked back in. The new room was bigger and brighter. I called room service and ordered myself two gin and tonics. I asked for extra lemon and extra ice. Perhaps that would encourage them to cough up a lone sliver of citrus.

Then I opened my laptop and got to work. The website for Habibi Farms Foods Company greeted me with a slogan similar to the one I'd seen on the packing crate: *Pakistan's Finest Produce. We don't make compromise on QUALITY.* They specialized in bananas, mangos, oranges, cucumber, guava, and something called chikoos. I clicked on the banana order page. Delivery time was four working days. Minimum order was a hundred dozen. Jesus. Nadeem had been ordering twelve hundred bananas a month? That meant eating forty a day. Even at the rate his landlady appeared to be freezing the overflow and converting them to banana bread, it seemed a tad excessive.

Under the CONTACT US tab I found an address in Karachi and a phone number.

I didn't expect anyone to answer. It must be past business hours in Pakistan. But I dialed anyway.

The phone rang a few times and then, sounding far away, a woman's voice answered, "Habibi Farms, how may I help you?" I recognized the singsongy, vaguely irritating accent of the subcontinent.

"Oh. Hello. I was calling to check on an order. A banana order. Placed by Mr. Nadeem Siddiqui."

"Yes, of course. To whom am I speaking?"

"This is . . . his secretary."

I could hear her tapping away at a keyboard. After a moment she said, "I'm sorry, what was the name on the order again?"

I spelled the name for her and she started tapping again.

"No, I'm sorry. There is no order record for that name."

"Well . . . I'm quite sure the deliveries have been arriving from you. There would have been one in the last month. Is it possible to search by destination? They would have been sent to Cambridge, England."

"Certainly, madam. One moment. I'll see if our shipping supervisor is still available." She put me on hold.

I couldn't imagine that Habibi Farms was shipping many crates of Pakistani bananas to Cambridge, England. Surely it wouldn't be too difficult to locate Nadeem's order.

After a good five minutes the woman returned. Her voice sounded completely different. Nervous. "What did you say your name was?"

I hesitated. Well, why not? "Alexandra James."

"And how did you get this telephone number?"

"What? Off your website," I said, confused. What an odd question.

"I'm afraid I have no information about an order for Cambridge, England." Before I could respond, she hung up.

I DIDN'T GET LUCKY UNTIL later that night.

I had tried the number Gitta Juette gave me for the research exchange coordinator. It rang and rang.

Next I did the obvious thing, which was to google Nadeem Siddiqui. A real estate agent in Detroit popped up, along with an obstetrician in New Delhi. Apparently it was a common name. Finally I found what looked like a match. A brief trade-journal item from three years ago mentioned that a Nadeem Siddiqui had taken up the position of assistant research director at Khan Research Laboratories (KRL) in Kahuta, Pakistan. Siddiqui had degrees from the University of Karachi and the Technical University of Hamburg-Harburg in Germany. His age was given as twenty-eight, which would make him thirty-one now.

That was it. There was no other information, no photo. No mention anywhere of his teaching stint here in Cambridge.

I sipped my gin and tonic. Tried to think if I'd missed any angle. Then it came to me. Mrs. Forsyth had said Siddiqui was into weight lifting.

I turned back to my laptop and quickly found half a dozen gyms with free weights around Cambridge. It was well into evening by now, but they might still be open to accommodate the after-work crowd. I started with the swankier-sounding gyms. L.A. Fitness Club and the Leys Sports Complex had no membership record for a Nadeem Siddiqui. Neither did the Kelsey Kerridge gym, where I vaguely remembered attending a ladies' Pilates class when I had studied here.

Then I tried Fenner's. That's the official university gym.

A man answered, "Fenner's, Dave here."

"Hi, I'm calling for a friend who's been using the weight-lifting room—"

"You mean the power-lifting room?"

"Um . . . that's where the weights and dumbbells and things are?" I was speaking a foreign language. I've never lifted a weight in my life.

"Yup. But I don't think you'll get in tonight. We close at ten and there's already a wait list."

"Right. No, no, that's fine. I meant I'm calling for a friend who's used the weight—the power-lifting room, rather—and he's had to leave town suddenly. And he wanted to make sure you had his forwarding address."

"I'm . . . not sure we would need any forwarding address, miss. But what's the name?"

"Nadeem Siddiqui." I spelled it.

"Hold on."

And that's when I got lucky.

"Glad you rang, actually," Dave said when he came back on the line. "Your friend owes a tenner in locker fines."

"Locker fines? He has a locker there?"

"He's overdue for this month. You say he's moved? We'll have to put his things in lost and found."

"No, no, I'm sure he'd want me to collect them," I lied. "I can pay the fine. I'll come right over."

Fenner's smelled of chlorine and sweat. Dave turned out to be a skinny, pimply guy in baggy shorts. He was lounging behind the reception desk eating a sports energy bar. He made me sign a piece of paper and pay him the ten pounds before he trotted off to the men's changing room with the master key.

He returned a few minutes later with a plastic bag.

I took it outside and sat down on the steps.

It contained a rank-smelling towel and a black T-shirt. Also an empty water bottle and a balled-up pair of socks. I was wadding them back up when I realized I'd gotten very lucky indeed. At the bottom of the bag was a cell phone.

21

It was a cheap-looking phone. Black plastic, the kind that flips open.

I switched it on. The little gray screen lit up. It showed an empty address book. There was no record of any text messages, nor of any incoming calls. But the call log showed two outgoing calls. Both were made one week ago. Both numbers looked to be in Pakistan.

I copied them into my reporters' notebook. Pakistan was four or five hours ahead of the UK. It would be past midnight there now. Still, if one of these was Siddiqui's number, and I could reach him and clear things up tonight . . .

I got my notebook and a pen ready and hit the redial button for the first number.

It rang six times.

Then a voice answered, "Malik?"

I froze. A moment passed.

"Malik?" Then several words in a language I did not understand. The voice—a male voice—waited for an answer.

"Hello?" I said finally. Then, sounding idiotic: "Nadeem Siddiqui?"

Silence. The man hung up.

I copied the word *Malik* into my notebook. Underlined it. Was it a greeting? A name? I stared at the phone. I wasn't even sure this phone was Nadeem Siddiqui's, and I definitely wasn't sure what any of this had to do with Thom Carlyle. All I knew was I'd just managed to piss off someone in the middle of the night in Pakistan.

But then I studied the second number. It looked familiar. I paged through my notebook, until I found the number for Habibi Farms. I compared them. They were almost identical. Just the last two digits were different, as though they belonged to different extensions at the same business.

So this must be Siddiqui's phone. There couldn't be two people with lockers at Fenner's university gym who were making calls to Pakistani fruit exporters. He had called just last week. Why? To give them a change of address? To cancel all further orders? The only way to find out was to call. But given my earlier, odd conversation with the woman who answered the main number, I wasn't confident I'd get anything out of them. I had no idea how big a company it was, and if the same woman answered, she would recognize my voice.

I thought about it. I needed someone to call on my behalf. Someone who would sound persuasive, someone good at getting people to do what he wanted.

I slid my own phone out of my pocket and dialed.

He answered on the fourth ring.

"Hello?" said Lucien Sly.

* * *

LUCIEN AGREED TO MEET ME at the hotel only after extracting promises that I would have a cold drink waiting and that I would be wearing a disgracefully short skirt.

I stopped at a liquor store named Oddbins on the walk back from the gym and picked up white wine and a bottle of gin. He would have to live with the knee-length dress I'd had on since this morning. Miniskirts and sexy lingerie hadn't exactly been high on my packing list when I was throwing clothes into my suitcase at home last Thursday. Not that I would have tarted myself up just because he'd asked me to. Not that I had any intention of sleeping with him again.

Lucien showed up at my hotel half an hour later. He strolled in and poured us each a glass of the wine. He didn't ask why I'd returned to Cambridge for another night. Instead he looked increasingly amused as I explained my predicament.

"So essentially, you've no idea who will answer the phone at this Habibi Farms place, or what exactly you're trying to find out, or how this relates in any way to your alleged assignment, but you want me to weasel as much detail out of them as possible? Is that the gist?"

I frowned. He sounded like Hyde. "Anything we can get about why Siddiqui was calling before. And if they know how to reach him now."

"And if they ask who I am and why I need to know about this Mr. Siddiqui's fruit orders?"

"Well, you could leave the vague impression that you're some sort of business associate of his. And sound a little intimidating. Haughty. As though you're quite important and pressed for time."

He flopped into an armchair. "You want me to pose as a self-important prick? Can't do it. Obviously. Too much of a stretch." He smirked.

I rolled my eyes. "Can we just get on with this, please?"

"All right, all right. Don't get your knickers in a twist. But you do know that it's got to be something like two in the morning there? Shouldn't we wait till morning? No one's going to answer now anyway."

I paused. That would of course be the sensible thing to do. But I only had a day until Hyde was going to yank me off the story, and I wanted to keep going.

I held up the phone. "Let's just try," I pleaded. "Someone might be there."

He sighed. "Fine. Hand it here."

I highlighted the second number on the phone and pressed redial. Then I leaned in so I could hear.

Sure enough, it was a recording. "You have reached the office of Mr. Aziz at Habibi Produce and Shipping," said a female voice. "Please leave a message and he will return your call." She repeated the message in a foreign language. Urdu? Pashto? What did they speak in Karachi?

I hung up and slumped onto the bed. "Well, that was a waste of time. Sorry for dragging you over here. I'm on deadline for tomorrow and now I can't get anything done until the whole damn country of Pakistan wakes up in the morning."

"Mmm. Luckily I have quite a good idea for what we could do to pass the time." Lucien leaned over and topped up my glass. "Let's get trollied and go to bed again."

I threw a pillow at him.

He started tickling me.

I tried to kick him and missed.

"That old-ninny dress you're wearing must be restricting your movements. Shall I loosen it and liberate those legs? Then you can kick all you want." He bit my ear, hard.

And you can probably guess what happened after that.

22

Thirty-three thousand feet above the Atlantic, Nadeem Siddiqui was squirming, trying to get comfortable in his seat. He was a compact man, five feet six inches and lean. But this was his third transatlantic flight in a week. His leg muscles flinched at being crammed under yet another reclining seat back and tray table. He stretched his neck and shoulders and then gave up, settling back against the greasy headrest.

What a disaster of a week it had been. To have topped it off by running into the girl yesterday was a stroke of such preposterously bad luck that it almost defied belief. He had frozen when he heard the lock turn and the door open. And then to find Petronella Black standing there . . .

As usual, he could think of nothing to say to her. She intimidated him. Most Western women did, but Thomas Carlyle's girlfriend especially so. She was beautiful. Bewitchingly so. The embodiment of everything he desired and despised about the West, wrapped up in one slender, silky package.

Luckily she had seemed as uninterested in him as ever yesterday, despite the odd circumstances of their meeting. He thought he had pulled it off, just. He had learned to keep quiet. Never say more than required in a situation. It would only come back to trip you up. So with Petronella, once he had recovered his wits sufficiently to speak, he had murmured his sympathies, and then a flimsy excuse about losing something. Ironically, this was the truth, and she had seemed to buy it. She had actually looked bored.

The British often were, in Nadeem's experience. The chattering classes who thrived at Cambridge were so thoroughly self-absorbed, so focused on their lager-soaked ambitions, that a quiet Pakistani man could move among them as a shadow. This was an advantage. He had been able to keep to himself. He focused on his own ambitions.

Still, he had hated his months in Cambridge. He hated the cobbles, the courts, the chapels, the colleges. He hated the cheery little tea shops, the medieval streets now clogged with belching tour buses. He hated the students whizzing past on bicycles, threatening to knock him down, their bright, stripy scarves flying behind. Most of all he hated the damp. It seemed to seep from everywhere—from his sheets and blankets, from underneath the floorboards of the room he rented near the train station. Every day he choked down the limp tuna-mayonnaise sandwiches that passed for a meal in that wretched country and counted the days until his escape. The only person who had shown him kindness was his ridiculous, plump little landlady, tutting over her loaves of banana bread. Nadeem snorted. He looked forward to never eating another banana as long as he lived.

He shifted position again and rubbed his leg where it had fallen asleep. He closed his eyes. He was still uncomfortable, but now another, unfamiliar sensation was creeping over him. Calm. England was receding behind him. He would not be going back. The most important work still lay ahead, but he was back on the right track. The lost phone was a distraction, nothing more.

The whole episode with Thomas Carlyle . . . well, he had taken care of it. There were bound to be hiccups in an operation such as this. Of course, it looked bad for him. His handlers had not been pleased. No, it was worse than that: they had threatened to delay the whole operation, to replace him and start again. He was compromised. They asked, over and over, what had Carlyle heard? Whom could he have told? How—exactly—had he died?

And Nadeem had assured them, over and over, it was nothing. Carlyle had told no one. There were no traces.

23

was jolted from sleep at five in the morning when my cell phone rang.

I groped around for it in the dark. "Hello?" I answered groggily.

"Hello? Hello? Who is this?" a man demanded. He had a strong accent.

"What? Who is *this*? You called *me*." I dragged myself into a sitting position and turned on the light.

"I— Yes. Excuse me. This is Dr. Syed Qureshi. My telephone shows I missed two calls yesterday from this number. But there was no message. To whom am I speaking?"

Syed Qureshi. The name sounded familiar. I was still half-asleep. Then it clicked. The exchange coordinator in Pakistan. The man Gitta Juette had told me to contact. I had tried him a couple of times yesterday, but he never answered.

"Of course, yes. My name is Alexandra James."

"And you are calling from America?"

"Well, no, actually. I'm in England. In Cambridge. I was hoping you might be able to put me in touch with Nadeem Siddiqui."

"Nadeem!" the man sounded relieved. "He is with you? We have been very worried."

"No, no. I am looking for him. The lab—Cavendish Laboratory— gave me your phone number. They said you could put me in touch."

"I do not understand."

I was getting frustrated. "I need to speak with Mr. Siddiqui for some . . . some research I'm working on. He's finished his program here, as I'm sure you know, and I wondered if you could help me contact him."

Qureshi was quiet for a moment. "But I was hoping you could do the same. You work at Cavendish, did you say?"

"No. But Dr. Juette there gave me your number. Listen, I just need to speak with him briefly—"

"But he is not here. I thought—I thought he might have stayed on in Cambridge a bit longer. His feedback from there was excellent. But he was expected back at work here last week. And he has not appeared. It is most irregular, Miss James. It reflects most poorly on my program." He sounded huffy, as though I were responsible in some way for Nadeem Siddiqui's truancy.

I was thinking fast, trying to recall the trade-journal blurb that had mentioned where Siddiqui worked. "So he was expected back at—um— back in Karachi last week?"

"No, at Kahuta," Qureshi said impatiently. "They will revoke his clearance, you know. They will do that. Even with his seniority now. An unexplained absence will not be tolerated. And I am really very worried this will endanger future funding for my—"

"If you could just give me his e-mail address, Dr. Qureshi. Perhaps I could speak with him."

"No," he said sadly. "No. I have tried that. Several times. He is not responding."

THAT LAST CONVERSATION MIGHT HAVE been the tipping point for me. The tipping point where I became irrevocably interested in the story of Nadeem Siddiqui, whether or not he had anything to do with the death of Thomas Carlyle.

But I think actually it was this next one that did it.

After I hung up with Dr. Qureshi, I nudged Lucien awake.

"Holy mother of God," he moaned. He opened one eye. "Unless you're in the market for another shag, it can't possibly be time to wake up."

"Time to call Pakistan."

He shifted his eyes to the clock on the nightstand. "Or we could call them at eight. Or nine even." He held out his arms to me. "Come back to bed."

"Lucien. Please. It will take five minutes. And then I will tuck you back in and you can sleep as late as you want."

"And you can't do this yourself, because . . . ?"

"Because they might recognize my voice. I told you that."

"Right. I'd forgotten you were so thick with the Pakistani fruit-export community."

But he rolled over and held out his hand for the phone. I think he could tell there was no use arguing. I reminded him what he should say. He groaned in a can-we-just-get-on-with-this kind of way, and then I hit the redial button.

This time someone answered right away.

"Mr. Malik? Good morning. Is everything all right?" It was a man. He sounded worried.

Lucien and I looked at each other. That name again. *Malik*. Who was Malik? And why did everyone who took calls from Nadeem Siddiqui expect to speak to him?

"Hello, Mr. Aziz," Lucien said crisply. Well done, remembering the name we'd heard on the voice mail yesterday. "Just calling to check in."

"Mr. Malik? Is that you?"

Mr. Aziz, whoever he was, must have caller ID. Either that, or else only one person ever used the number we'd just dialed. From the way he'd answered, Aziz was clearly expecting a specific caller.

Lucien raised his eyebrows at me questioningly, then pressed on. "This is Lucien Sly. I am an associate of his. He asked me to check on the status."

Lucien was good. His wording was perfect. *The status* could refer to anything, after all. He was fishing.

But the voice on the other end sounded uncertain. "I don't know you. I deal with Mr. Malik."

"Of course," Lucien said soothingly. "But Mr. Malik is—is traveling right now, as I'm sure you know. That is why he gave me your name and number. And why he asked me to use this phone, his phone. So I could check the status."

Aziz hesitated. Then he cleared his throat. "But the status is the same as when I last spoke to Mr. Malik. We shipped on the twenty-first."

"Yes, yes, the twenty-first," said Lucien, still winging it. "Do you have any update though on the arrival date?"

"I believe it's still due to arrive later today."

"Splendid! Mr. Malik will be pleased. Yes. But he did also ask me to reconfirm the delivery address. Could you just read it back to me?"

"But it's the same address as I discussed with Mr. Malik," protested Aziz. "He said he would be there to meet it."

He would be there to meet it? I had no idea who this Mr. Malik was, or what shipment we were talking about, but it suddenly seemed urgent to find out where it was headed. I made frantic little hand gestures at Lucien. He batted me away.

"I'm well aware that you and Mr. Malik have discussed this," he said sternly into the phone. "But you will appreciate the importance of confirming these details? It is in everyone's interest, certainly yours I would remind you, to ensure that everything goes smoothly. Now let's go over this again."

When Aziz spoke again, he sounded rattled. He read Lucien a tracking number. And an address. An address in the United States. An address just outside Washington, DC.

I WENT FOR A LONG run that morning, or a long run by my standards— the reverse of my Sunday loop, sprinting out across Parker's Piece and then several slow miles tracing the banks of the Cam.

I was trying to collect my thoughts. What did I actually know at this point? Often it helps if I try to write the news story in my head—figure out what my lede is, and what evidence and quotes I have to support it. Right now I had nothing remotely worthy of filing for the paper. My assignment was to investigate the death of Thomas Carlyle, and since last week I'd managed to accomplish very little on that front. I'd met his girlfriend. I'd seen where he lived. And I had learned that a man who had no reason to be in his room had possibly broken in and rifled through Thom's things, five days after he'd died.

But so what? That might have absolutely nothing to do with Thom's death. And it hardly made Siddiqui a murderer. Maybe Siddiqui really had left something in Thom's room. Maybe Petronella had been mistaken about the door's being locked. And maybe Siddiqui—a respectable Oxbridge lecturer, after all—had decided to take a spur-of-the-moment-vacation, and that's why no one could track him down just now. Again, no crime there.

It did seem strange that he'd bumped into Petronella in Emmanuel College two days ago, when his landlady was under the impression that he'd left Cambridge. And I couldn't think of how this Malik character fit into the picture. Who was he? A friend of Siddiqui's? A workout buddy? Maybe an American, since he was having deliveries shipped to Washington.

Lots of things didn't make sense. But nothing seemed overtly illegal.

I sighed. Hyde was right. I didn't have anything, really. Only . . . how had he put it? A half-baked conspiracy about a Pakistani banana fiend.

24

Elias was already up and on the treadmill when I called. Eleven in the morning my time, 6:00 a.m. for him in Washington.

Elias and I started at the *Chronicle* the same week. We were summer interns together, competing over stories like shark sightings on the Cape and the sinkhole that swallowed a professor's car in the MIT parking lot. A few times over that long, sticky summer we would buy cheap seats for Red Sox games and bike over to Fenway after work, to drink beer and eat hot dogs and complain about the metro editor. There was never anything remotely romantic about our friendship. That was why it worked, and why it has lasted. And why now, when I had no idea what to do next, and Hyde was probably preparing to scalp me alive, I called Elias.

Around the same time I finally got promoted to cover the universities, he got the chance to fill in for a few months down in the Washington bureau, while the regular White House reporter, Nora Cooke, took maternity leave. He thrived. He filed stories nearly every day, often for the front page. He even managed to scoop the *Washington Post* and the *New York Times* a couple of times. The news managers noticed. When Nora came back from leave in a huff two weeks early, to reassert her seniority, they kept finding excuses to keep Elias in Washington. He managed to secure a Pentagon hard pass and became a fixture at the Defense and State Department briefings. He somehow weaseled an interview with the head of the CIA, a man who rarely gave interviews. After a year, management bowed to the inevitable and named him national security correspondent. Elias says the secret is to get to the newsroom first and then work harder all day than anyone else. That, and always to have an important-sounding but vague series in the works, the better to dodge dull daily assignments.

"Hi, Ginger," he panted now, picking up on the third ring.

"Good grief. Only you would already be in the gym. Or at least I hope that's why you're panting. How many miles?"

"Two to go. What's up?"

I smiled. Leave it to Elias to have already accomplished as much as I had today, when thanks to the time difference I had a five-hour head start on him.

"It's the Thom Carlyle story. I'm still in England."

"I know. That didn't go down so well yesterday on the three p.m. call."

The three p.m. call would be the daily conference call among editors planning the next day's front page. "It didn't? How do you know?"

"Because the Washington bureau got dragged into figuring out how to cover the funeral today when it turned out you weren't going to be there. I think they're going to leave it as a White House story."

"A White House story? Why?"

"POTUS and FLOTUS are going, you know." The president and the first lady. "Nora managed to get in the press pool on the plane up with him. So she'll write the story with a Boston dateline. The Silver Fox was ranting about it, but I guess there was only so much he could say, since he's the one who let you go to England in the first place."

I nodded. "Hyde thinks I'm on a wild-goose chase over here."

"Actually, I gather his language was somewhat more colorful than that."

"Ouch. Did he say I should be chasing the goddamn bastard goose?"

"What?"

"Nothing. Forget it. But I do actually need your help."

"Okay. Shoot."

"This wild-goose chase I'm on has to do with a guy named Nadeem Siddiqui. He was at a party Thom threw the night before he died. And then he may have broken into Thom's room last weekend. And now he's gone missing."

"Gone missing how?"

"Well, I don't know if he's missing exactly, but he was supposed to have gone back to work in Pakistan and he hasn't. He's not replying to e-mail"—I'd finally gotten Syed Qureshi, the exchange coordinator, to give me the address—"and nobody seems to know where to find him."

"Well, maybe he's on vacation."

"Maybe. There's this other weird stuff, though, about a package that's getting delivered to the States. The point is, I really need to talk to him, and I'm wondering if there's a way to find out if he's left the UK. What's the Homeland Security–type agency for the UK, do you know? If we could find the right person, could they give us a steer, just as to when and where his passport last scanned?"

"I would say that's a *veeery* long shot. I have no idea where even to start calling in the UK. And there would be privacy issues involved.

They're not going to just check up on a private citizen and leak his travel plans to a reporter, Alex."

I took a deep breath. "Well . . . okay, fine then. What about trying to track him down through his employer. He's a nuclear physicist. He works at someplace called . . . hang on . . ." I flipped through my notebook. "Here we go. Kohuto."

"Kahuta? In Pakistan?"

"Yes. I think that's right."

"That's the big nuclear facility. The headquarters."

"I did say he was a nuclear physicist."

"Right, but, I mean, it's famous, Alex. A. Q. Khan and all that."

"Oh."

"Only the biggest nuclear-proliferation scandal in history. How can you not have heard of it? Have you actually read my byline in the last several years?"

"Darling, you know I live for your byline," I said sweetly. "So, do you have any sources there? Anyone who could help me track down our friend Nadeem Siddiqui?"

"Sources at Kahuta," snorted Elias. "Obviously, sure. They're coming out of my ears. Those guys just won't stop hassling me. Jeez. Hang on." Elias was huffing and puffing now. The treadmill machine let out a series of beeps as he slowed it down to a walk.

"Seriously, Alex, they don't exactly let you just fly to Pakistan, wander around the nuclear labs, and chitchat with folks. But let me think. . . . I tell you what. There's a guy here in Washington who used to be a military attaché to Pakistan. He works Pak nuke issues now for INR—the intel guys at the State Department. And then there's a very good source of mine out at Langley. Proliferation, Pakistan, some Iran stuff too, I think. He's pretty high up. I can run your guy's name past them, see if it raises any flags. But, Alex, these are good sources. I don't want to embarrass myself. Do you really need this?"

"I really need this."

"Anything else I can use? To drag these conversations out to sixty seconds before they hang up on me?"

I told him the address where Nadeem had been renting, upstairs at Mrs. Forsyth's. "She says he's really into weight lifting. And what else . . . oh, he ordered bananas there. From Pakistan. Like, thousands of them."

"Bananas, huh?" Elias burst out laughing. "Yeah, that'll get 'em talking. I've noticed that about spooks. Give them a Chiquita angle and they just can't stop blabbing."

I glared at my phone. "If you're quite finished with the sarcasm, I'll let you go now."

"Oh, man." He was wheezing now, whether from laughter or the treadmill, I couldn't tell. "I needed that. I was just reading something interesting about bananas, actually. Can't think what it was. Or where." He giggled again. "Probably some article my mom forwarded, telling me to eat more fruit. Anyway. I'll keep you posted on what I hear back. Talk soon, okay?"

"Okay. Bye, Shorty."

"Bye, Ginger."

25

Two hours later, at the US embassy in London, the phone rang. Jake Pearson answered on the second ring.

He was glad for the interruption. It had been an unusually slow day so far, and the prospect of spending the afternoon sorting through the paperwork piled up on his desk did not excite him. He had already fit in a long session at the embassy gym, three sets of pull-ups, squats, and free weights followed by half an hour on the StairMaster. He took pride in maintaining the physique of his college-football days. He was now approaching middle age, and long days sitting at a desk had added a bit more . . . *substance* to his frame, but he liked to think it made him look imposing.

Pearson worked in the embassy's commercial-affairs office. He was senior manager, charged with promoting exports of American goods and services into the UK market. At least, that is what it said on his business cards. In reality, Pearson knew little about trade issues. When he reported to work at the great hulking building on Grosvenor Square each morning, he took the elevator straight down, to the windowless, underground floors that housed the CIA's London station.

He had worked here for three years. It wasn't entirely clear what his job was—the responsibilities kept evolving—but essentially he was a logistics guy. He organized planes and passports for colleagues heading off to more exotic destinations. He knew where the safe houses were, and how to move money in ways that no foreign spy service—or US congressional committee—would ever see. He knew how to get things done. And he had one other key attribute, which was that he had no scruples. He did as he was asked, efficiently and quietly, because that was his job. He left the legal and ethical dilemmas to his bosses. Jake Pearson was that rarest of creatures at the CIA: a man who slept well at night.

Now, as he listened down the secure phone line to this latest request, he did allow himself briefly to wonder, Why me? It seemed a task better directed at one of his cloak-and-dagger colleagues. Pearson might serve on the operations side of the CIA, but he was a facilitator, not a spy. He used his real name at work. It was on the buzzer at his apartment building. But for this one assignment, the caller was suggesting he use a false identity. Anything would do. He would only need to use it for a few hours, and the cover did not need to stand up to scrutiny.

Pearson shrugged. It was really not in his nature to ask questions. The request was clear enough. He finished listening, nodded, and hung up the phone. He was about to have quite a different afternoon than he had planned.

26

That afternoon found me wedged into a blue plastic chair at the Cambridge train station.

I was waiting for the 2:35 p.m. express back down to London. Even I couldn't think of any good reason to stay on in Cambridge. Or England at all, for that matter, not when I seemed to be spending all my time on the phone either to Pakistan or to the United States. I'd made up my mind to catch the first flight back to Boston in the morning. I could keep working the phones from there. And it would be better to face the wrath of Hyde in person.

Meanwhile, I was hatching a plan to do a bit of shopping in London this afternoon. There's a little shoe shop on Marylebone High Street that I make a point of visiting every time I'm in London. It's just opposite my favorite place for afternoon tea, Patisserie Valerie. My mood was already improving at the prospect of a new pair of heels and a pot of Darjeeling.

I was pondering whether to try to squeeze in a stroll through Regent's Park after tea when my phone rang. I shifted my notebook and my copy of the *Guardian* onto the chair next to me and pressed the button to answer.

"Miss James?" came the voice.

"Yes, speaking."

"Oh, that's great. Excellent. Glad I caught you." It was a man. Friendly sounding, American. A touch of a southern accent, perhaps. "I'm calling from the US embassy in London. I understand you're looking for some information, and I thought I'd get in touch and see if we might be able to help."

I raised my eyebrows in disbelief. "I'm sorry, what did you say your name was?"

"This is Crispin Withington." He sounded rather pleased with himself.

"Crispin . . . Withington?"

"Yes, ma'am. I wonder if you might have a moment to meet me."

"And . . . where exactly did you say you're calling from?"

"I'm with the embassy," he repeated. "It's come to my attention that you have a few questions you'd like answered, and I'd love to talk them over with you."

I sat still for a moment, puzzling this over. Then it came to me.

"Elias, for Christ's sake, if this is supposed to be funny . . ."

"Miss James, I assure you, no one's playing with you here. Your colleague conveyed your questions, and since I'm local, they were conveyed to me. Shall we meet in, say, half an hour?"

I fell silent again. Was it remotely possible that this guy was for real? That Elias's feeble inquiries on my behalf had already been relayed to the American embassy here in England? And that someone there thought they were enough of a priority to set up a same-day meeting? I didn't have much experience working sources inside the federal government bureaucracy, but this seemed implausibly efficient. Maybe Elias had more clout than I realized.

"I'm not quite sure what to make of this, Mr. . . . Withington," I managed finally. "But, yes, I'm trying to find out whether Nadeem Siddiqui—"

"Hold on, hold on. It really would be so much better to do this in person. How about we meet at Claridge's Hotel, the main lobby on Brook Street?"

"Or—why not at the embassy?"

"Oh, no need to make this complicated. Kind of a hassle to get you cleared in through security and all that. Claridge's is pretty close by. Shall we say in twenty minutes?"

"No. I could—I could make it by four o'clock or so."

"Actually, now would be good, Miss James," he said, sounding a bit less friendly than before.

Then again, so was I. First Petronella, and now this guy. What was it with the last-minute summons to mysterious meetings in London? Also—and I realize this is pathetic—but I was irritated at the prospect of my shoe-shopping splurge slipping away.

"I'm not *in* London at the moment, just so you know, so that's impossible," I said coldly. "I can be there by four. As I said. And, yes, I know where Claridge's is. I'll look forward to seeing you there."

"I'll be waiting," he said, and hung up.

AND SO HE WAS. HE'D obviously done his homework, too, because he recognized me the instant I walked through the door.

"Alexandra," he said, smiling and holding out his hand. "Great to meet you."

I was caught off guard. I'm not sure what I'd expected Crispin Withington to look like, but this wasn't it. I suppose I'd imagined someone who worked at the embassy would look more . . . diplomatic. Sophisticated, slender, fluent in five languages, that sort of thing. Instead he was built like a bouncer. Beefy. He looked utterly, unmistakably American. Withington was wearing a yellow polo shirt that strained around his biceps. It was tucked tight into a pair of neatly pressed, front-pleated, slightly too short khakis. His hair was short and sandy and his teeth were perfect. Crispin Withington would have fit right in at a meeting of the Wichita Kiwanis Club. In the lobby of a posh hotel in Mayfair, he stood out.

"How do you do, Mr. Withington." I shook his hand.

"Great." He flashed the perfect teeth. "How about we go for a walk? It's a nice day. By London standards, anyway. It'll give us a chance to stretch our legs while we talk."

He had his hand on my back and was steering me back toward the front door when I had the sense to object. I had no idea who this man really was. No way was I leaving a well-lit, public space.

"You know, I'd rather not. I've got my bag and everything." I nodded at my suitcase. "And it's easier if we sit down so I can take notes."

"Well. Let's just start by talking, why don't we?"

"Let's just start by ordering tea." Before he could answer, I grabbed my suitcase and headed straight back into the hotel. He had no choice but to follow me.

The room where they serve tea at Claridge's is legendary. I'd been there before, years ago, with one of my Scottish aunties. If it is possible for a place to be ostentatiously tasteful, Claridge's succeeds. Everything gleams in ivory and cream. The silver sparkles. The waiters manage to convey both fawning politeness and the absolute certainty that they are superior to you. I suspected it was usually impossible to get a table, but by this hour of the afternoon, the ladies-who-lunch crowd had moved on, and only a few Chinese tourists dotted the tables.

A waiter swept over. If I couldn't have my shoe splurge, I would at least get proper afternoon tea. I waved away the menu. "A pot of Darjeeling, sandwiches, scones, and clotted cream." I glanced at Withington. He looked lost. "For two," I added, and smiled at the waiter. He bowed decorously and backed away. Then I took out my notebook, opened it to a clean page, wrote *Crispin Withington* and the date across the top, and looked up. "Did I spell that correctly?" I pointed at his name.

He stared at the words as if he needed to consider the question.

"And can you give me your full title? You're from the press office? I don't know quite how it works here in London."

He leaned over, took the pen from my hand, and quietly tore the piece of paper with his name out of my notebook. "Let's just talk. Off the record."

I shook my head. "No. Let's at least start on background, meaning I can quote you, just not by name. We can figure out whether I identify you as a 'US official,' or something more specific. Otherwise this meeting isn't really much use to me."

"I'm afraid you're not grasping the point of this meeting." His tone had changed. He moved his arm close to mine on the table, not quite touching it, but the message was clear: I was not free to go.

"We are off the record, Miss James. I'll give you any guidance I can. But let's do this by my rules. Now, I understand you're interested in a certain gentleman from Pakistan, and what his current whereabouts might be. Have I got that right?"

I didn't have much choice. "Yes. That's right."

"And who exactly is this gentleman, and how do you know him?"

I wasn't sure where to begin, or how much to tell this man, whoever he was. It seemed a good bet his real name wasn't Crispin Withington. Elias had failed to answer his phone or respond yet to my e-mails asking if he knew Withington and why he'd invited me to tea. So I started with a basic summary: that in the course of my reporting the name Nadeem Siddiqui had popped up, that Siddiqui might have useful information for a story I was working on, but that he had disappeared and I needed to find him.

"And what do you know about Siddiqui? What do you want to ask him?"

Again I weighed how much to say. Then again, what did I have to lose? And journalism is like any business. There's a give-and-take; to get information sometimes you have to give some.

"Well, he is a scientist. Pakistani, as you know. He seems to have been one of the last people to see Thomas Carlyle. The White House counsel's son? Who died at Harvard last week?"

"Yeah, I remember. You've been writing about him. I read your stories before I walked over. But what's the connection to Siddiqui?" Withington looked genuinely bewildered.

"I don't know. That's the point. Just . . . Siddiqui was in Thom Carlyle's room. Twice. The night before he died, and then again just this past weekend. I don't know why. He also seems to have some . . . strange habits. And some loose ends back in Pakistan."

That seemed to get Withington's attention. "Such as?"

"No, my turn now. You haven't told me what *you* know. Or why any of this is of interest to the US embassy."

"Just trying to help. It's one of the embassy's missions to do press outreach to US reporters abroad."

I sighed. "With respect, give me a break. I've dealt with my share of press officers. And I would bet money that's not what you are. For starters, you haven't tried to present me with a souvenir memo pad or a coffee mug with the embassy seal on it yet."

This got a small smile. "I was saving them for the way out."

"Seriously. If you're not going to let me quote you, or tell me anything, why are you here?"

Withington stared into the far corner of the tearoom. He picked up a watercress sandwich, chewed it slowly, swallowed, then spoke quietly. "Nadeem Siddiqui is a person of interest. That's all I can tell you."

"But why is he of interest?"

"Oh, lots of people are of interest. For all kinds of reasons. You wouldn't believe the number of people the US government takes an interest in. See, that's your tax dollars at work."

"Come on. If you're here meeting with me, you must have some idea what makes Nadeem Siddiqui so bloody fascinating."

"You come on. You seem smart enough. I wouldn't think it would take a wild leap of imagination for a reporter to figure out that since 9/11, nuclear scientists from Siddiqui's part of the world might be of passing interest."

"Oh. So is he on some sort of nuclear watch list?"

"To be completely honest with you—and I'll admit it's an unfamiliar sensation—I don't know. There are so many different watch lists these days that it's a full-time job just trying to keep track of them."

I tried changing tact. "And what about Thomas Carlyle? What's the connection?"

"I have no idea. I don't know that there is one. Swear to God, that's a new one." He raised his right hand as if he were taking an oath. I studied him. Either he was a terrific liar or he was telling the truth.

I took a deep breath and let it out. "Fine. Let's just talk logistics then. Is Nadeem Siddiqui still in the UK? Or has he left the country?"

Withington cocked his head to one side. I wondered whether he was also weighing the universal rule of doing business: *to get information, sometimes you have to give some.*

Finally he spoke. "Just to make sure we're crystal clear. We are off the record, Miss James."

"Yes. You've been quite clear about that."

"This meeting did not happen. As far as you know, I don't even exist."

"Oh, for God's sake. Has he left the country or not?"

"There is . . . there is nothing to indicate him leaving Britain.

Nadeem Siddiqui's passport hasn't scanned since he flew in from Islamabad in March."

We were both quiet for a minute.

"Well, I guess that's something," I said finally. "At least I know where to look for him." I pushed my chair back and laid several bills on the table, to cover my share of the check.

"Hey, one last thing," Withington said. "You said Siddiqui had some strange habits. Like what?"

What the hell, I thought. "Like power lifting, whatever that is. And he likes bananas. I mean, he *really* likes bananas. He's been ordering huge crates of them. From Pakistan, every month. But I thought he must be traveling, because the latest order . . ."

"The latest order . . . ?"

I decided I'd said enough. "I guess we'll have to see. It could be . . ." I fumbled, trying to backtrack. "It could be useful if he turns up to sign for it."

"But why did you think he's traveling? Did he suspend his usual order or something?"

"How on earth would I know that?" I lied.

"Do you have a tracking number? The name of the company he orders from?"

"Nope," I lied again.

He narrowed his eyes at me, and his tone changed once more. Now he sounded menacing. "Miss James, you normally cover higher education, if I'm not mistaken. I gather Pakistani scientists and banana shipments are a bit off the beaten trail for you?"

I nodded.

"You might want to think about keeping it that way."

27

nside Harvard's Memorial Church it was hot and stuffy. The morning had dawned unusually warm for Massachusetts in June. Several hundred people sat crammed into the pews, perspiring and sneaking glances at their neighbors to gauge whether it would be rude to fan themselves with the order of service.

There had been some discussion over whether to have Thomas Carlyle's funeral here or in the church the Carlyle family attended. Thom had been baptized at Christ Church on Garden Street and had been dragged there to Christmas and Easter services all though his childhood. But there was the question of numbers: the Carlyles had many friends, they all wanted to pay their respects, and Memorial Church simply held more people.

Among those in attendance now, in the second row, sat Petronella Black.

She looked exquisite. Her creamy skin, her pearl choker necklace, and her white-blond hair all caught the morning light. Everything else was black: black sheath dress, black kid-leather Chanel pumps—but lower than she usually wore, only three-inch heels. Petronella had been born knowing what to wear. It was the emotion she had to fake.

It was a bit awkward, being seated here in the family section. She was right behind Thom's parents and sisters, next to an aunt to whom she'd been introduced earlier this morning. Thom had occasionally spoken of his family. But she had never paid much attention to the details, and now she was struggling to keep the sisters' names straight. The Carlyle clan, on the other hand, all seemed to be under the impression that she and Thom had practically been engaged. This morning when she had met Anna Carlyle, Thom's mother, Anna had embraced her and wept. Then Anna had reached down, touched the bare fourth finger on the younger woman's left hand, and smiled sorrowfully, as if to acknowledge the diamond that would now never be placed there. Thom had apparently told his family he was going to propose. And he had apparently not had the chance to tell them that she had broken things off. Even Petronella had the decency to feel mildly ashamed.

She sat now with her hands folded primly across her lap, her face arranged into the mask of a grieving fiancée. So many people had approached her this morning, patting her arm and murmuring condolences, that she was managing to convince herself that she did perhaps feel something approaching grief.

She watched Anna Carlyle's shoulders ahead of her shaking with sobs. Petronella fluttered her lashes. Slowly a tear formed in her own eye. Her handkerchief was poised. It wouldn't do to muss her mascara; it would look sloppy. Petronella did not own waterproof mascara. She had never needed it. She never allowed herself to cry.

She was trying to pay attention to the words the priest was speaking, truly she was, but it was so bloody hot in here. Her stockings itched around the ankles. She could feel her hair going flat. Also, she longed to turn around and ogle the president and the first lady. There had been a murmur when they slid inside, moments before the service began. They were sitting near the back, on their own, although she guessed Secret Service guards must be posted at the doors. Their presence lent a frisson of glamour to the otherwise mournful proceedings.

The priest droned on and on, and now it appeared there was to be another musical interlude. Was it her imagination or could she actually see heat shimmering up around the candles on the altar? A fat fly buzzed along the tops of the hymnals. Petronella fought the urge to sneak outside for a smoke. Her mind flitted in random directions. She thought of Lucien Sly. He had not returned her calls yesterday, and when she had finally reached him last night, he sounded odd. Distracted. They had exchanged pleasantries for several minutes, and it occurred to her they didn't actually have much to say to each other.

Petronella watched the lips of the priest moving in prayer. Her gaze wandered across the center aisle and settled on Joe Chang, Thom's old roommate. His cheeks were ashen and he was slumped over in what appeared to be true misery. When they had been introduced this morning on the steps of the church, he had appraised her unsmilingly and blinked in a way that seemed to say, *Now I get it.* Then he had turned and walked alone into the church.

In front of her, Anna's shoulders had stopped shaking. She was resting her head against her husband's arm, as he kissed the top of her head over and over. Lowell Carlyle had been polite to Petronella but more distant than his wife. He seemed an earnest man, more serious than his son. Making small talk with the woman his only son had loved was perhaps more than he could bear.

They were singing a hymn now, and it seemed the funeral might at last be drawing to an end. Petronella mouthed the words. The voice of one of Thom's sisters carried. Which one was she again? It was a pure, rich voice, but it trembled on one of the high notes as she began to cry.

Petronella's own eyes were dry. So many people here had loved Thom.

It was not her fault that she had not been one of them.

OUTSIDE THE CHURCH, MARCO GALLONI scanned the crowd.

He had chosen a sober black suit and tie for the occasion. Unfortunate given the heat, but it wouldn't do to stand out. He had positioned himself near the bottom of Memorial Church's wide stone steps.

Harvard police were providing basic security, steering tourists away. And of course, a Secret Service team was escorting the president and the first lady. Galloni's role was simply to watch. You never knew what you might glean from the people who turned up for a funeral, what furtive glances or snatches of conversation you might catch. If Thom Carlyle *had* been murdered, chances were he knew the person who killed him. And it followed that that person might turn up here today.

Mourners were now pouring out of the church. They formed sad little clusters on the steps, exchanging greetings and sympathies. He watched Petronella Black sweep out from the double doors and step daintily to the side. She pulled a mirrored compact out of her handbag, checked her lipstick, and fluffed her hair. Then she glanced around and disappeared around the corner of the church.

Interesting. Galloni followed her. What he saw made him shake his head. Petronella was standing in a beam of sunlight, a microphone in her face, granting an interview to an excited-looking TV reporter. The logo on the side of the camera read ABC NEWS. She must have made the arrangement earlier, figuring she could squeeze in a few minutes between the church service and the funeral cortege to the cemetery.

Tacky, thought Galloni. But then nothing about Petronella was to his taste. He had met and interviewed her briefly last night, at her hotel. She was a knockout, no question. But brittle. Snooty. And skinny, too narrow in the hip-and-ass department to hold his interest.

Not like Alex James. Galloni swatted away the thought of her. Since their brief encounter last week, he had dreamed of Alex. Erotic dreams that left him thrashing beneath his sheets. When he snapped awake, he was sweaty with pleasure and embarrassment. Yeah, he liked her. Annoying that she wasn't here today to cover the funeral. He could have suggested a drink afterward, under the pretense of hearing more about what she'd uncovered in England.

But enough. He had work to do. He left Petronella to her tawdry television chatter and walked back around to the front steps of the church. The crowd was beginning to thin. Galloni wiped the perspiration off his face and noted that the Feds he'd had to put up with for the last two days hadn't showed.

Lowell Carlyle had apparently called in a favor. Word had it he was not happy with the investigation's progress—or lack thereof—and had asked the FBI director to take a personal interest in his son's death. A flurry of phone calls around Washington had resulted in a pair of taciturn Feds swooping in. They had insisted on spending hours up in the Eliot House bell tower, taking photographs and dusting again for prints. At the station they combed through Galloni's notes. It was a nuisance. There was no reason for the FBI to take the lead, no reason not to leave the case to the Cambridge PD, other than Mr. Carlyle's status as a Washington big shot. But that wasn't what bothered Galloni. No, it was something about the two Feds themselves.

It was the questions they asked, and the way they handled evidence. They were simultaneously thorough and oddly careless. Yes, that was it. Thom Carlyle had likely been murdered, and Galloni saw his job as collecting evidence that would lead to an arrest. And then to a trial, and then eventually to a conviction. He was supposed to find the bad guy and put him behind bars. It was the way police were trained to think, the way they built a case. But these men were trained in something else. They did not appear interested in the wheels of justice.

He hadn't been sure until yesterday. The duo had deigned to join him for a drink after work, in a bar around the corner from the station. Galloni had ordered a pitcher of beer. And they had ordered . . . Chablis. *Chablis?* At happy hour in a police hangout in Kendall Square? No. No self-respecting cop went in for dry French wine. Not in public, anyway. These guys clearly worked for some federal agency. But Galloni was convinced it was not the FBI.

28

The heat got worse the farther south you went.

In Washington, DC, that day, it was insufferable. The city's notoriously swamplike summers seemed to arrive earlier every year. Local forecasters had already dubbed this first heat wave of the summer the "Beltway Meltaway"; stepping outside felt like getting slapped with a hot, sticky towel.

But inside the rooms of the Key Bridge Marriott, air-conditioning was blasting great gusts of arctic air. And Shaukat Malik was feeling good.

He liked having his own hotel room. Room 609 was near the vending machines and had two queen beds. Both were swathed in navy-

and-orange-striped fabric, as were the matching curtains, obligatory armchair, and bathroom shower curtain. He had a view out over the muddy currents of the Potomac River. And if he stood at the corner of his window and pressed his cheek to the pane, he could glimpse the tall needle of the Washington Monument.

Mind you, he was not in Washington proper, but across the river in Arlington, Virginia. A disappointment. The website had promised "a premier Georgetown location." But this was a trifle. He would see Washington tomorrow, the real insider's Washington. He would see a room few people ever laid eyes on in person. And in that room he would complete his last critical assignment.

Today, though, he had nothing to do except wait for a message that the shipment had arrived. The confirmation would arrive on his new phone. He was expecting an automated, computer-generated e-mail from the shipping company, which he would forward without comment. And that would be that. The wheels were in motion.

Malik surveyed the brown water below. He wondered what kind of birds lived along the banks of this Potomac River. He liked birds. Perhaps he would take a walk and find out. No reason not to. Let them find him if they needed to. After all, he was an important man now. An indispensable man. He clasped his hands behind his balding round head and savored the feeling: Shaukat Malik was a player.

29

taxied from Claridge's to my own—considerably less well-appointed—hotel in a state of supreme irritation. The Heathrow Comfort Lodge in Slough was as depressing as it sounds. The *Chronicle* travel agent had given up on me and my ever-changing itinerary and told me to book my own room. Ordinarily I would interpret this as carte blanche to check into the Ritz, but that seemed a bit cheeky given that I hadn't filed a story in three days now.

So the Comfort Lodge it was. At least it would be convenient for my flight in the morning. I checked in and got my room key, but there was no point rushing up to what would surely be grim quarters. Instead I flounced into the bar and ordered a double.

Then I sat brooding. This Crispin Withington character. Who the hell was he? And his parting shot—*You might want to think about keeping it that way—* What the hell was that supposed to mean? The whole encounter left me feeling unclean. I'd been outmaneuvered so thoroughly I hadn't even understood what game I was supposed to be playing.

What I wanted now was to vent to someone who would listen and not judge. I thought for a moment and then pulled out my phone and rang Lucien.

"Hallo, lovely lamb chop," he answered. "You've caught me headed to dinner. How's London?"

I glanced around the seedy little bar. "Well, I'm drinking cheap gin in a cocktail lounge, which is empty except for me and an off-duty flight crew for Aeroflot, and the sound track here appears to be Michael Bublé's greatest hits. So, you know. A promising start to the evening."

He chuckled. "Sorry it's not up to the high standards of the Eagle. And what about the banana sleuthing? Any developments on the Pakistani fruit front?"

"Umm-hmm. I spent a bizarre afternoon at Claridge's with a man purporting to be from the US embassy. He says Nadeem Siddiqui is still in Britain."

"The plot thickens!" Lucien whispered delightedly.

"Well, but I couldn't get anything else out of him. He didn't seem to think there was any connection between Siddiqui and Thom Carlyle. He wouldn't tell me anything else, not that it matters anyway, because the whole conversation was off the record. And I don't even know who this source really was, and I haven't filed a story in days, not that I even know what the story is anymore—"

"All right, all right, it's not as bad as all that," said Lucien, cutting across my ravings.

"Actually, it is."

"If you say so. Now, listen, I need to hop off—I'm just walking in to dinner with Mum and Dad—but how about I ask Dad tonight if he can help. If you think this Siddiqui chap is in Britain, and you say the American embassy is watching him, maybe Scotland Yard is too. I could ask Dad's people to make some calls."

"What do you mean 'Dad's people'?"

"His staff. He must be on some committee that has clearance for this sort of thing. God knows they sit around doing bugger all else all day."

"Sorry, I'm not following you."

"Westminster, silly. Parliament. Dad's in the House of Lords."

"Your father—you father is in the House of *Lords*?"

"Of course. Along with eight hundred other pompous old gits with titles. Not that I can think of the last time he bothered to show up and actually, say, vote on anything."

I was dumbstruck.

Lucien interpreted my silence as acceptance of his offer. "So what did you say this embassy officer's name was? Might be useful to know where the information is coming from."

"Er—I hadn't. He was a bit funny about it. Didn't want to be quoted or anything. But his name is Crispin Withington."

There was a pause.

"*Crispin Withington?*" repeated Lucien.

"Ridiculous name, I know."

"Complete bollocks name is what it is."

"What?"

But now Lucien was roaring with laughter. It was a full thirty seconds before he could pull himself together to speak.

"Let me take a wild guess here and assume that you don't closely follow British sport?"

"British—sport? What are you talking about?"

"Only that Crispin Withington"—he had to stop here and chortle again—"only that Crispin Withington is wicketkeeper for the England cricket team, Alex. He's in the papers quite often. And it's, um, rather a distinctive name. So unless our man Crisps is exploring a radical career change, I very much doubt he's now spokesman for the American embassy."

For the second time in this conversation I was stunned into silence. Then, slowly, I began to smile. The ludicrousness, the sheer absurdity, of the last few days hit me with force. Hyde was right. I was on a goddamn bastard wild-goose chase. I was meeting men masquerading as English cricket players for tea, and swapping banana-bread recipes with loopy landladies, and stalking fruit exporters in Pakistan. And none of it was yielding a single scrap of news about my alleged assignment, Thomas Carlyle.

"Alex? Are you still there?" Lucien sounded worried.

I began to giggle.

He began to laugh again.

Soon the two of us were cackling away like a couple of demented hyenas. What can you do?

THE SITUATION DID NOT SEEM so funny later that evening when I finally dragged myself up to my room, opened my laptop, and typed in the website address for Habibi Farms.

I had decided to go back over everything I knew. I wanted to write it all down in one place and see if the fragments added up to something. Otherwise I would have to call Hyde back in the newsroom and admit defeat.

The company that had been selling Nadeem Siddiqui his bananas seemed a reasonable place to start. But when I tried to pull it up to check for any details I might have missed, the page was gone.

Safari can't find the server, my computer announced. I tried again. Same result. Then I googled it. Nothing. Not a single hit. I flipped through my notebook to where I'd written down the phone number, the one the nervous woman had answered. I called and listened to its ringing. No answer.

A little chill went up my spine.

Next I pulled up FedEx and tapped in the tracking number that Lucien had managed to extract from Mr. Aziz. At least the FedEx website still appeared to exist, which after the last couple of minutes felt like a minor victory. *Locating transaction record,* the computer reported. I held my breath. Then, a message: *Your item was delivered at 11:09 am on June 29 in DULLES, VA 20166. Find another item?*

There was no other information. Nothing about the contents or the billing address or the intended recipient.

I stared at this information, my mind ticking. Then I copied it down.

I needed to do one more thing. Something I wished I'd done before I went to Claridge's. I pulled up the phone number for the press office at the US embassy. It went straight to voice mail. But the message included an after-hours cell phone number. I called.

"Hello," answered a grouchy American voice.

"Hi. This is Alexandra James calling from the *New England Chronicle.*"

"Okay."

"Am I through to the duty press officer?"

"That would be me. Sally Harlow."

"Great. Sally, hi. Sorry to bother you after office hours. But I had a meeting today with someone from your office, and I want to make sure I was speaking with the right person. I mean, I'm not sure I got his name right. I'm on deadline."

She made a little tutting sound. "That's why you're supposed to double-check these things at the time of the interview. So what's the name?"

"Well, he said it was Crispin Withington."

"Never heard of him."

"Not in the press office?"

"Definitely not."

"Listen," I persisted. "Part of what I'm confused about is exactly what his title is. He may be—he may work in another part of the embassy. It's pretty big, right? Do you have some sort of embassy directory we could check?"

"That's what I'm doing." I could hear her typing. "Not there . . . not there . . . Spell the name for me?"

I did. More typing.

"Nope," she said finally. "Definitely, definitively no one working at the embassy by the name of Crispin Withington. You can quote me. Maybe somebody from the State Department in Washington? They'd be the ones more likely to be dealing with American reporters, anyway."

"Right. I'll check there," I mumbled. "Thanks very much."

"No worries." She hung up.

I'd known it already, of course. But it was still eerie hearing the confirmation. If the man I'd met for tea wasn't from the American embassy, then who was he? How had he gotten my cell phone number? And how did he know I was interested in Nadeem Siddiqui?

I shook my head. None of the pieces of the puzzle fit together. I didn't know whether to feel intrigued or exasperated.

30

Deep in the bowels of the embassy, Jake Pearson sat typing up his report.

Evening was his least favorite time to be stuck in the office. He was a morning person, and the hustle and bustle of the early hours suited him. He could roll with the middle-of-the-night emergencies too, when a terse phone call from Langley would hurtle him from slumber out into the night, and to the car outside already waiting to drive him to Grosvenor Square. But the hours after 6:00 p.m., when most of London had spilled out into the pubs or crammed onto the Circle Line—these wearied him. It was a shame that the nature of his work meant he was tied to his physical desk, with its secure phone lines and encrypted databases. Such was life with a top-secret clearance. You couldn't exactly conduct business from your cell phone in the supermarket checkout line.

Tonight he felt particularly annoyed as he watched a cloud of cigarette smoke rise from the cubicle just outside his office door. Jake hated cigarettes. Smoking was technically forbidden in the office, and he had already complained to this particular offender more than once. But the guy was just back from a TDY—sixty days temporary duty in Yemen. Smoking was probably one of the least objectionable habits he'd picked up. The men who thrived in the clandestine service were, by definition, professional rule-breakers. Guys who've been trained to target terrorists with Hellfire missiles don't tend to fret over violating the office smoking policy.

Jake scowled and turned back to the task at hand. It shouldn't take too long. Just a couple of pages to crank out. And then, if the phone lines would just stay quiet, he could slip out.

He was sure the girl had held some information back. Based on her questions, he thought he'd gotten most of it, though. He had had the advantage of knowing exactly who she was and what she was looking for. He smiled to himself. The name Crispin Withington had been an amusing touch. It was so deliciously British. Risky, of course. But he had correctly guessed that Alexandra James was about as likely to know the lineup of England's cricket team as his granny back in Charlotte.

She was sharp, though. She would have googled him by now and figured it out. He'd been surprised when she'd first stepped into the hotel lobby. The photo on the *Chronicle* website didn't do her justice. In person she was . . . not beautiful exactly, but riveting. Long, strong legs and more than a hint of feminine curves. And that crazy red hair.

Pearson cracked his knuckles and kept typing. Just about done now. He had included the question of a possible link with the White House lawyer's son, Thomas Carlyle, since she'd seemed obsessed with it, although he wasn't sure what it had to do with anything. Same with the banana orders, which again might or might not be relevant. The beauty of his job was he didn't have to figure these things out. Just get the job done, check the boxes, clock in, clock out. He almost never knew the full picture of the tasks he was asked to carry out. It was better that way.

He hit SAVE and forwarded the report as an attachment to a Hotmail account, as he'd been instructed. There. It was unusual to bypass the regular system and instead use a personal e-mail account. But it was simply not in Jake Pearson's nature to ask questions. His passivity would have made him a lousy spy. But it made him an excellent administrator of their affairs. Now he meticulously wiped the file from his own machine and logged out through several layers of security. He stood up and turned off his desk lamp. Then he shut his office door and walked out, glaring in passing at the puffs of smoke still rising toward the fluorescent lights.

31

I t was very late in Islamabad.

Dr. Syed Qureshi sat in his moonlit study, staring at his computer screen in shock. He sucked on his cigarette and tried to take in the news.

Nadeem Siddiqui was dead. The letter from the supervisor at Kahuta was short but definitive on this point. The family had written to inform the lab of the news, and to inquire whether any personal effects could be sent home to Karachi. A burial ceremony was still to be arranged. That was it. Nothing else. There was no mention of how he had died, or where—still in Britain? Back home in Pakistan? Somewhere else?

Dr. Qureshi had met the younger man only once, during the formal interview for the overseas exchange program. Now he was struggling to recall which of the hopeful faces had belonged to Nadeem Siddiqui. He pulled out his file. Yes, he vaguely remembered him now. He checked Siddiqui's medical records; there was nothing to suggest he had been ill. He had been nervous, the doctor remembered. And smart. They all were. It was a selective program, a chance for Pakistan's top young scientists to spend a term at Cambridge, Oxford, or one of the elite London colleges. Britain's Foreign Office picked up the tab. According to the brochure that Dr. Qureshi had helped write, the idea was to "enable in-person collaboration with foreign colleagues," as well as "encouraging the global reach of Pakistan's scientists and scholars in the network of academic colleagues across the UK." A jumble of jargon, thought Dr. Qureshi now, sucking hard again on his cigarette. The reality was it was a pleasant and not particularly taxing way to spend a few months in Europe.

He always worried, of course, about the potential for disaster. Many of the candidates had never traveled outside Pakistan before. You never knew how they would cope when surrounded by the vices of the West. But Siddiqui had already proven himself resilient. He had done his postgraduate work in Germany, three years in Hamburg, and emerged with glowing references and a dissertation worthy of publication. He seemed a serious young man.

So what had happened? Qureshi wondered. And most important, from his point of view, how would it reflect on him? The doctor had found running the program an advantageous sinecure. He had the power to bestow prestigious fellowships on the sons and the daughters of Pakistan's elite; the parents channeled perks his way to ensure their offspring were among the chosen.

Nadeem Siddiqui had been unusual in this regard. He didn't come from an upper-class family. And he was old by the standards of the group, already in his early thirties, already settling into a career in Pakistan's foremost nuclear facility.

It was all a very strange business, Dr. Qureshi reflected. That lady who had called—he had thought she was from the Cavendish Laboratory in Cambridge. But she had said no, and she had sounded American. What day had that been? Was Siddiqui already dead when she had called? Had Siddiqui ever seen the messages from Dr. Qureshi, inquiring with increasing shrillness these last few days about where he was and why he had not returned to work, an explicit requirement of the exchange program?

The doctor scanned the message from Kahuta one last time. He noted with relief that no action appeared to be required from him. He hoped there was a sad but simple explanation. A car accident, or a fall. Or perhaps the boy had been ill after all. Yes, it would be something like that. Nothing that would tarnish the reputation of Qureshi's program. He stubbed out his cigarette and prepared to head up to bed. He would be happy to close the book on this one.

32

I PUT OFF CALLING HYDE for as long as I could, pottering around flossing my teeth and shaving my legs. Eventually the dank little hotel room ran out of distractions and I forced myself to pick up the phone. It was well past six back in the newsroom—pushing midnight for me here in London—and I wondered whether he would answer.

Surprisingly, he did. And even more surprisingly, he didn't bite my head off. Perhaps he was already nursing his end-of-the-workday glass of wine. He inquired politely whether I'd seen the video from Thom's funeral. I hadn't. Apparently it had been running all day on CNN. Cameras hadn't been allowed inside, but they had turned out for the president and the first lady and then filmed the Carlyle family leaving the church.

"You didn't miss much," Hyde said. "Nora did fine covering it from the press pool. We're running the photo front page tomorrow, but we're putting the copy inside. You were right. It wasn't worth rushing back for."

"Oh. Well—er—good," I said, not quite sure how to proceed. Hyde in a raging temper I could handle, and I was used to his mood swings between gallant charm and cutting sarcasm. But a mellow Hyde? This was a new phenomenon.

"Hyde," I tried again. "For what it's worth, I think you were actually right. About this wild-goose chase over here. The more I'm finding out, the less any of it makes sense, and the less it seems to have to do with Thomas Carlyle."

"And the Siddiqui character? Anything worth writing up there?"

"I—I had a very strange interview today, or meeting I guess you would call it . . ." I trailed off. I just didn't have it in me to recount the day's adventures with Crispin Withington. It would only bolster the view surely solidifying in Hyde's mind that I was a bumbling nincompoop he should never have let within a mile of a big story.

"Anyway," I mumbled, "I can fill you in when I get back to Boston. I'm on the first BA flight tomorrow morning. If everything's on time, I could swing by the newsroom midafternoon. And I can pick up trying to work my police sources, and—"

"Fine, fine," interrupted Hyde. "I've got meetings tomorrow in Washington, so I won't be around anyway. Why don't you check in with David when you get back? And we'll catch up soon."

David was the editor for education stories. My regular editor. I realized with a lurch that Hyde was releasing me from the special status I had been enjoying—that is, lead reporter on a big story, reporting directly to the managing editor and bypassing the usual management chain.

Shame washed over me. Hyde had trusted me—had let me follow my instincts all the way to England—and I had come up with nothing. Nothing printable, at least, which was as good as nothing.

"Oh, and if you happen to have a minute to make a call or two," Hyde was continuing, "you may want to look at the story ABC News just posted to its website. They've got a good write-through about Carlyle being depressed, screwing up the exams to get into law school, that type of thing."

"But I had all that! Remember? From Thom's roommate."

"Yes. But we didn't run it. He didn't want you to quote him, as I recall. And you said you wanted more time to report it out. Also, ABC isn't quoting the roommate. Their source is Petronella Black."

My mouth fell open. That bitch.

"It looks like their White House reporter managed to corner her outside the funeral," Hyde concluded. "Anyway, take a look. It's strong stuff. Definitely moves the story forward."

"I don't suppose it mentions the fingerprints being wiped clean?" I asked bitterly. "Seeing as that was my scoop, and seeing how it totally undermines the whole Thom-Carlyle-got-depressed-and-killed-himself theory?"

"No, I don't believe they mention that. So—you'll take a look?"

"Sure," I said through gritted teeth.

"Lovely. Then get some rest, Ms. James." Hyde hung up.

I threw the phone down onto the bed and cursed. Goddamn ABC News. No, more to the point: goddamn Petronella Black.

It took me half an hour to reach Joe Chang and cajole him into putting the quotes he'd given me last Friday on the record. He agreed after I pointed out that thanks to Petronella, Thom's lousy LSAT score was now public record anyway.

Then it took me another hour to write and file a short update story for tomorrow's paper. The evening update editor carved out space so it could run as a sidebar to Nora's funeral story. Hyde had alerted him I might be calling in. The editor insisted on inserting this line:

The LSAT score was first reported by ABC News . . .

And I insisted on keeping this one:

But sources close to the investigation say many questions remain, such as why no fingerprints were found in the tower room from which Carlyle fell.

Finally I turned out the lights and climbed into bed, still furious. At myself, at ABC News, at Petronella, at Crispin Withington or whoever he was . . . At sodding Nadeem Siddiqui too. I was determined to find that creep, if only to wring his neck for behaving so strangely.

I burrowed under the covers. Tomorrow I would call the shipping company and see if I could find out anything about the package they had delivered. But I decided to keep this to myself for now. Hyde had sounded bored by the whole Nadeem angle, and who could blame him? Still. I wanted to find Nadeem. I'd invested too much time in him and his stupid bananas to quit now. I would not mention him to Hyde again, not until I had something real to report.

I KEPT SOMETHING BACK FROM Hyde that day five years ago in the newsroom too. I've never told anyone the whole truth about what happened. Not even my mother. Especially not my mother.

It is true that I had a daughter, and that I lost her. What I've never told anyone is how.

The summer I was seventeen I developed a hopeless crush on a boy from my school. A senior. I spent my afternoons prancing around the pool in what I considered my most fetching bikini, trying to catch his eye. He ignored me. So it went for weeks. Then summer ended, and I half-forgot about him when he left in September for college.

But when he came home for Thanksgiving break, I bumped into him at a party, and miraculously, he smiled at me. My head was spinning from warm beer and cheap tequila—this was well before my serious gin days—and he teased me about my red hair. It was dark and loud, and I remember the electric feeling as he refilled my plastic cup at the keg and let his hand graze the curve of my jeans. I felt beautiful and reckless and very drunk. We must have left together at some point. A lot of that night is a blur, but I do recall with absolute clarity looking out at the night stars from his car window, my seat pushed all the way back. I remember being sweaty and cold at the same time, my jeans peeled down, my back stuck to the vinyl upholstery, and my knee jammed painfully against the emergency brake. He didn't have a condom. I pretended to be too cool to care. It was my first time.

Now, surely the gods weren't spiteful enough to let a girl get pregnant the very first time, from a quickie with the boy she was sure was the love of her life? Oh, but they were. It was such a cliché. My period wasn't regular in those days, and there was no morning sickness. I waited more than three months before I sneaked to a pharmacy across town and bought a pregnancy test.

When I finally took it and saw the definitive proof, I bawled and then began swinging between terror and denial. The practical thing would have been to quietly get an abortion. But I wasn't thinking practically. I was thinking of how my parents would kill me. And I was secretly hoping—I know this is awful—that I might miscarry and the whole thing would take care of itself. Weeks somehow went by, then months. I wrote to the boy—the *father*—and fantasized that he would show up at my front door, ask me to marry him, and the story would have a fairy-tale ending. It didn't happen.

I was seriously skinny back then, and it was winter and then a chilly spring. I pulled off the leggings-with-a-baggy-sweater look for a long time before anyone noticed how much my waist had thickened. My mother gave me long, questioning looks at breakfast for most of April before she said anything. When she finally confronted me, I was nearly six months along.

The scene with my parents was even more excruciating than I had imagined. But it was also a relief to let them take over and tell me what to do. By then it was too late for an abortion. Instead a "family emergency" was hastily concocted and sold to my teachers to get me out of the last three weeks of school. And my mother and I packed our things and left for a rented cottage in Maine. The plan was simply to hide me for three months. Then deliver the baby, give it up for adoption, and head back to school for my senior year. The timing actually worked beautifully. I was due on August 16.

It all sounds terribly old-fashioned. But people in my parents' social circle just don't have unwed, pregnant, teenage daughters. Don't get the wrong idea. My parents weren't monsters. They were trying to protect their daughter. And I agreed with them. A baby was the last thing I wanted.

I remember that cottage in Maine as idyllic, strangely enough. It was cozy and I had nothing to do but lounge around reading and watching movies. No one knew us up there, but I still wasn't supposed to go into town, just in case. So my mother made grocery runs and went for long walks while I lay about feeling sorry for myself. In the evenings she would crack open a bottle of Scotch, pour herself a tumbler, and cook aggressively healthy meals. Kale and cabbage gratin. Spicy, scrambled tofu. Fennel and seaweed slaw. She urged me to eat for two. Why? Some impossible-to-repress grandmotherly instinct, even though she would never hold this grandchild in her arms?

My dad came up once for a weekend visit. And every couple of weeks my mother would go home for a night or two, to see my father and to keep up appearances. It was on one of these weekends that my water broke. July 12. Exactly five weeks early. At first I ignored it, convinced the trickle of clear liquid between my legs was just one more indignity, proof that my last remaining vestiges of bladder control had gone. When the contractions began, I tried to ignore them too—surely just false labor, my body practicing for the big day. The doctor had told me this would happen. The pain cinched across my lower back, making my knees shake and the sweat bead across my lip and forehead.

I waited until the clenching came every few minutes, until it was too late, too late to call my mother, too late to do anything but roll back and forth on the kitchen rug, sweating and panting and terrified. It was quick. Not like the war stories you hear. Only an hour or so of the very worst pain. I rocked my spine along that rug and screamed and then— *sweet Jesus*—there it was. A little girl. She slid onto the floor between my legs. She was covered in blood and wet. I looked at her. She was tiny.

I lay there trembling. Blood was still pouring down between my legs. I wasn't sure what to do. Clean her off, warm her up? There were supposed to be nurses helping me. The doctor. My mother. I hadn't expected to do this alone.

I picked up the child and put her to my shoulder. Clapped her back. I waited for a cough or a whimper. But she was quiet. I looked at her again, more carefully. Rubbed her little legs. Squeezed her. She was limp. She did not move.

And then I was frantic. I hooked my finger and swept her mouth, pressing her warm tongue down, trying to clear her airway. *Come on.* I covered her mouth with mine and breathed, quick little puffs, hoping she would pink up. Hoping she would cry.

When the ambulance arrived, I was sitting on the floor, rocking her. She was so light. So still. I am told they had to pry her from my arms.

She never even opened her eyes.

* * *

IN THE DAYS THAT FOLLOWED, everyone spoke in whispers. They told me in low voices how sorry they were, so very sorry, and how brave I had been.

The doctor explained that my daughter's oxygen supply had been obstructed during her premature delivery. There was nothing I could have done. She would have felt no pain. He hoped I had gained some comfort from getting to hold her. He kept me in the hospital for the night and then sent me home with phone numbers for a women's crisis hotline and a bereaved-parent support group.

I never used them. Weeks went by and I began to feel better. I wrote in my diary, and that helped. By the time school started back after Labor Day, I had developed a mental trick: every time my thoughts turned to my daughter or to what had happened, I imagined a screen fading to black. It worked. Oh, I did feel sadness. And shame, plenty of it. But it would be accurate to describe my prevailing emotion as relief. It was over, it was for the best.

Over time I thought of her less and less. I never talked about what had happened. No one at school knew, and my parents were only too happy to avoid the subject. And so for a long time, I just got on with things. I rejoined the lacrosse team, aced my final exams, and headed off to college.

Not until some years later did I begin to have trouble sleeping. I was living on my own for the first time, trying to get promoted off the *Chronicle* night shift. The hours were brutal. I was bad at the job. I lived on a stream of coffee and microwaved ramen-noodle bowls. One night I was sent to interview the mother of a kid who had gotten shot up in a Charlestown housing project, and as she sat weeping, and I sat taking notes, something inside me broke. Her grief was so raw. I couldn't see how a person could recover from such sadness. As I drove back to the newsroom, my hands shook. I sat trembling in the parking garage for a long time.

After that I began a kind of mental pacing, back and forth between two truths that did not seem able to coexist: I had had a daughter. And I had killed her. Not literally perhaps, but as good as. I had wanted her dead, and she had died. Did it not amount to the same?

The precise details of that day began to torment me. I should have gone straight to the hospital when my water broke. I should have called the ambulance sooner. I should have tried to breathe for her for longer, for hours, for days, for however long it took. My doctor had been wrong. There was plenty I could have done.

I started the scratching thing around then, raking the pale skin inside my elbows. It didn't help exactly, but it was clarifying to feel pain that had nothing to do with my daughter. To have a wound that I could see. At my worst I ripped out handfuls of my own hair. I would reach up and grab a hunk and tear it out from the roots. Then I would press my fingertips, hard, against the tingling patch of bare scalp. The handfuls of red looked so soft and fine, fanned out over my white sheets. Like the hair of a baby.

33

WHEN I WOKE, I REACHED for Lucien.

It took a moment to remember he wasn't there, that I wasn't likely ever to wake up beside him again. Depressing. But probably just as well. If the warm curve of his body were pressed against mine, we would no doubt find ways to occupy the next hour, and I would wind up missing my flight.

I kicked off the covers, grabbed my phone, peeked at the messages that had arrived overnight. One of them provided encouraging news: Lowell Carlyle was finally consenting to an interview. I'd been trying to get Thom's father for the past week; every day I fired off a fresh request, and every day I got back a frostily discouraging response from his secretary. But now, here it was, at the top of my e-mail in-box: a message inquiring whether I would be available today to do the interview. Mr. Carlyle was willing to give me twenty minutes, in person at the White House. The window was between five and six this afternoon. I was about to type back that I was in transit and propose tomorrow instead, when I realized—why not? If I flew to Washington instead of Boston this morning, I could be there by late afternoon. Surely there must be a Washington flight leaving around the same time.

It didn't take long to sort out. British Airways did indeed have a Dulles-bound flight leaving from Heathrow that morning. The first reservations agent I reached, on speakerphone as I packed up, informed me that my only option was to buy a new, full-fare business-class ticket. I thanked him and hung up.

In person I had more success. The Terminal 5 ticketing desk was staffed by an implausibly helpful manager. He nodded enthusiastically when I explained that I had business at the White House and really, really needed to switch flights. For fifteen minutes he tapped away at his keyboard, making reproachful, little tutting noises when it refused to let him do what he wanted. Finally he looked up triumphantly.

"Done. Sorted." Then he looked sheepish. "I couldn't find a way to get around the change fee, I'm afraid. So that's a hundred pounds. I'll just put it on your credit card, shall I? I do apologize. But if I may—here's a pass for our Galleries Club lounge, so at least you can get some tea after you clear security. Will that be all right?"

I grinned at him. He appeared to be laboring under the impression that I was someone hugely important, a cabinet secretary or something, rushing back to restructure the economy or overhaul health care.

I decided to push my luck. "That'll be fine. Thank you. Now, could you direct me to the lost and found? I left an item on the flight over, and I'm hoping someone might have kept it for me."

* * *

HALF AN HOUR LATER I was sitting in the British Airways lounge, sipping champagne and skimming the *Guardian*. A tan Burberry coat was folded over the seat next to me, a man's size forty-two long. It smelled brand-new. Life was looking up.

I wrote an e-mail to Hyde:

Headed to Washington sted Boston. Got the Lowell Carlyle interview. Can have it for you for tomorrow. Will touch base when I land. Maybe see you in DC?

Yours in chasing wild geese,
Alex
P.S. There's a Burberry here with your name on it.
P.P.S. Sorry about everything this week.

I wondered which of these Hyde would be more excited about, the interview or the raincoat. Either way I would be back in his good graces.

Next I wrote to Elias:

Coming to Washington today. Lowell Carlyle intvu at WH. How annoyed will Nora be? (She asks gleefully). Also: any chance I could crash at yours? Would love to avoid having to submit yet another hotel bill for reimbursement.

I had a mysterious interview yesterday on the Nadeem Siddiqui angle. Will tell you about it. And there's this package delivery I need to check out. Don't suppose you've heard back from your guys at CIA, or was it State Dept? Hyde has lost interest, but I still think there's something there. Talk soon.

Love,
Ginger

All around me in the sleek lounge, people were typing away on laptops. I noticed more than a few were joining me in a midmorning tipple. Maybe it was the champagne, but I was feeling mischievous. I tapped out one last message:

Why yes, I do keep crossing and uncrossing my legs in a rather clingy pencil skirt in the first-class lounge . . .

I scrolled through my address book, found the number, and hit SEND. Ninety seconds later my phone rang.

"I thought that might get your attention."

"You saucy minx," growled Lucien. "Do you know what a message like that does to a man?"

"Sorry? I couldn't quite hear you. Just that this lace bustier I'm wearing keeps rubbing and making such a loud rustling noise . . ."

I could actually hear him groan. "That's it. I am *so* coming to bite you—"

"Promises, promises," I said airily. "Actually, I just called to say good-bye."

"Right," he sighed. "So you're headed back to Boston?"

"Washington, actually. Change of plans. Thom's dad finally agreed to talk to me. So I'm headed to the White House tonight."

"Ah. May I offer a word of advice? If any men claiming to be international cricket stars approach you on the plane today, it's a ruse. Just say no. Tell them you're taken. Tell them Crispin Withington will personally take his bat and wallop them if they come within three feet of you."

I smiled.

"You know, don't take this the wrong way or anything," he continued, "but I think I'm going to miss you."

"Well, not to worry. Petronella will be back soon to keep you warm at night." I tried and failed to keep the cattiness out of my voice. *Petronella*. The sheer, bitchy cheek of that girl.

"Hang on—was that a note of jealousy I just detected?"

"Hardly," I sniffed. "Just I know how much you must be looking forward to a happy reunion with the little trollop."

Lucien sucked in his breath. I heard him smother a laugh. "Right. No jealousy at all there, then. To tell you the truth, Alex—and I admit this is ungentlemanly—she's rather boring. I mean, she's stunning to look at. But . . . she's not exactly a laugh riot. So. The thing is—"

I was barely listening. I was too busy relishing the thought of Petronella as a boring old trout.

"The thing is," Lucien persevered, "speaking of changing travel plans, I did have a thought. How about, once you file this interview or whatever you need to do, how about you take a break and we meet for a weekend somewhere? Maybe Bermuda. Then we'd be meeting in the middle, nearly. My treat. Just some sand and some sun and good wine and fun. And you in a bikini, obviously."

I jerked back to attention. "You and me? Go away together?" I was startled. It had honestly never occurred to me that I might ever see him again after this week.

Lucien Sly was a great fling. He was fantastic in bed. And he had made me laugh like . . . well, like I hadn't laughed in years. But he was too young for me. He couldn't be more than twenty-three or twenty-four. And he had a title, for God's sake—*Lord* Lucien Sly. Not to mention that he was obviously a cad and incapable of an exclusive relationship.

"I don't know if that's a good idea," I said slowly. "I mean, I just—I'm older than you and what we want is—is—well, I don't know if you're mature enough for me." I paused momentously. It was the truth and I meant it and I was about to press the point when I realized how incredibly snooty I must sound.

"I see," he said huffily. "It's true that I can only dream of ascending to the dizzying heights of your wisdom and maturity—"

"I just meant you don't seem to want a serious girlfriend—"

"Your banana-busters crusade, for example—"

"And I'd really rather not be two-timed—"

"Your penchant for Michael Bublé sing-alongs in dodgy bars in Slough—"

At this I nearly choked on my champagne and am afraid I let out a loud snort. A few of the better-behaved guests glanced over with arched eyebrows.

"Stop it. Enough," I gasped.

"No, no, I'm warming to the subject now. Let's not forget your fondness for afternoon-tea trysts with preposterously named prats like—wait for it—*Crispin Withington*—"

"But there is an actual person really named that!" I protested.

"Yes, but not that you've ever met!"

By now I was doubled over with giggles. Lucien was too, great waves of laughter bellowing down the phone line.

By the time they called my flight, he had made me promise to meet him in Bermuda in two weeks' time. I couldn't stop smiling as I stood in the queue waiting to board. I had to fight the urge to wink at the flight attendant as she scanned my boarding pass.

Today was shaping up to be a very good day.

MY GOOD LUCK DID NOT, alas, extend to an upgrade out of economy class.

But I was relieved to note as I brushed down the aisle that I'd been given a window seat. And when I arrived at 38A, I was amused to find my seatmate for the flight looked as if she could be my sister.

Tiny lines around her eyes suggested she might be a few years older than me. Probably in her early or midthirties. She was a few pounds heavier too. But she had the same milky skin and freckles, and copper-colored hair, cut shorter than mine. She stood up to let me in and smiled as she registered my appearance.

"This must be the redhead ghetto, then." She sounded Irish.

"Yeah. They must think it's safest to herd all us Celts together." I hoisted my carry-on bag into the overhead bin and squeezed past her to the window seat.

"You're American, then? Heading home?" she asked conversationally.

"Eventually. I live in Boston now. But I've got a meeting in Washington."

She nodded. Looked me up and down. "Brilliant shoes," she said, inclining her head down toward my Manolos.

"Thanks. They're killing me, actually. I can't wait to take them off and slip on those free little plane socks I'm hoping they're about to hand out." I glanced around to check if flight attendants were making the rounds yet. "But I've got to dash straight to this meeting when we land, and I'm not sure if I'll have time to change, and half the time the checked luggage doesn't make it. . . ."

She nodded again. "They better not lose mine this time. I'm off on holiday. Couple of days in Washington and then hiring a car with my mates to drive down to Florida. Should be a laugh." She fished around in her handbag and pulled out what looked like a prescription bottle of Ambien. "Just to warn you, I'll be popping one of these as soon as we take off. I'm dead tired and hoping to sleep like a baby the whole way."

"I've never tried those. Gin seems to do the business for me."

She laughed. "Aye, gin works fine too."

"Well, I've got work I need to get done. And I may be up and down a bit. If you like, we can trade seats once we're up in the air. So you can sleep and I won't be having to crawl across you the whole time."

"That'd be lovely. Thanks for that."

She flicked open a magazine. I leaned back and stared out the window.

It was only five days since I'd landed at Heathrow from Boston. I'd managed two bylines, if you counted the silly LSAT-score-first-reported-by-ABC-News driblet that was running in today's paper. Not exactly setting the world on fire, but not a disaster either. I would score another story tomorrow—knock on wood—if the Lowell Carlyle inter-view went according to plan. And this Nadeem Siddiqui thread might turn into something yet.

The curious development was this twist with Lucien. There is no point jinxing a good thing by overanalyzing it. But here is a fact: I felt lighter now than when I'd stepped off the plane last week. Physically lighter. A woman who floats rather than plods. Great sex two nights in a row can do that, I suppose. But this felt less about sex and more about rediscovering an ability to belly-laugh.

It was as if, without my quite realizing it, something like a stone had grown heavy and cold inside me. I imagined it nestling against my lungs, stooping me over a little. Had it been with me all these years since the summer of my daughter? Or had it hardened slowly, a calcification of the soul? Either way, I had lived with it long enough that I only noticed it now, now that—just an inch—the stone was shifting. Loosening. I had been unhappy for so long. It was strange now to feel myself, if this is the right word, *unclench*.

THE IRISH WOMAN WAS TRUE to her word. She popped a sleeping pill right after takeoff, pulled a blanket tight around her, and passed out. Once she mumbled something in her sleep and nuzzled in closer to the window. Then she was still again, her hair falling like a curtain across her face.

Meanwhile I watched the first half of a movie, got bored, then pad-ded around some in my cozy socks. I went to the bathroom, then over to pester the stewardess for tea and some crisps. Finally I forced myself to work a bit. I sketched out five questions and follow-ups for the Car-lyle interview. I wrote a to-do list for myself of leads to follow up on and drafted several e-mails to send once we'd landed and my phone had service again. By the time the final food trolley came rumbling down the aisle, hawking an unappetizing spread of cheese sandwiches and stewed tea, I was feeling in good shape.

I glanced at my seatmate to check if she might want a tray, seeing as she hadn't eaten the whole flight. Nope. Still out like a light.

I sipped at the tea. Reluctantly slipped off the socks and forced my swollen feet back into the Manolos. I touched up my lipstick, ran a brush through my hair, hesitated, then nudged her. The captain had announced we were landing shortly, and she looked as if she might need a few minutes to pull herself together.

I nudged her again. "Hey," I said gently.

When did I first suspect something was wrong? I shook her arm. It flopped against her side. I shook her again, harder. I glanced around for the little bottle—*how many of those pills had she taken?* Tentatively I reached for the curtain of flaming hair and brushed it away from her face. Her eyes were closed. I slapped her cheek. Not hard, but hoping the sting would jolt her awake. That's when I saw it. A fat drop of blood. It had stained her collar. I forced myself to touch it. Wet. Fresh. My eyes traced its path back up her neck. In the hollow below her jaw, the tiny circle of a puncture wound was just visible. A bruise the size of a fingerprint was spreading purple across her white skin.

I stifled a scream. What was happening? Was she dead? My breath was jagged, my thoughts racing very fast. This woman—this woman with blood staining her neck—looked quite like me. *She had been sitting in my seat.* I had given her 38A, the seat printed on my boarding pass, the seat anyone searching my name in the airline database this morning would have pulled up. No no no no. This couldn't be.

I felt a jolt and nearly cried out. It was the plane landing. I hunched my shoulders up close to my ears and twisted my hands in my lap. The nerves in my own neck twitched. All around me people were sliding on shoes, stuffing newspapers into seat pockets, gathering up their things. No one was staring at us. No one else looked worried.

I wanted nothing more than to leap up and run. But from the chaos of my mind two thoughts were gelling. This was no accidental overdose. Someone had tried to kill this woman. Perhaps had succeeded at killing this woman. Had they been trying to kill me? But why? I shivered. It made no sense.

The second thought was even worse. We were locked inside an airplane. Whoever it was, was still on this plane. My breath came in frantic little pants now. I should press the button for the flight attendant. I should call out for a doctor. Or an air marshal—did they have them on international flights? I looked at her again. I forced myself to reach for her wrist. My own hands were shaking so badly, it was hard to hold on to her. My lips moved, praying. *Please, God, please, God.* It took a minute before I was sure: she had no pulse.

I needed to unravel this—needed time to think it through—but first I needed to get off this plane alive. Whoever had done this must think I was dead. I looked around again. Bored faces, tired faces—no one who seemed to be paying attention to me. As the plane started to empty, I stood and checked the overhead bin. My laptop bag was gone. I closed my eyes and pictured it: my *Chronicle* business card, laminated and dangling from the strap. Fortunately I kept my wallet, phone, and reporter's notebook in my handbag, which had never left my side. I stole one last look at her, still primly bundled in her blanket, her hair disheveled and lank now across her face. She looked like a passenger who had greedily grabbed too many minibottles of wine and needed to sleep it off.

Quickly, head down, one foot in front of the other, I knifed down the aisle, making eye contact with no one. Off the plane now. Just keep going. I felt, if anything, more vulnerable in the vast open atrium of the terminal. My knuckles were white on my handbag strap. I felt a brief moment of security at passport control—at least cameras were everywhere—then sped past customs, out through swinging doors, and into a sea of faces in the arrivals lounge. I started to jog and then to run. I left my suitcase spinning on the baggage carousel. I darted down a ramp and into daylight and to the front of the taxi line, repeating hoarsely, "I'm sorry—it's an emergency—I've got to get—please—I'm so sorry—"

People grumbled but let me through.

The driver turned languidly around, thrust a pamphlet at me, and began explaining the fares to the District, to Maryland, to Virginia.

"Go. Just go, go," I hissed. I thrust a $20 bill at him. He rolled his eyes, but pocketed it and pulled away from the curb. I slapped down the door lock with my elbow and clutched my handbag tighter across my chest. I turned around. Looked back. Was it my imagination, a trick of my frightened eyes? Or was a woman holding up her phone as if to snap a picture as we sped away?

THERE WAS A WOMAN, HER name was Jane, and at that moment she was staring at the retreating taxi in horror.

How could it be? Jane wondered. How on earth could this have happened?

The assignment had come in at the last minute. Nothing unusual about that. And then the plan kept shifting. Even as she had navigated the snarled traffic to Heathrow Airport, a text arrived directing her to switch her ticket to a different flight, headed to a different city. But there was nothing particularly unusual about that either. Jane—not her real name, but the one she used with this particular client—was a professional. By the time she pulled up at the Heathrow terminal, she had the information she needed. The target's name, her seat assignment, and her photograph. The photo was grainy. It showed the target in profile, twentysomething, red hair.

Jane had managed to change her ticket to a business-class seat on the Washington plane. She could have planned everything better if she'd had more time. But the client was quite specific: the hit must be accomplished before the target arrived on US soil. Absolutely no flexibility on this point. Otherwise things would get complicated.

On the plane it had been easy to swish back from business class to the main cabin. The target was obligingly asleep in her assigned seat, her red hair slanting over her face. There was even an empty seat next to her. Yes, it had been easy to glide in, administer the injection, grab the satchel from the overhead bin, glide out. No one had noticed. The nearby passengers were engrossed in their in-flight entertainment; the target herself had barely stirred. Done. Jane felt a certain satisfaction in her professional competence. She might be in a loathsome business, but she was exceedingly good at it.

So then—who was this woman who had just streaked past her in the taxi line, panicked and pale and *looking exactly like the target*? And if it was—if the woman who'd just sped away in a taxi was Alexandra James—then who, exactly, was slumped dead in seat 38A?

34

W here to?"

I snapped my head around, startled. The driver was staring at me in his rearview mirror.

"Where to?" he repeated.

A reasonable question. I had no idea. Where to, when someone has just tried to kill you? I stared back blankly as if he were speaking alien gibberish.

The driver glanced at the oncoming traffic and then looked back intently at me. "Lady?" He appeared to be making up his mind that the best destination for me might be the loony bin.

"Yes." I sat up and tried to pull myself together. "Let's go downtown, into Washington," I said, fluttering my fingers vaguely in what I thought was the right direction. "I'll get you the address in a minute."

He sighed and turned his attention back to the road.

We were speeding along the bank of a river that I assumed was the Potomac. I don't know Washington well, but I was pretty sure it only has one river. Soon the silhouettes of the Jefferson Memorial and the Washington Monument appeared on the far bank.

I pulled out my phone and tried to figure out what to do. It was still two hours before my appointment with Lowell Carlyle. If that even mattered given what had just happened. Whom should I call? Hyde? Elias? The police? And tell them what, exactly? That a passenger sitting next to me on a plane had died, and that I feared it was meant to be me instead. It made no sense. Almost nothing that had happened these last couple of days made sense.

I screwed my eyes shut. The red-haired woman on the plane was already starting to seem unreal. Perhaps I had dreamed her. Perhaps . . . the blood on her collar was a mosquito bite she'd scratched, perhaps she really was just sleeping.

But no. My laptop bag. It was gone. It had not disappeared on its own. I tried to remember what was in there, what information I had on the computer. And my checked suitcase. I wondered in a detached way whether it was still circling on the baggage carousel, or whether a porter would have lugged it away by now. It would find its way back to me eventually. My phone number was on a tag on the handle.

My phone number. A chill went down my spine. It was entirely possible I was imagining all this, that I was losing my mind. But if I was not—if that puncture wound had really been intended for my neck—how had someone known to look for me on a British Airways flight to *Washington*? I had only changed plans this morning. The only people I'd told were Hyde and Elias, when I e-mailed them from Heathrow. And Lucien, when he called me in the lounge.

I had no idea how these things worked. Would someone who knew what they were doing be able to break into my e-mail account that easily or listen in on my calls? This was more Elias's world than mine. My typical workday—at least until recently—involved trying not to doze off during faculty meetings. It was Elias who ran around meeting sources in trench coats and signaling for meetings by moving flowerpots, or however they did things on the intelligence beat. He was the one who reported on classified code words and wiretapping and warrants. Not that someone into murdering people would likely pause for a warrant, mind you. For Christ's sake.

I considered my phone again. A terrible, paranoid thought occurred to me. I tapped on Google maps. A message appeared: *Mapping would like to use your current location. Allow?*

A couple of seconds later, there I was: a flashing red dot, moving down the bank of the river. If I could see this, who else could? I felt nauseous. We were turning. I looked up. The taxi had swung right on to a wide bridge. The square façade of the Lincoln Memorial loomed straight ahead. I rolled down my window and breathed in the humid air. Toward the middle of the bridge, I flicked my wrist and threw as hard as I could. The phone sailed out across the water.

The driver looked back at me with alarm.

Where to?

"Take me to the White House," I told him.

LOWELL CARLYLE'S SECRETARY LOOKED ONLY mildly surprised at my turning up an hour and a half early.

I'd been pre-cleared through security into the White House. It still took a few minutes for the guards manning the checkpoint outside the West Wing to examine my passport, consult their list, and shepherd me through the X-ray and metal-detector machines. I was directed to cross the lawn. A wall of TV cameras was lined up in what looked like a permanent formation on the right. Cameramen stood smoking and drinking coffee in pairs, waiting for correspondents to rush out to do their live shots. The door to the West Wing swung open and a couple of reporters shot past, chasing a woman I recognized from TV as the president's press secretary. No sign of Nora, thank God for small favors. Inside was a large and dimly lit waiting room. The receptionist took my name again. Aides scurried past.

Ten minutes passed before Mr. Carlyle's secretary appeared. She offered me tea and coffee.

I declined. Instead I smiled politely, thanked her for working me in, and asked whether I might see him earlier than scheduled. Like, how about now?

She raised her eyebrows in an expression that meant *You've got to be kidding me.*

"He's in with the president just now, as it happens," she said, stretching her lips into a thin smile. "And it's amazing he's here at all, what with the funeral and Mrs. Carlyle still in Cambridge. So terrible." She shook her head. "Anyway, so far he's running on time for your interview. Anything else I can get you while you wait?" She had already turned and begun sidling away.

"Actually, a phone. If there were somewhere where I could make a couple of calls?"

A few minutes later I was installed in a cupboard just outside the briefing room. All the major news organizations keep cubicles somewhere in the press warren. The few remaining newspapers with national ambitions were clustered in one corner. The network television and cable-news channels shared their own hallway, cleaner and reeking of hair spray. Closest to the briefing room—and thus to the news—were the wire services. An aura of panic and deadline pressure radiated from behind the half-shut doors. I could hear keyboards clicking frantically inside. Mr. Carlyle's secretary tried to usher me into the *Chronicle's* booth, but thankfully it was locked tight and Nora was nowhere to be found. So now I found myself in what appeared to be a general-use/transient space. The closet-size cubby contained a buzzing fluorescent light, the curling transcript of a speech the president had given three months ago, and several chewed-on styrofoam cups in which stewed the remnants of God-knew-how-old coffee. All that, and a phone. Hallelujah.

I picked up and dialed Hyde's cell phone. No answer. Then I tried Elias.

"Hello, Elias Thottrup," he answered, sounding harassed.

"Elias. Thank God."

"Hello?" A pause. "Alex?"

"Hi. Yes. It's me. I need—"

"Hey. Are you in DC yet? Listen, I'm on deadline. But I got your message—"

"Never mind that. I'm at the White House. I'm going to do this Carlyle interview, but I really need to find Hyde—"

"I got your message," he continued, as if he weren't listening to a word I said, "and I've got to go now, but I wanted to tell you—"

"Elias!" I shrieked. "Please—is Hyde there in the newsroom?"

"What? No. He was before. You can stay tonight, by the way. But what I was going to tell you—"

"Please, can I just—"

"Shut up, Alex, for once," he barked. "What I was going to tell you is, I remembered the banana thing."

"The banana thing?"

"Your Pakistani guy ordering all the bananas. And it was bugging me that I'd just heard something interesting about bananas."

"Elias—"

"It was at this big Homeland Security conference the other week," he pressed on, ignoring me. "They get waved past radiation detectors. Because of the potassium. I was at this panel talking about dirty bombs, and how the screening systems at ports in places like Newark and LA are basically useless. Because all kinds of stuff apparently emits low-level radiation. Kitty litter and denture cleaners and, let's see, manhole covers. And bananas. The detectors can't tell the difference between fruit and a nuclear bomb. Unbelievable, huh? This one guy on the panel, from Los Alamos, he said they just wave banana shipments right through."

He paused. "Alex?"

"Yeah."

"I thought it was funny. I mean, funny in a freaky kind of way, right? Since this banana baron of yours actually works on nuclear weapons at Kahuta."

I was gripping the desk in front of me tightly. I felt sick and quite cold at once.

When I didn't reply, he added, "Anyway, I've really got to run, okay?"

"Listen to me," I said finally, and my voice was shaking. "I don't quite know what is happening. But something is wrong. Very wrong. I need to talk to Hyde. And to the police. In that order, I think."

"The police?"

"I don't have my cell phone anymore. Or my computer. Can you— can you get a message to Hyde? Tell him the interview with Lowell Carlyle might be about to go in a very different direction. Tell Hyde I need to see him, in person, tonight."

I hung up and sat staring at the phone. I was starting to get a bad feeling about why someone on that plane might have wanted me dead.

LOWELL CARLYLE LOOKED JUST LIKE you would expect the president's lawyer to look. Gray hair, gray suit. Patrician.

He stood up from his desk to greet me, and as we shook hands, I could see the exhaustion sketched on his face. He sat down again heavily.

"I'm very sorry for your loss, Mr. Carlyle."

He nodded. Even this small movement looked as if it caused him pain. "Thank you for your reporting, Miss James. It's been . . . thorough. I wasn't planning to give any interviews. But after the funeral yesterday, Anna and I—we felt it was time to do one. To share how we will remember Thom. The *Chronicle* is our hometown paper. And so it felt fitting. Thom grew up reading the *Chronicle*. Well, the sports pages anyway." Lowell gave a small, sad smile.

I nodded. "I gather he was quite an athlete, sir."

"Yes." He cleared his throat loudly. I thought I saw moisture in his eyes, and I looked away while he collected himself. "Yes, he was. That's relevant here, actually. It's what I want to talk about. Anna and I have decided to establish a scholarship in Thom's memory. At Harvard. To honor and encourage student-athletes. When Thom was a boy . . ." And he was off, launching into a long story about Thom's Little League triumphs.

I scribbled down some notes and let him go on until I couldn't stand it anymore.

"Mr. Carlyle, I—forgive me for jumping in. It's just that I know your time is limited. And there are some other things I need to ask you about."

His jaw tightened, just for a moment. He was not a man accustomed to being interrupted. But he nodded and leaned back. "Go ahead."

"As far as I've been able to find out, the police are still trying to figure out how Thom died. I mean, why he fell from the bell tower. I know this is painful, but I wonder whether you've learned any more detail about what happened that night?"

He shook his head. "I was going to ask you the same."

"Did your son ever mention a man—a man named Nadeem Siddiqui? They would have met in England."

He frowned. "No, not that I can recall. Why?"

I took a deep breath. There was no going back now.

I told Thom's father about how Petronella had found Nadeem rummaging around in Thom's room. Thom's *locked* room, and after Thom had died. I told him that no one had seen Nadeem since then, that he seemed to have disappeared. I told him about the massive banana shipments. That the latest one had landed here in Washington yesterday.

Lowell Carlyle listened to all this carefully.

"Now, here's where it gets weird," I said.

He shot me a look that suggested he thought we'd already crossed that threshold.

"Please. Just give me two more minutes and then you can throw me out," I pleaded. "A woman was killed today, and it is somehow connected to all this."

This seemed to get his attention. He put his left hand to his temple and started rubbing little circles.

I kept going.

I told him about Nadeem's work at the nuclear lab in Pakistan. I told him how bananas would slip past a nuclear detector (I prayed Elias had his facts straight on this one). I told him about my odd encounter with Crispin Withington, and how he had warned me to back off. And finally I told the White House counsel about the redheaded woman on the plane today, the drop of blood on her neck, her pulseless wrist, how she'd been sitting in the seat assigned to me.

Lowell Carlyle shot up in his chair. "Are you quite sure she was . . . dead?"

"Yes."

"What was her name?"

"I don't know."

"And you've given all this information to the police?"

"I—er—no. You're the first person I've told."

His eyes opened wide. "What? Why?"

"I came directly here from the airport. I wasn't sure if I was still in danger—I mean, if whoever killed her would realize their mistake. That they'd gotten the wrong person. If they did get the wrong person . . ." I suddenly felt very stupid. "It would have taken so long to explain everything to the airport police. And I didn't think I'd get another chance to speak with you if I didn't show up this afternoon."

To my relief, he nodded. "It's—quite a story, Miss James." He sat appraising me thoughtfully.

"You're trying to figure out if I'm insane."

He was too polite to answer directly. "I'm trying to figure out how any of this might fit together. Or whether there might be reasonable explanations for most of what you've told me. The only thing clear to me is that if a woman really did die, and you were the last to see her alive, then you need to tell what you know to the police. Immediately. I'll call the Secret Service in and they can help you sort it out.

"As for the rest of it . . ." He shook his head. "I'm sorry. It's been a long few days. I was planning to spend this time talking about my son. And instead—" He spread his hands. "I'm not sure what any of this has to do with Thom. Perhaps . . . perhaps you should speak with someone on the NSC. The National Security Council. While you're here. You can tell them what you've told me, and they can pass it on to the appropriate channels. Yes, that might make the most sense."

He picked up the phone and began making arrangements. He looked even grayer and more tired than when I'd first sat down. He seemed a decent man. I wondered what his and his wife's nights had been like, whether they'd slept since they'd gotten that terrible phone call.

I know something about sleepless nights. About missing a child . . . *Stop it.* I dug my nails deep into my palms. That wasn't the point right now.

The point was I had stumbled onto something. I was sure of it. Whether Lowell Carlyle believed me or not, I wanted to find out what it was.

35

Exhaustion was setting in by the time I finished telling the police everything I knew about the red-haired woman. Mr. Carlyle's phone call had almost instantly produced two Secret Service officers. They steered me into a small, plain room and asked me to wait. Eventually two other men appeared to question me—FBI, I think, although it wasn't entirely clear. I went over what had happened on the plane, twice. I promised to make myself available for further questions. They refused to answer any of my questions—whether her body had been found, who she was, whether anyone had been arrested.

Instead they showed me back into the main waiting room for the

West Wing, where I'd started two hours before. The same receptionist was still on duty. Aides still scurried through, though it was now past seven o'clock.

I closed my eyes, slumped in my chair, and let the jet lag wash over me. I was past caring who came to question me next. Then I heard a voice I recognized.

"Fancy meeting you here."

Hyde. I was so happy to see him I wanted to hug him.

Instead I gave his wrist a squeeze. "What are you doing here?"

"Hello, Ms. James. Funny thing, that. Your boy wonder Mr. Thottrup tracked me down at almost the exact same moment as the National Security Council did. I had no idea you've been having so much fun. You can imagine how delighted I was"—he looked hard at me—"how absolutely delighted I was to get a call from an NSC spokesman, begging me to hold our story until we'd all had a chance to sit down and talk. Now, would you like to fill me in on what story he's talking about?"

"Yes. Okay. I—"

"Because, Ms. James, the last story I remember assigning you was to investigate the death of Thomas Carlyle. How, pray tell, has that led to the two of us sitting here waiting to see the deputy national security adviser for combating terrorism?"

I blanched. No one had told me that was who I was waiting to see.

"It's just a small thing, but it is *irksome* to have to hear secondhand about my reporters getting mixed up in murder investigations. Or to learn that the president's lawyers seem to know far more about what my reporters have been up to in the last twenty-four hours than I do. Or to find out that you've had Elias calling around the CIA and the State Department on your behalf . . ." Hyde's voice remained ominously low during this monologue, but his face had turned purple.

"Alex," he finally spat. "Start talking and tell me everything. Quickly, before they call us in. I can't protect you or the newspaper if I don't have the facts."

AN HOUR LATER HYDE AND I were tucked into a corner table of the closest bar.

From the beeline he made straight out from the West Wing gate, I guessed this wasn't his first visit. He stalked across Lafayette Square toward an expensive-looking hotel, then down a set of narrow steps. A brass lantern lit up the name on the awning: OFF THE RECORD BAR. I glanced at Hyde and decided now might not be the best time to point out the irony. He had not spoken or looked at me since we'd left the White House.

Hyde took the better seat and immediately ordered himself a bottle of Grgich Hills sauvignon blanc. He did not look inclined to share. I asked for my usual Hendrick's and tonic. Silence hung between us.

Not until the wine had arrived and Hyde had taken a long sip did he finally look up at me. "I want you to swear that you will never, never, *never* pull a stunt like this again."

"But I—"

"Now."

I sighed. "I promise."

"Good." He drained his glass and poured himself another. When he looked up again, his features had rearranged themselves into a relatively pleasant expression. "So what's your lede?"

"My lede?"

"For the story you're going to write. You seem convinced there's a story here, although damned if I can figure out what it is."

"Well, that's reassuring. Thanks a lot. How about . . ." I drummed my fingers on the table. "How about this? 'A mysterious fruit delivery, a missing Pakistani scientist, and a dead Irish tourist all converged Wednesday to spark alarm at the highest echelons of Washington's political establishment. . . .'"

Hyde raised his hand to hide a smile. "Yes, that's colorful. Captures the drama. But try again."

"Let's see. Wait, I got it: 'White House officials raced yesterday to stay ahead of a fast-moving situation that may—or may not—involve nuclear smuggling, international terrorism, and the death of a Harvard man, not to mention a beautiful but bitchy London heiress. . . .'"

"Catchy. But aren't you underselling the story now?"

"Hyde, seriously"—I pouted—"I have no idea how to write the lede to a story when I have no idea what the story is. That's the point. It's all too convoluted."

He clicked his tongue in a scolding sound. "Good stories are always convoluted. If you sit around until they're crystal clear and you know every goddamned detail, you'll never write anything."

I nodded glumly. "I was hoping the NSC guy would have told us something. Anything. Anything that would help me figure out how all these crazy pieces fit together. If they even do."

"Well, he must think there's something there. Senior administration officials, in my experience, aren't prone to talking to people they think are wasting their time. He wanted to meet you. He must think you're onto something."

"He wanted to meet me because Lowell Carlyle told him to," I countered.

"And I suspect the White House counsel is also not a man prone to wasting time," Hyde said calmly. "You know my golden rule: just write what you know and how you know it. Do that, and do it again the next day, and then keep doing it every day until you get somewhere."

"I know, I know."

"You might also want to think about getting a good night's sleep. And enough of that for now." He slid my empty glass away from me to the far edge of the table. "I have the feeling tomorrow might shape up to be another challenging day."

Normally I would have bristled at the suggestion that I'd had enough to drink. Especially from a man who skipped right over the wines-by-the-glass list in favor of his own bottle. Tonight, though, I was too tired to protest. I also felt rumpled and smelly and desperately in need of a shower and fresh clothes. Then I remembered.

"Oh, no," I moaned. "My suitcase. I left it at the airport. All my clothes. I don't even have a toothbrush."

"Where are you staying tonight?"

"At Elias's. In Georgetown."

"Well, hurry up then." Hyde checked his watch. "The shops on M Street should still be open for another hour."

I hesitated. I felt nervous wandering around on my own. But perhaps the doorman here could hail me a taxi. I could hand the driver a twenty to wait at the curb on M Street and then deliver me straight to Elias's door. Yes, that would work. I stood up and kissed Hyde's cheek. "Thank you. For everything."

He looked embarrassed. "Don't be silly. Check in with me first thing in the morning."

"Right. Oh, and, Hyde? I didn't forget."

He looked at me quizzically.

"Your Burberry. But it was in my carry-on. The one that got nicked. Sorry."

He smiled. "That's the least of your concerns, surely. I wouldn't think— Wait, hang on. Did you say it was in your carry-on bag? Along with your laptop?"

"Yes."

"But that's brilliant," he said, beaming. "The airline will have to compensate you for everything that went missing. I wouldn't think they'd quibble, what with you already having to put up with the inconvenience of the passenger next to you getting *murdered*. No, they'll want to just pay up and keep quiet that you were robbed on top of everything else. Splendid. A spot of good news in an otherwise rather wretched day."

I stared at him, astonished. The man was extraordinary.

"Good night, Ms. James," he said, as if this had been a perfectly normal evening out on the town with a colleague. As I left, he was pouring himself the last glass of wine.

36

Elias looked ready to pounce when I finally staggered into his apartment at half past ten that night.

He lived on a surprisingly lovely block of Dumbarton Street, one of the posher addresses in Washington's poshest neighborhood. In the cab up from M Street, I passed well-kept gardens, gas lanterns, and historical plaques. Through the windows I caught glimpses of antiques and trays of polished silver. Many of the parked cars were expensive and German. This was clearly not the studenty part of Georgetown.

At the corner of Thirtieth Street we turned left. Elias rented the garden flat at number 3027. It was hard to pick out house numbers in the moonlight. At last I found the door and knocked. His was the last in a row of tall brick Victorian houses.

"Nice place," I said when he opened the door.

"Ginger! Tell me *everything*," he breathed, pulling me inside. "What the hell is going on?"

I looked at him fondly. Elias isn't a big guy, maybe not even as tall as me. Hence his nickname. He has shaggy, dark blond hair and a budding potbelly and looks permanently disheveled. He's also maybe the friendliest, genuinely nicest person I've ever met. Reporters use different tactics to get sources to talk to them. Some flatter their sources; some try to intimidate them. I've seen male reporters play the old-boy-network card, going golfing with the people they want to talk to. Pretty females flirt. They won't admit to it, but they do. In Elias's case, I think people tell him their secrets because he's just so damn likable.

I glanced around his apartment. No gleaming trays of silver here. Elias's bike took up a quarter of the room we were standing in. Behind him stood a navy futon piled with copies of *Sports Illustrated*, the *Economist*, a Stanford sweatshirt, and an assortment of remote controls. "Just tell me you have a hot shower somewhere and a bed with marginally clean sheets waiting for me. Otherwise I may really lose the will to live."

"Yep. I can even dangle the prospect of leftovers from my Chinese take-out dinner. As soon as you tell me everything."

I reeled off the highlights of the last twenty-four hours. He stood gaping. I held up my hands before he could start firing questions.

"I'm going to take a shower now. And then I'm going to eat your Chinese leftovers. And then I'm going to bed. Oh, and I need something to sleep in."

Twenty minutes later I was sitting at his kitchen table in the Stanford sweatshirt, scrubbed clean and wet hair dripping down my neck. I felt like a new woman. Shrimp in black-bean sauce had never tasted so good. Elias was raining questions down on me, most of which I couldn't answer. Soon I was fading again, my eyelids starting to droop, when the kitchen phone rang.

It was past eleven. Elias raised his eyebrows and answered.

"Hi. . . . Yes. . . . She's here. . . . Sure, hang on." He passed me the phone. *"The Silver Fox,"* he mouthed.

I raised my eyebrows back at Elias.

"Hello?"

"Ms. James." I heard the familiar voice. "We'll need to look at getting you a new phone. And did you find somewhere to buy clothes?"

I cocked my head to the side and considered this. Hyde Rawlins, the managing editor of the *New England Chronicle*, was sitting up late in his hotel room, fretting about the state of my wardrobe?

"Yes," I ventured. "I found a J.Crew on M Street that was still open. Why are you—"

"Lovely. I'll see you at the West Wing gate again at eight tomorrow morning. Be on time, please. They're asking for a meeting at eight thirty, but I'm trying to push it to nine, in case Jill can join us."

"Hang on, hang on. What are you talking about?" Jill, if it was the Jill I thought he was referring to, was the Washington bureau chief of the *Chronicle*.

"I got a call from our friend on the Security Council a few minutes ago. He said he didn't have a good phone number for you. He would like to see us again, along with his boss—the national security adviser—and the White House press secretary." Hyde paused. "It appears they're pulling out the big guns to try to persuade us not to publish. I thought it best not to mention you haven't actually written a single sentence yet."

"But—what story do they think we're about to run with?"

"It seems your visit this afternoon triggered quite the extraordinary chain of events, Ms. James. He told me—this is strictly off the record— he told me they've identified the woman beside you on the plane. Her name was Polly Murphy. Irish citizen, thirty-five years old. She worked at a bank. No criminal record. Nothing out of the ordinary about her.

The proper autopsy will take a bit, but they know what killed her. Her blood samples came back swimming with barbiturates and potassium chloride. That's—well, obviously—it's deadly."

I gave a little gasp. "Potassium chloride? Isn't that the stuff they use . . ."

"In lethal injections, yes." He paused again. "You do realize why they told me this? And why I'm telling you now?"

"Because I was the one who discovered her?"

"Yes, and because it does seem likely, as you've already suspected, that the injection was intended for you."

I swallowed. It felt very cold suddenly in Elias's basement kitchen.

"That's not all, I'm afraid. The man you've been chasing. Nadeem Siddiqui. He was on a US counterproliferation watch list. They keep tabs on the people who work at Pakistan's nuclear labs when they travel. Standard practice. I suspect so they can try to recruit them to spy for us. I don't know if it worked in Siddiqui's case. Or if he'd done anything in particular to arouse suspicion. At any rate—" Hyde stopped for a moment. "At any rate, he's dead. Nadeem Siddiqui is dead. His lab in Pakistan apparently reported it yesterday."

37

Shaukat Malik leaned into the Oval Office and smiled.

He was delighted to find it looked as he'd imagined it, as he'd seen it so often on TV. Through long windows he could see the Rose Garden and beyond it the emerald lawn unspooling. Inside, carefully arranged, stood emblems of power: the thick carpet with its presidential seal, a pair of richly decorated flags, and of course the famous desk. He couldn't help a little shiver of excitement from traveling down his spine.

"Very nice, very nice," he said respectfully, catching his guide's eye. "What a great honor."

This was his last task. The last time he would personally face danger.

All the hours, all the sweat, all the roads, had led to here. He and the man posing tonight as his grandfather would be engaging in an elaborate performance. They each had specific roles to play. This morning they had rehearsed in Malik's hotel room, practicing where to stand, what to say. Malik was cast as the eager tourist, the older man as the senile patriarch of the family. It was all scripted. If they could pull this off, the rest would be out of Malik's hands.

He had held his breath on the way into the White House, as guards inspected his passport photo and scanned the bar code into their machine. He willed himself to look casual, to keep the beads of sweat from appearing at his temple. No matter. It was a hot night. Everyone was sticky. He felt rivers of sweat roll down his back.

"What a scorcher, huh?" asked one of the guards, motioning him through the metal detector and then handing back his wallet and belt. The guard was sweating too. Malik nodded. Everything was in order. They made him leave his cell phone behind. No electronic gadgets or cameras allowed on West Wing tours. Not even these private, after-hours, friends-and-family visits.

But he had known about this. It was taken care of. Another phone was already waiting for him, inside. He found it right where it was supposed to be, taped under the seat of the second-from-the-left chair in the West Wing waiting room. Easy. He made as if to tie his shoe, leaned over, unpeeled the tape, and slid the phone into his pocket.

He wanted to test it, and this proved easy too. He waited until their guide appeared and introduced himself as Daniel. Then Malik made an embarrassed gesture and asked for the men's room. Inside the stall he tapped in the password he'd been given. The phone lit up. He clicked on the camera and selected VIDEO. The recording light glowed. He hit pause and stuffed the phone back in his pocket. He was ready.

Daniel turned out to be disconcertingly eager and chatty. This, despite the fact that giving after-hours tours couldn't rank among his more thrilling duties as a White House aide.

"Well, you two excited? Here we go," Daniel chirped. "Now, we're not going to be visiting any of the fancy formal state rooms. That's for the regular tourists. The hoi polloi." He winked and led them to the press briefing room, then steered the men to seats in the front row. Daniel ducked behind the podium and mimed the daily ritual of the grilling of the White House press secretary and other senior officials. Malik nodded politely. What a strange country.

"All right, down these stairs now." Daniel swept ahead of them. "Here we are. The White House mess. They do a mean breakfast taco here. At least I hear they do. Only senior staff eat here. Anyway, where you guys from? How you liking this heat?"

Malik marveled at the seemingly bottomless American capacity for small talk. "We're from Baltimore," he replied. "Not originally, but that's where we live now. The whole family's there." This was the cover story they had rehearsed.

Daniel seemed to buy it. "Cool. Baltimore. The harbor there is really cool. And your grandfather? He, uh, doesn't speak much English, I guess?"

Malik looked at the elderly man. He was smiling in a vaguely demented way and studying a lunch menu tacked to the wall.

"No, but Grandpa picks up more than he lets on." Malik hoped this was the case. Before this morning, he had never actually met the man now playing his grandfather.

"But, so how did you guys get on an insiders' tour?" Daniel persisted. "These are pretty hard to get, you know. You must know somebody high up."

"It is my grandfather's dream—since he became an American citizen—to come see the president at his home, and thank him," Malik lied smoothly, ignoring the actual question that had been asked.

Daniel laughed. "Yeah, well, I don't know if we'll be meeting the president tonight. But we'll get you close."

Malik and the old man feigned interest at the locked door to the

Situation Room ("Sorry—even I can't go in there"), and then, finally, they were headed back upstairs. Daniel led the way down a corridor and around a corner. They passed the stately Cabinet Room, then the Roosevelt Room. Malik pretended to admire the portraits on the walls. Daniel waved hello to a Secret Service agent tucked behind a workstation.

At last they stopped. "All right," said Daniel. "Time for the grand finale. The most famous room on the tour. Are you two ready?"

Behind Daniel's back, the old man cocked his head and raised his eyebrows at Malik. Malik nodded, almost imperceptibly. Grandpa nodded back. Together they turned and looked into the room.

The Oval Office was brightly lit, immaculately neat, and empty. A velvet rope prevented them from actually stepping inside. But that was no matter. Malik could see everything he needed from the doorway. His fingers closed around the phone in his pocket. He would only have a minute, perhaps less.

Just as they had rehearsed, the old man began to mumble, *"Maaf karna . . ."* Then, louder: *"Maaf karna,* my wallet, must have dropped . . ." Grandpa shuffled with surprising agility back toward the Cabinet Room.

"Hang on, you can't—" Daniel streaked after him. The Secret Service guard stood up. As he rounded the corner the old man dropped to his hands and knees, cursing loudly in Urdu. Daniel and the guard swore in surprise and followed.

Now.

Malik yanked the phone from his pocket. He undid the pause button, and the video began recording. He swept the camera around the room behind him, so there would be no mistaking where he stood. Then he zoomed in and locked the picture tight on his face. There was hatred in his eyes. He had memorized what he would say, timed it so he would not stumble and lose his place. He spoke quickly now, in a low voice and directly into the microphone.

"As-salaam alaikum. My brothers, my sisters, do you see where I am tonight? Do you see where the mujahideen have reached?

"America, do you think you can send your spies into our country, send your drones to kill our people, send your assassins to kill the great sheikh inside his own home? Well, here we are inside your home. Inside your White House. Who is powerful now?

"*Inshallah*, we will take our revenge. You will see the power of a Muslim bomb. God willing, Islam is coming to the world."

As he said the last words, he heard the crash of something being knocked from a table and hitting the floor. The old man was still cursing loudly, a calculated attempt to mask the sound of Malik speaking. It sounded like he was being pulled to his feet. Malik was out of time. He hit stop and shoved the phone deep into his pocket. He prayed the file would save correctly.

Daniel appeared red-faced at the door. "I think we need to go now. Your grandfather's had quite enough for one night." The Secret Service agent had the old man's arm twisted underneath his own. His radio was crackling. Two more guards appeared.

"This old geezer?" one of them asked.

The two were whisked back to the main waiting room. The guards stepped aside and conferred. There appeared to be some discussion as to whether the commotion in the Cabinet Room required follow-up. Daniel stood tensely off to the side.

Then the old man began to chuckle softly. He held up his hand in the air. He was clutching a wallet.

Malik played along. "In your pocket, Papa? The whole time?"

"But different pocket, wrong pocket," the old man croaked. He shrugged his shoulders in an apologetic way and let the glazed look creep back over his eyes. His mouth hung slack. He looked ancient, feeble.

The guards appeared to reach a decision. "Enough already," one of them snapped. "Thanks very much for coming. Out you go. This way, thank you, gentlemen . . ."

Malik caught Daniel's eye and mouthed a thank-you. Then they were walking back down the driveway. There was no security check to exit the White House. Malik dropped his temporary ID in a bin and collected the phone he'd had to check on the way in. He put it in his pocket next to the new one. They spun through a revolving gate and walked together in silence down the block to Seventeenth Street, just in case anyone was watching. At the corner they turned and faced each other.

"You recorded the video?" the older man asked in perfect English.

"Yes."

"Good." He turned and walked swiftly away.

Malik stood still and looked up at the starry night sky. It was still warm outside. The smells of bus fumes and fresh-cut grass hung in the air. A few tourists wandered past.

He allowed himself a small smile. He had done it.

38

Lucien Sly hunched over his desk and studied the contents of the folder. This latest assignment was bizarre, even by the standards of his line of work.

Photographs of Alexandra James were fanned across his work surface. They captured her smiling in her official picture on the *Chronicle* website . . . in profile walking into a terminal at Heathrow Airport . . . sitting two days ago outside a café on Old Compton Street in London. In this last one she was staring in the direction of the camera, a feisty look on her face, as if she knew she was being photographed. It was disconcerting.

When the classified file on Alex James had landed in his in-box yesterday, his first thought was that it must be a joke. Some of the blokes down at Vauxhall Cross taking the Mickey. Perhaps someone had spotted them together at the Eagle pub the other night and decided to have a laugh.

But this had turned out not to be the case. Incredibly, Alex appeared to be a legitimate surveillance target for MI6. Awkward to be asked to monitor someone when you were in fact already sleeping with her.

What was not clear from the file was *why* she had been singled out for surveillance. Yes, she had been asking questions about Nadeem Siddiqui. And, yes, Lucien had stupidly made a few phone calls for her. Trying to impress her, showing off. But it had seemed a lark, calling the fruit company, not something that touched on Lucien's real work. Siddiqui was leaving England, going home. His folder was about to be closed. Honestly, who cared why the Pakistani liked his bananas?

Spying on an American civilian was not something British intelligence would enter into lightly, so Lucien could only assume the CIA was involved or at least being kept informed. But again, why? His request for further information had been rebuffed; the answer that came back from headquarters boiled down to *You don't need to know so could you just shut up please and get on with it.*

He frowned and switched on his espresso maker. It was so bloody typical.

His father had warned him that a career with the Secret Intelligence Service would prove frustrating. It was a bit . . . common. And the history of the service was riddled with scandal and failure. Remember that whole sordid business with the Cambridge Five spies, his father had argued—who wants to get mixed up with that lot? But then, his father was a duke. It wasn't as if he were ever actually going to work for a living. The same was true for Lucien's eldest brother, and arguably, even the middle one. But the third son of a duke . . . well, he could find himself with time on his hands.

And so it had come as a relief when the master of Lucien's undergraduate college had discreetly invited him for tea during his final year. He had glided through university, was about to finish with a first in languages, but he had no clear idea what to do with his life. The master had quizzed him in French, then Italian, then German—then asked how he might feel about picking up Arabic. Love to, Lucien replied. Good. There were some gentlemen he should meet in London, the master had said. Things happened quickly after that.

Two years later, life as a spy for MI6 was proving nothing like Lucien had imagined. He was aware, thank you very much, that James Bond was a work of fiction. But was it too much to ask for a small crumb of adventure, given that all over the world *at this very moment* arms deals were probably being struck, terrorist plots hatched, dictators covertly toppled? And here he was, stuck in rudding Cambridge, where the most radical idea put forward all week was whether to banish the Latin blessing at formal hall.

Lucien longed to travel. It was what MI6 did, for God's sake; the agency's raison d'être was to collect *foreign* intelligence. Affairs on British soil were supposed to fall to their rather less glamorous sister spy service, MI5. And Lucien had traveled a bit, in the beginning. But it became apparent that he suffered an unusual disadvantage: He was too well connected in London society. He could move in circles no other recruit could penetrate. His assignments soon trended toward dinners in Belgravia with Russian oligarchs, Saudi princes, German financiers. Lucien moved with ease at their parties because they were the type of parties he would have been invited to anyway. He was simply too valuable at home to be sent abroad.

His cover was not exactly creative. He was supposed to be a graduate student at Cambridge, pursuing his PhD in the department of Middle Eastern Studies. His Arabic was coming along quite well, not that it looked as if he would ever have the chance to use it. And from this post he was free not only to travel regularly to London, but to investigate the many people of interest who passed through the university.

Pakistani nuclear scientists, for example. He had been asked to watch Siddiqui months ago. Standard operating procedure. Pakistan was currently generating terrorists and nuclear weapons at equally alarming rates. Despite their public protestations of confidence, neither London nor Washington were at all convinced that Pakistan's weapons were safe. Thus almost anytime someone with knowledge of the nuclear program traveled to the West, he was monitored. Probably approached too, with an eye to persuading him to sell his country's secrets. Whether this had happened in Nadeem Siddiqui's case, Lucien did not know. That was above his pay grade. He was just supposed to keep an eye on the guy.

This had not been difficult. Siddiqui kept a low profile. He got up to little worth reporting. Lucien had noted his budding friendship with Thom Carlyle. It seemed an unlikely pairing, the golden-boy jock from America and the taciturn Pakistani. The two had met for lunch a couple times. Lucien did not know what they had discussed. He began keeping tabs on Carlyle as well. That had had the fringe benefit of bringing Petronella into his orbit. An enjoyable if not entirely professional detour. Lucien had felt guilty the first few times his job had led to trysts. But he was learning that MI6—an agency that broke the law in other countries as a matter of routine—did not pass judgment when its officers indulged in the occasional moral lapse.

Now, though, Thom Carlyle was dead. And the whole situation with Alex—it was one twist too many. It was one thing to meet someone through your work and end up in bed with her. It was quite another to meet someone through your work, end up in bed with her, and then have her photograph appear on your computer screen as your next surveillance target. He was having trouble sorting through the ethics implications. No, forget the ethics—he was having trouble sorting through the basic mechanics of what was going on. The Crispin Withington encounter, for example, struck Lucien as extremely odd. Who had that man really been? The choice of such a clumsy cover identity seemed amateur for an intelligence agency. But who else could it be?

He reached for his coffee. It had gone cold. Then he looked again at the file. Now that Alex had left the UK, he was supposed to submit a short final report on where she had gone and whom she had spoken to while here. Tricky, given that she'd spent half her time in bed with him. He was also required to provide his professional assessment of the subject's state of mind.

Lucien pulled back his shirt and regarded a purplish bruise flowering across his collarbone. In the middle was a ring of small, pink, horizontal lines. Teeth marks. It had hurt in a searing, wonderful way when she bit him. *Her state of mind?* Assertive, definitely. Determined. Funny. Really, really sexy.

He sighed and stared at his blank screen. He was mad to be carrying on with her. Stark, raving bonkers to have asked her to Bermuda. He could always get out of it, he supposed.

But here he was forced to confront an uncomfortable fact: he very much liked Alexandra James. He quite wanted to go to Bermuda with her. It was ridiculous, obviously, but there it was.

And, really—how much of a problem could it turn out to be?

39

WHEN I WAS A LITTLE girl, my mother used to wake me by singing.

It is one of my earliest memories. Her entering the dark room, walking to the window to pull back the curtain and let the sun shine in, humming "Amazing Grace." When she was reasonably confident I was awake, she would drop the humming and burst into full-throated song. She has a deep, warm, honeyed voice and is partial to old hymns, though she's never been much of one for church. Old hymns and Broadway choruses and Scottish lullabies.

"Amazing Grace" is one of her favorites. As she sang, she would lean down to kiss my cheek and pull the blankets back, and I could smell tea and warm milk and love on her breath. Outside the thrum of New York traffic would be roaring to life. She would coax me to the mirror and wash my face with a warm rag, then brush my curls into pigtails. Singing the whole time. *I once was lost, but now am found. Was blind, but now I see. . . .*

It's been years since my mother has woken me with song, and it took me a minute to work out why the memory was washing over me now. It was the first gray light of morning. The only sounds came from pipes moving water in the house upstairs and a bird chirping in a nearby tree.

Then I realized. Something in my subconscious must have been yearning for that voice, and everything it conveyed: a sense that everything in the world was fine, just fine, and that, yes, a hot bowl of porridge did lie in my immediate future.

I turned over in Elias's bed—he had gallantly taken the sofa—and tried to knead the knots out of my neck. Jet lag and exhaustion had mercifully combined to allow me several hours of sleep. But I had apparently slept with my neck twisted and my pillow in a kind of death clutch. Everything in the world was definitely not fine. I felt, to put it bluntly, petrified.

I dragged myself out of bed and down the hallway toward the kitchen. Heavy doses of either coffee or gin were going to be required to get me through the morning. Coffee seemed the more socially acceptable route at six in the morning. Coffee. I registered with fleeting interest that for the first time in days I was craving coffee, not tea: my internal switch had already flipped upon crossing the Atlantic.

In the kitchen I couldn't help cracking a smile. Last night I had not noticed the enormous, barista-style coffeemaker on the counter. It was one of those contraptions that costs $1,000 at Williams-Sonoma and can grind your beans, froth your milk, and probably toast you a bagel while it's at it.

One of the many lovely things about Elias is that he drinks espresso the way Italians do. Which is to say, like water. He is notorious in the newsroom for disappearing on deadline, driving his editor into an apoplectic fit, and then casually reappearing with a steaming thimble of black sludge. He does not believe in milk. Or sugar. Why dilute perfection? I've seen him grimace at people emerging from Starbucks with twenty-ounce, venti pumpkin-spice lattes in hand. It seems to offend him on some deep, personal level.

I clanked around the kitchen for a bit. My second cup was brewing and I was buttering toast when Elias appeared in the doorway.

"Morning, Shorty. Coffee?"

"Um-hmm. I'm amazed you managed to figure that thing out." He nodded toward the espresso machine. "How'd you sleep?"

I hugged my arms tight across my chest. "Okay. Considering. How about you?"

He looked ruefully back at the futon. "Okay. Considering."

I smiled. "Any chance I could check my e-mail? I lost my laptop yesterday, as you know, and my phone too. I am officially"—I paused for effect—"off the grid."

He regarded me with the stunned expression of a man who has not ventured out without a cell phone for the entirety of his adult life.

"Uh—sure," he said, recovering. He left the kitchen and reappeared a minute later carrying his laptop.

I set his espresso thimble in front of him and waited. Minutes passed. Elias clicked and typed, clearly checking his own in-box, his face screwed up in concentration. I stared at him and drummed my fingers.

"In your own time," I finally grumbled. "I mean, I've just got this little old meeting at the White House, nothing important. Wouldn't be useful at all to check the headlines and my messages beforehand."

"Yes, okay, okay, but listen. There's an e-mail to both of us from Hyde—"

"What's he saying?" I pounced toward the screen.

"It's so weird. He's asking what we know about UTN. Well,

really asking me, I suppose. No reason you should have heard of them. But if it's the UTN I'm thinking of . . . I haven't heard that name in years."

He looked puzzled. "Hyde says he reached an excellent source of his last night, and the guy told him there's a lot of buzz about UTN. They were these crackpot nuclear scientists from Pakistan. The leader was a real nut job. . . . What was his name again . . . ? But I thought they got shut down after 9/11. Nobody's written about them for years."

"Let me see." I tried to elbow Elias over so I could share the screen.

"Hang on. Just want to check . . ." He was typing furiously. "Let me bounce this off a couple folks. At least get a steer on whether Hyde's source is right. I am so *not* loving being one step behind the boss, not to mention you, on my own beat."

I sighed. He ignored me. He was clearly not going to let me near the laptop.

"Fine," I said. "I'm going to take a shower. And in half an hour, I am going to reappear so you can give me a primer on UTN. And let me check my mail. Okay?"

He continued ignoring me. I flounced off to the bathroom.

In fact I was ready in less than fifteen minutes, a personal record. I'd had to pull my damp hair into a knot, having discovered that Elias— being a boy—didn't own a hair dryer. The only makeup I had was what had been in my handbag, mascara and a tube of plum lipstick. My reflection in the mirror looked pale and severe. It suited my mood.

Still, the cream sheath dress I'd picked up last night fit remarkably well. And thank God I'd worn my Manolos on the plane. I slipped them on and instantly felt a little better. Some women report that lipstick has this transformative effect on them. My friend Jess swears by a certain shade of Chanel red. For me, it's always been about the shoes. I felt dressed for battle.

Back in the kitchen Elias was scowling. "No one's gotten back to me yet."

"Well, it has been all of, like"—I consulted my watch—"seventeen minutes."

"Yeah, but these are guys who check their e-mail every ninety seconds. Anyway, I scanned the wires. Nothing on them about UTN or even Pakistan, except there's flooding in some town I've never heard of, and there was another suicide bomb in the tribal areas."

"A bomb?"

"Yeah, but that happens every day just about. They barely even register anymore, unless somebody important gets killed or there's a big death toll."

"How lovely. Anything else I need to know?"

He gave me an overview on UTN. And he finally relinquished the computer so I could log in. There was the message from Hyde. Elias had already fired off a one-word answer—*Checking*—and since I had nothing to add, I left it. There were various invitations to press events, a reminder from news admin to fill out my time sheet, and a note from Jess asking if I wanted to have dinner on Sunday. Then I got to one that made me blush. The subject line of Lucien's e-mail read, *Good Morning, Luscious Legs.*

Elias, reading over my shoulder, smirked. "Should I ask?"

"Nope," I said firmly, and logged out before he could read further. I stood up. "I need to get going. Could you call me a taxi?"

"No need. M Street is crawling with them."

I looked dubiously at my four-inch-high heels, remembering the brick sidewalks and the steep hill the taxi had navigated to get here.

"Anyway," he continued, "I'm coming. Give me ten minutes."

"I'll give you five," I said, although secretly I was relieved. It felt safer not to go out alone.

HYDE MET ME OUTSIDE THE White House with a new cell phone.

"It's a loaner from the bureau," he said. "I had the IT people program it so calls to your desk in Boston will forward automatically. Your old cell number should forward too."

I eyed it suspiciously. "Do you know whether the GPS—"

"I asked about that," interrupted Hyde, reading my mind. "I confess I didn't quite understand all the technical mumbo jumbo. I think the takeaway was that they've tried to disable the GPS. But I must say the overnight team didn't inspire my complete confidence. So treat it with caution."

I nodded. "Thanks. You've been busy."

"That I have, Ms. James. And you? Did you get some sleep?" He studied me. "You're looking . . . if I may say . . . a touch seasick."

I pinched my cheeks to put color in them. "Never better, actually. Is Jill coming?"

The paper's Washington bureau chief was not among my favorite people. Jill Hernandez possessed a vicious temper and strangely large nostrils, which opened wider still when she was angry, which was often. It was enough to make you steer well clear. Still, I figured the more people in this meeting who were at least supposed to be on my side, the better.

"She is. Now, Mr. Thottrup." Hyde turned to Elias. "Have you been able to confirm any of the information I've been passing along? About the unfortunate Nadeem Siddiqui no longer being with us? Or why everyone's hair is on fire over this UTN outfit?"

Elias seemed to shrink. "Still working it. I've got lots of calls out. No one's getting back to me. Even the ones who usually do. I don't understand it."

"Um-hmm. Perhaps you could keep working the phones while we're in this meeting. Perhaps you could even trouble yourself to work the hallways at the Pentagon or State? Between espresso breaks, obviously. It would be so useful, truly, to have someone besides myself producing new information."

Elias nodded miserably.

He was saved by the arrival of Jill. She came clomping down Pennsylvania Avenue toward us, a Dunkin' Donuts Dunkaccino mug in hand and a nylon laptop bag slung across her chest. She wore a navy suit at least two sizes too big. This was set off by beige pumps and support hose. Was it just me, or did women in this town go out of their way to look unattractive? Incredible, really, that so many sex scandals unfold in Washington, when everyone walks around dressed like suburban Sunday-school teachers.

"Good morning," Hyde called out. "So kind of you to join our merry band."

"Hi, Hyde," she said curtly, before turning on me. "Good morning, Alex. Any more surprises in store for us this morning? You have no idea exactly how unpleasant you have made my last twenty-four hours."

I smiled thinly and considered various responses, mostly along the lines of *And you have no idea exactly how unpleasant the sight of your ankles straining those granny tights is.* But both Hyde and Elias were shooting me urgent looks that meant *Zip it.*

I bit my tongue.

Jill, however, pressed on. "I sure as hell hope the two of you know what you're doing, because I certainly don't," she spat, eyeing Hyde and me. "What a complete fucking fiasco."

"Thank you, Ms. Hernandez," Hyde cut across her. "That'll be enough."

"Well, it's not as if you—"

"I said enough."

"With *respect*, Hyde," she said acidly, "I am the one who will be fielding phone calls for the next month—"

"With respect, Jill: Shut up."

Elias sucked his breath in and muttered, "Whoa." Jill must have heard it. She rounded on him. The nostrils flared. "What are you doing here? You weren't invited this morning, were you?"

Elias shook his head, his humiliation complete. "I just wanted to make sure Alex made it here okay. Off to the bureau now."

He was turning to slink off when Jill held out the Dunkaccino mug. "Carry this back for me, will you? I don't think they'll let me take it in."

I watched Elias fight to suppress a shudder. Then, sweet boy that he was, he reached out his hand.

That's when Hyde snapped. "For Christ's sake, Jill, you'd be bloody lucky to have them confiscate it. Vile plastic crap." He snatched it from her hands and started marching toward the White House gate.

"Let's go then, both of you," he called over his shoulder. "'Once more unto the breach, dear friends, once more—'"

I rolled my eyes.

"Oh, come on," said Hyde. "This is going to be fun."

40

The president's national security adviser is an ex–Marine Corps general with ramrod posture and one lazy eye.

Mike Carspecken had a reputation for being difficult. I remember reading that he'd needed quite a lot of persuading to take the job because it required retiring his uniform and stepping down from active duty. He sat facing me now in a charcoal-gray suit and red silk tie. Both the tie and his cuff links flashed the Semper Fi crest. Apparently he was prepared to take the civilian look only so far.

After we were shown into his West Wing office, he had shaken our hands and then motioned us toward a bristly, blue sofa pushed up against the wall. Hyde, Jill, and I sat down uncomfortably side by side, three ducks in a row. General Carspecken and the other White House officials took chairs facing us across a low table. Coffee was offered and politely declined; the general and Hyde exchanged pleasantries in a stiff way that suggested they had crossed swords before.

Finally the general smoothed his red tie and leaned back. "Let's get down to business, shall we? We have what appears to be a small situation on our hands. My understanding is it's under control, but it would be useful not to have inflammatory or inaccurate media reports circulate while we try to wrap things up."

Hyde gave a snort.

General Carspecken ignored him. "As I was saying, I need to ask you to keep this matter quiet right now. For national security reasons. That has to be the utmost priority, naturally, for all of us. So what I would propose is that you hold your story for now, Alexandra." He looked at me. "In exchange, I can give you a bit of context today, to enhance your understanding of the issues at hand. We can also discuss the possibility of your sitting down at a future date with senior administration officials, doing some exclusive interviews with them." The general cocked his head toward the White House press secretary.

She nodded vigorously. "The SAOs would be on background, obviously. But they could fill in details that would put you well ahead of your competitors—"

"Oh, please," interrupted Hyde. "Can either of you explain to me exactly how our story is supposedly going to damage national security?"

"Well, obviously, I can't comment on national security matters," General Carspecken began testily.

"But what argument are you making, Mike? That we'll damage sources and methods? Disrupt an ongoing operation?"

"Yes, both of those. And it always complicates things once wild rumors start flying around in the press. You know it as well as I do."

"I couldn't agree more," Hyde said pleasantly. "Which is why, instead of wild rumors, we were thinking instead of publishing facts. For example, the tracking number of a large fruit shipment that just landed from Pakistan. Or the fact that yesterday someone tried to kill the reporter who's been asking questions about that shipment. Or, let's see—the fact that the man who placed that fruit order, a member of Pakistan's nuclear establishment, has just been reported dead." Hyde paused and looked down at his fingernails. "Frankly, Mike, we have so *many* fascinating facts to relate to our readers that it's hard to know quite where to start."

The room fell silent.

General Carspecken cleared his throat. "I'm sure I don't have to explain why matters such as the ones you're describing might be . . . sensitive at this particular point in time."

"No, you don't," said Hyde. "And I'm sure I don't have to explain why matters such as the ones I'm describing add up to a pretty interesting news story. Or why—given the financial pressure I'm under to shut down the DC bureau completely—it would be nice to have the *Chronicle* out front on a major national story. So you're going to have to give us a better reason than 'things are sensitive' to get me to sit on one."

Silence fell again.

I had to hand it to Hyde. I might be out of my depth on national-security matters, but I had wheedled information out of enough reluctant officials to recognize a master at work.

After a moment Jill spoke. Her nose had twitched when Hyde made the threat about shutting the Washington bureau, but otherwise she hadn't entered the fray. "Why don't we start with what's happening now. When Hyde asked just now whether our publishing might disrupt an ongoing operation, you said yes. Can you be more specific?"

The general sighed. He must have been wishing he could order us to drop and give him fifty push-ups. Instead he smoothed his tie again, crossed and uncrossed his legs, and finally looked up at me. Or at least I think he looked at me; it was hard to tell with his lazy eye.

"Alexandra," he said in a patronizing tone, "I suspect you've never had reason to have heard of an organization called the Ummah Tameer-e-Nau."

I pretended to think for a minute. "UTN, you mean? The group headed by Sultan Bashiruddin Mahmood? He's the guy who talked to Al Qaeda about selling them nuclear weapons technology. But I thought they'd been effectively dismantled. What's UTN got to do with anything?"

Jill stared at me. Hyde looked away, trying not to smirk.

The general shot a furious look at the press secretary, then turned back to me. "You seem well-informed for someone who usually covers the education beat."

"I try to read widely, sir."

"Of course you do," he said coldly. "And you are correct that they were dismantled after 9/11. But there is some . . . evidence . . . that suggests perhaps offshoots remained active. And may remain dedicated to the original goal. Of course, we do not remotely believe they're capable of procuring or detonating an active weapon." The general stopped, as if that pretty much covered things.

"What does that have to do with Nadeem Siddiqui?" I asked.

"He is someone we have monitored."

"Why?"

"We always worry about extremist links."

"But did you have a reason in his case?"

"He . . ." The general hesitated. "We fear he may have been doing trial runs."

"Trial runs? For what?"

"Siddiqui was ordering large crates of bananas."

"I know. I saw one of them."

"It was quite large?"

"Almost as big as a car."

"Yes. I gather you've learned that among the unique qualities of a banana is that it produces radiation. Low levels, obviously. They're quite safe to eat. But enough that bulk shipments don't get inspected. They set off the sensors, and then they get waved through. Literally hundreds of tons of them every day. An ideal hiding place, isn't it, if you were trying to shift radioactive material?"

"And so you think—"

"What I think is we would very much like to find and inspect that shipment that arrived at Dulles on Tuesday. And I think it would *not* be helpful for you to sow mass panic by writing about events that you know little about."

Hyde rolled his eyes. "As it happens, she appears to know a good deal more about them than you do, Mike."

Before the two of them could start bickering again, I cut in. "General, forgive me, but I'm still trying to get my head around this. Say for argument's sake that it's true, and somebody is trying to smuggle a nuclear bomb inside boxes of bananas. I mean, it's ridiculous sounding, but on top of that—how would they get it? Doesn't Pakistan keep that stuff locked down? Surely someone would notice if a nuclear weapon just walked out the door."

The general shrugged. "You would think. A complete weapon would be very challenging to steal, I would hope. But weapons-usable material turns up fairly often on the nuclear black market. No one ever seems to notice it was missing until it gets seized."

"But that's crazy. I guess I can see it for old Soviet weapons, rusting in a warehouse outside Kiev or something. But for an active program in a country like Pakistan? With terrorists running around? I thought I read that we were spending all this money to help them with high-tech launch codes and security protocols and stuff. Isn't someone supposed to be keeping track of where everything is?"

The general leaned forward. "Young lady, without confirming or denying the existence of any funds that may—or may not—have been appropriated to aid Pakistan's nuclear program, consider this scenario. The right person, placed inside the right laboratory, underreports just a little every day how much nuclear material has been produced. Or how much is in storage. Over time you could have quite a sizable little stockpile that just . . . disappeared."

"And you think—you think Nadeem Siddiqui was that person?"

"No comment."

"But you're talking some sort of inside job. You're not suggesting the complicity of the Pakistani government, are you?"

"No. I don't think they're quite that insane. But given that you read so widely," the general added mockingly, "you'll be aware that Pakistan's recent history doesn't suggest great success at detecting or thwarting threats from inside the military and nuclear establishments."

I thought about this for a moment. Then I took a chance. Elias had suggested a couple of long-shot interview requests, and this seemed as good a time as any. "I'd like to meet with the head of the CIA. Get a full briefing on UTN and other radical offshoot groups."

Everyone in the room, including Hyde and Jill, looked at me as if I were cracked.

"No," said General Carspecken.

"Why not?"

"Why not? Well, let's see: he's a busy man, he almost never gives interviews, and we're speaking here off the record about classified information. Anyway, the CIA handles his press requests, it's got nothing to do with us."

The press secretary bobbed her head in agreement.

I narrowed my eyes. "You're asking me to sit on what would appear to be the story of a lifetime. I'm asking you for an interview. An *on*-the-record interview."

Back came the patronizing smile. "As I said, he's a busy man. I'll see what I can do."

"Thank you. One last thing. What does any of this have to do with Thomas Carlyle?"

"With Thomas Carlyle?" The general looked blank. The press secretary leaned over and whispered in his ear. "Ah, yes. I heard you asked Lowell about that. A bit heartless to trouble him with this nonsense when he's just lost his son, don't you think?"

"Heartless? I'm not trying to trouble him or not trouble him. I'm just trying to understand the connections."

"There is no connection. Not that I know of. What would it be?"

"There is no connection?"

"Yes, that's what I just said, Alexandra," the general said irritably. He looked around. "Okay. Are we good?"

Hyde stood up. "Just so we're clear, Mike. We're going to continue to aggressively pursue this story. I'll check in with you this afternoon to let you know where things stand and whether we intend to publish tomorrow. We'll obviously give you the opportunity to issue a statement on behalf of the administration."

"You do that," said the general, looking as if he sorely missed the days when people shut up and saluted when he gave them an order. "But just so we're clear too. I will use every tool at my disposal—including the full legal power of the White House—to prevent you from publishing."

"Of course. Good luck with that," Hyde replied. "I haven't been sued yet this week, I don't think. But, hell—it's only Thursday."

41

Later that morning I got two interesting phone calls.

The first was from a spokesman for the CIA. He told me they had received my request and that they would be able to offer me a background briefing that afternoon.

"With the director?"

"No, I'm afraid he won't be available today. With Edmund Tusk."

"Who's that?"

"The associate deputy director of the National Clandestine Service."

"I had asked for an interview with the director."

"Again, he's not available. Between you and me, you're better off with

Tusk," the spokesman added conspiratorially. "Former chief of station in Islamabad and Kabul. Amman too, I think. He speaks Dari, Pashto, God knows what else. He's the one who knows all the people worth knowing over there."

"Well, I'll need it to be on the record."

"Sorry. Can't do it. Not the way these guys roll."

"But—"

"Listen, you gotta understand, this is a guy who's probably never talked to a journalist in his life. He only just got his cover lifted back in February."

"He—what?"

"He was working undercover until he got called back to HQ a few months ago."

I sighed. Nothing about this experience was making me envy Elias the intelligence beat. Did no one ever use a real name or speak on the record? Still, I couldn't see I had much of a choice. Maybe once I got out there and met the guy I could persuade him to give me a few quotes I could print. I agreed to a time and hung up.

The second call was from Marco Galloni.

It felt like years since I'd thought of him; it actually took me half a second to place the name. Was it only last week we'd been flirting and trading threats in the Eliot House courtyard?

"Alex," he said urgently. "Hi. You okay? What are you mixed up in? I shouldn't be calling. But the weirdest alert just came across. About increased vigilance at border crossings, and new orders for highway patrol to stop produce-delivery trucks for random searches—"

"No. Are you kidding me?"

"No, they just came out this morning."

"But from where?"

"Let's see . . . NCTC. The National Counterterrorism Center. You know, we're supposed to all be partners now, a whole new world of information sharing, yada yada yada. Sometimes stuff even trickles down to lowly local law-enforcement guys like us. But, Alex, the memo mentions you."

"*What?*"

"Yeah. It's in the increased airport-vigilance section. Something about a security incident yesterday on a British Airways flight?"

I laughed darkly. "A security incident. That would be one way of putting it. The woman sitting next to me was murdered. And it appears it was actually me they were after."

"But you're okay?"

"I appear to still be among the living, yes."

Galloni made a whistling noise as he exhaled. "Jesus. Why would someone want to—want you dead?"

"I don't know. The last few days have been extremely strange. Listen, Lieutenant—Marco—sorry, I'm not even sure what to call you—"

"I think we can go with *Marco* at this point."

"Okay. Marco. No one seems to believe me about this, but I think it's somehow all mixed up with Thom Carlyle. I think he was involved in something big. I don't know exactly what, and I can't tell you everything I do know. But this wasn't—this wasn't just a guy who fell out of a bell tower because he was depressed or got clumsy after a couple of beers."

"Yeah. I think we were in agreement on that point last week. I just can't prove it."

"No. Me either."

At that moment, a truck beeped its horn loudly behind me.

"Alex? Where are you?"

"Washington. Just walking down K Street. Trying to find a decent sandwich."

"But I called your desk."

"It's auto-forwarding calls to my cell phone. I had a meeting at the White House this morning. And I'm off to the CIA this afternoon. Quite the glamorous life I'm living down here."

Galloni was quiet for a moment. "Alex, two thoughts. I want you to listen to me, okay? You should switch to Skype. Stop using the cell."

I stopped walking. "Why?"

"Because I can't tell you everything I know either. But trust me, it's not that hard to eavesdrop on a cell phone once somebody knows the number. Skype is harder to intercept. Still not hard, mind you, but harder."

"Okay, but—"

"You just told me somebody tried to kill you yesterday. What makes you think they've stopped trying? And this morning your name went out in an urgent memo to every metropolitan police department on the East Coast. I'd say making yourself a little tougher to find might be a good idea."

"Fine. No more cell phones. What was the second thing?"

"Are you staying somewhere safe? Don't say the name out loud."

"Now you're making me paranoid! Yes, I am staying somewhere safe."

"Good. I'm going to call a buddy of mine down there. He's in the Secret Service. You going back to the White House?"

"Not that I know of."

"Still. His name's Ralph. Ralph McNamara. He's a good guy. Solid. Actually, he owes me a beer next time he's in Boston. I'm gonna tell him to keep an eye out for you."

"Thanks. I'm touched. But I'm fine."

"No, you're not. Remember. Ralph McNamara. You see him, you tell him Marco Galloni said to take care of you."

42

They say the best spies look like Midwestern dentists.

Or accountants.

Meaning they have bland, easy-to-forget faces. People too handsome or too ugly or too distinctive in any way could be a liability. They stand out.

If true, Edmund Tusk made an excellent spy.

He was neither tall nor short. He could have been forty or sixty or anywhere in between. He was portly, but not excessively so. His hair was colorless and thinning and he spoke in a flat, accentless voice. Tusk's only distinguishing characteristic was a pair of enormous glasses, with lenses so thick it was hard to make out the color of his eyes.

I had been swept through the main lobby, where the huge CIA seal looked exactly as it does in the movies. The lobby was gray and white marble. Oppressive. And dated, the way you'd imagine an elite spy head-quarters looking in the 1970s. Past a row of metal turnstiles I could see a glass wall and sunlight from an inner courtyard. A few Agency staffers were hurrying past. But the place felt strangely deserted. I had expected fierce security—metal detectors, X-ray machines, body-cavity searches, who knew? But there was just one uniformed guard behind a big desk. In front of it stood the spokesman who had called me earlier. He instructed me to leave my phone in a cubby behind the desk. Then he steered me away from the turnstiles and up several stairs to the left, into a small, antiseptic conference room.

Edmund Tusk was already there waiting.

He stood up to greet me, adjusted his paunch above his gray suit trousers, and sat back down. The spokesman looked nervously from Tusk to me and cleared his throat.

"So, just to reconfirm the ground rules we discussed—"

"We're good," I interrupted. "No quotes, no recordings, no photos, no nothing. Got it."

"And actually, you're free to go," added Tusk, to my surprise. "I think Alexandra and I will get along fine on our own."

"Oh, no, I'll stay. I'd prefer to."

"I insist."

"But Agency policy—" The spokesman tried to protest, but Tusk was now making a shooing motion with his hands.

"Out you go. I promise not to give away any state secrets. Just leave the door open a crack, will you? For the cat."

The cat? I wanted to inquire, but Tusk had leaned back and was studying me with great concentration, his eyes swimming behind the huge glasses. A button strained against his belly. I wondered vaguely whether it would hold. Then he smiled.

"So. Alexandra James. It's good to meet you. You're doing wonders for morale around here, you know. We always enjoy watching someone else ratchet up the stress levels of our brethren over at the White House. I gather you worked the good general into quite a rage this morning."

"I thought he was always like that."

"True. Not the gentlest soul. Was he wearing the Semper Fi tie?"

Now I smiled. "And the cuff links."

"Excellent. Something so exquisitely . . . *insecure* about that, isn't there? But I digress. How can I help you?"

I took a breath. "I've been reporting on a man named Nadeem Siddiqui. I understand US intelligence was interested in him too, so I'm assuming you know who I'm talking about and also that he's dead. Can you tell me what you know about him? How he died? Who he was associating with?"

"No. I can't get into individuals. Just broad themes, that sort of thing."

"But would you steer me away from—"

"I don't play that game, Alexandra."

I tried another angle. "This group UTN. Everyone thought they had gone away after 9/11. Are they active again? Why is the administration so concerned about them?"

He answered my question with one of his own. "Was it Carspecken who told you there's concern about UTN?"

"My meeting with the general was off the record, so I can't say."

"Mike Carspecken wouldn't know his UTN from his arsehole," Tusk snorted. "He can't keep many acronyms straight in his head at any given time, so he just latches on to one and runs with it. Sure, UTN is running around in Pakistan. So is Hizb ut-Tahrir, and Lashkar-e-Taiba, and half a dozen Taliban factions, not to mention the Haqqani network, and Hekmatyar's guys . . . You've got all kinds of crazies running around. Of course, unfortunately, the most dangerous ones are completely sane.

"Here's how I summed it up for the president the other day," Tusk added, a tad pompously. "Pakistan has more terrorists per square mile than anyplace else on earth. And it has a nuclear weapons program that is growing faster than anyplace on earth. What could possibly go wrong?"

He gave a strange little giggle. For all his blandness, there was an effeminate quality about Edmund Tusk.

"You—you mentioned the nuclear weapons program," I said. "This banana shipment that Nadeem Siddiqui had delivered. That you guys are now looking for. Is that really because there might be nuclear material inside?"

"Again, I can't comment on any specific situation."

"But would it actually be possible to steal a nuclear weapon, hide it inside a fruit crate, and just mail it to America?"

"Can't go there."

I was getting frustrated. "Okay. Hypothetically speaking—"

"I don't indulge in hypotheticals."

"Fine. Broadly, *thematically* speaking—how small can a nuclear weapon be? Would one fit inside a crate the size of a car?"

He shifted in his chair as if considering how to answer. "You know," he said finally, "it's difficult sometimes to remember what's classified and what's not. Isn't that funny? So many not even remotely interesting things are top secret. And so many important ones lie right there in plain view." He paused. "But I think it's fairly common knowledge that you can build a sweet little bomb these days with less than forty pounds of HEU."

"HEU?"

"Weapons-grade uranium."

"That's it? Forty pounds? But that's—that's the size of a child."

"Well, that's not counting the explosives, the electronics, the casing, what have you. But no, it needn't be large. And then you pop it inside a lead bag and you can move it wherever you want, no worries."

"It can't be that easy. I mean, hasn't Iran been trying to build nukes for ages? And they haven't managed, and they've got a whole country working on it?"

Tusk summoned his patience visibly. "You miss the point, my dear. Pakistan already *has* nuclear weapons. You're just talking about plucking one off the shelf. Anyway, Iran—well, the whole analogy just doesn't work. Iran is trying to build a nuclear *program*. If you're a terrorist, you don't need a program, you just want one bomb. It doesn't have to be reliable, does it? Even if it fizzles and doesn't work that well, you've still succeeded at producing a complete fucking catastrophe."

I considered this. Then I jumped.

A large, gray cat had sprung onto Tusk's lap.

"There's a good boy. How's my baby?" Tusk stroked its ears and it began to purr.

"A cat?" I asked stupidly.

Tusk went on fluffing its fur.

"You—you bring your cat to work?"

"Oh, no. He lives here. One of the milder eccentricities around here, believe me."

He patted his leg. "Here, Philby." The cat stretched, gave a long yawn, and curled itself around his ankles.

"Where were we? Nearly done?" Tusk checked his watch. "Yes. Nearly done."

I searched my mind for what else to ask. There was so much I wanted to know; very little that he was likely to comment on.

"Targets," I blurted. "If there really were a bomb inside that crate . . . If terrorists had managed to steal one and get it into the US . . . What would they use it on?"

"You can't possibly believe I'm going to answer that."

"An alert went out this morning from NCTC. Calling for increased vigilance and random searches of fruit trucks. There must have been some intelligence that led them to do that. What was it?"

He raised his eyebrows. "Really? You're really thinking I might answer that?"

"Listen," I said, trying not to yell. "I get it. You're the CIA. And this is all very sensitive and top secret and hush-hush. But if you guys think there's even a remote possibility that somebody has smuggled a nuclear *bomb* into the country, don't you have some responsibility to inform the public?"

"Inform the public? That's your job, not mine."

"You're not exactly making it easy."

"No. But then I help run the clandestine service. *Clan-des-tine*. You do see the difficulty? Trust me, Alexandra. There are very good reasons why I can't answer your entirely reasonable questions. Now, let me give you this."

He peeled a Post-it note off the table in front of us. On it he wrote a number.

"My personal mobile number. I am not in the habit of giving it out. Please don't do anything foolish like entering it into your newspaper contacts database."

I shook my head.

"Good. Perhaps we can be of use to each other at some future date. I'll see you out."

He stood and walked me out of the conference room and around the corner, until we could glimpse the uniformed guard at the main desk. Then he waved at the guard, pointed at me, and indicated that I was to be seen out.

"Lovely to meet you, Alexandra. Best of luck."

"Thank you," I said stiffly, and shook his hand.

As he moved away, he spoke again in a quiet voice. "If you were a terrorist and you had just one—you're not going to waste it, are you?"

I spun to look at him but he was already headed for the turnstiles. He scanned his badge and disappeared into the building without looking back.

The cat followed him.

43

Shaukat Malik was lounging on the bed at the Marriott when his phone chirped to announce the arrival of a new text message.

Odd. Communications were supposed to have gone dark.

Malik pressed mute on the TV remote. He had been watching a cooking show, homemade lamb meatballs in three easy steps.

The message made the hairs on his neck prickle:

Status change. New date. We go TOMORROW, July 2. Stand by.

But this made no sense. The date had been agreed on weeks ago. Why move it up? Malik sank back onto his pillow, confused.

Perhaps someone important had changed his travel schedule.

Or perhaps the plan had always included shifting the date at the last moment. To keep people off guard. To make sure that any leaks or betrayals would give away only outdated information.

Malik did not know how many people knew details of the operation. He did not know, for example, how many people had received the text he just had. He assumed the circle to be small, for obvious security reasons. But even Malik knew only fragments. The precise delivery mechanism had been kept from him. As had the identities of the men funding the operation. They were rich. They must be. But where they lived, and what drove them to want to dictate history in this way—such was not for him to know. This was the way the network operated. Everything was compartmentalized. You were provided the information you needed to accomplish your specific task, and only that.

Malik read the message over again, as if he could discern a hidden meaning from the sparse words. Well. Whatever the reason, if the date was now tomorrow, it was time for him to move on.

His part was done. The video was uploaded, ready for release. He had always planned to leave the night before. He had not signed up to be a martyr.

Malik pulled his suitcase from the closet and threw it on the bed. There wasn't much to pack. Clothes, sandals, his toothbrush. From the windowsill, he gently lifted the souvenirs he had purchased. Tiny white plastic models of the Capitol, the White House, and the Washington Monument. He had arranged this last one in the window so that it lined up perfectly with the real Washington Monument, just visible outside across the Potomac. The vendor had tried to sell him the Pentagon and the Supreme Court too; he wondered whether he should go back. No, probably impossible to find the man again. And he had gotten the best ones: the Capitol in particular had a paper American flag attached to its miniature dome that appealed to him enormously. He rolled them all up inside a pair of pajamas and tucked them into his case.

The phone chirped again as he stood taking a last look around the room.

This message, clearly, was intended for him alone:

One more task for you. Stand by. Details tomorrow.

Shaukat stared at the phone in his hand. Details tomorrow? But tomorrow was . . . He began to pace nervously. What could it be? What was left to be done?

AT THAT MOMENT LUCIEN SLY was also nervously pacing.

To be precise, he was carving laps around an office conference table, pausing every so often to pound the table in frustration. Outside the windows a steady rain beat down, pricking the gray surface of the Thames River.

Lucien had been summoned to Vauxhall Cross, MI6's fortresslike headquarters in London, as it became clear the situation was deteriorating from merely bad to outright awful.

Yesterday had brought two pieces of surreal news: first, that Nadeem Siddiqui had been reported dead. Lucien was staggered. And then, even as he raced down the M11 motorway from Cambridge to London, his bosses had called to report an even more bizarre development. An Irish tourist had been murdered on a British Airways flight to Washington. On *Alex's* British Airways flight to Washington.

He had managed to catch her on the phone earlier today. An awkward conversation, with Lucien unable to share what he knew and forced to feign surprise at Alex's breathless updates. He needed to warn her; she seemed still not to grasp that she was in real danger. But when he urged her to take greater security precautions, she had laughed him off. Of course she would. She knew him only as a rich university student with a taste for the ladies. It was unbearable.

And that was all before the latest twist. The most surreal news yet had arrived today. The MI6 head of station in Islamabad had sent a cable, relaying that a security team at Nadeem Siddiqui's lab had searched his desk. What they had found was chilling. Maps, diagrams, photographs.

MI6's leaders were still trying to digest the new information. For now, it would not be shared with any foreign liaison partners, not even the CIA. Lucien was among the small number of people who'd been briefed. He had sat through the meeting feeling increasingly sick. Alex James had come up several times by name; Lucien's report on her was included among the PowerPoints.

Holy mother of God. Lucien whacked the conference table again and then raked his hands through his hair. He was caught.

He could not tell Alex he worked for MI6.

He could not tell MI6 he was sleeping with Alex.

Meanwhile dark forces appeared to be in motion, and he had no clue how to stop them.

Lucien had longed for action. This was not what he'd had in mind.

44

After my encounter with Edmund Tusk, I took a taxi straight to the *Chronicle*'s Washington office.

The next few hours were a blur.

Elias had convinced someone at the FBI to pass him a copy of the memo that went out this morning. It didn't say much more than Galloni had already told me, but with my being up against so many unknowns, it was comforting to have a physical document in hand.

Meanwhile Hyde had apparently spent the day alternating between shouting at the *Chronicle*'s in-house lawyers up in Boston, and shouting at the national security adviser's staff. The former were balking at giving us the green light to publish anything at all; the latter were balking at giving us a quote on the record. Both sides calmed down around 5:00 p.m., when General Carspecken consented to our using one of the more innocuous quotes from this morning's meeting—the one about everything being under control—on condition that we attribute it to an unnamed "senior administration official."

It wasn't much, but it was enough for Elias and me to sit down at adjoining desks and hammer out a story that began like this:

WASHINGTON—They say they don't know exactly what they're looking for.

But police and other law enforcement officials up and down the East Coast stepped up security measures Thursday, in the wake of an urgent memo issued by the National Counterterrorism Center here in Washington.

The memo—a copy of which was obtained by the Chronicle— urges extra vigilance at border crossings into the country. It also calls for food-delivery trucks to be stopped and searched. Administration officials declined to comment on whether information about a specific threat had prompted the memo.

"My understanding is [the situation] is under control," a senior administration official told the Chronicle. . . .

It was tricky when we knew so much more than we were able to say. The word *nuclear*, for example, didn't appear until the very bottom of the article:

The possibility of produce deliveries as a security concern was raised at a recent conference organized by the Department of Homeland Security.

Officials described how nuclear sensors installed at major ports and airports are designed to detect radioactive material. But certain cargoes—including bananas—are rarely stopped. The potassium in bananas routinely sets off the sensors, according to one former official from the Los Alamos National Laboratory.

As a result, he added, "They just wave them right through."

"Good," said Hyde, when we finally leaned back from our keyboards. He had been standing behind me, reading along over my shoulder and making suggestions as we typed.

"Not great, but good. At least we'll have put a marker down on the story. Now, why don't you two go get some rest? We'll reconvene here in the morning and figure out our next line of attack."

I stretched my arms above my head and nodded. I needed to do another emergency shopping expedition so I would have something to wear tomorrow. My plan was to force Elias to accompany me. He wasn't obvious bodyguard material, but he was better than nothing.

It was after 9:00 p.m. when we trudged up the hill again toward Dumbarton Street. I felt bone weary and I was lugging two shopping bags. I'd grabbed the first dress that fit, a silky wrap with a caramel-and-ivory swirl pattern. Also a buttery-tan pair of Tod's ballet flats: after marching around all day in high heels, my toes were screaming for mercy.

Back at his place Elias produced a well-thumbed pile of take-out menus.

"Your call, Ginger. Thai or Mexican? I think the Mexican place might deliver faster."

I kicked my Manolos off beside the door and plopped down beside him on the futon.

"I don't know. I don't think I can face a burrito. Any chance we could just throw together something here? I feel like I haven't eaten anything besides plane food and takeout in weeks."

I got up and rummaged around the kitchen. The refrigerator held slim pickings, but I found half a loaf of bread, a dozen eggs, and a few wilting vegetables.

"Tell me you have butter and salt somewhere, and I can whip us up an omelet," I called through.

"Sure. Breakfast for dinner. Love it," he yelled back.

A few minutes later I was cracking eggs into a bowl. Elias found a frying pan for me, then settled on a stool and launched into an impersonation of a constipated-looking Jill outside the White House this morning.

"'Carry this back for me, will you, Elias, you ignorant twit?'" he mimicked. "I nearly gagged when she handed me that grotty mug." He wrinkled his nose. "Did you see there were teeth marks on top, where she'd gnawed the lid?"

"Eww. What a cow. But you should have seen her once we got inside. Barely said a word. Hyde, though, he was great. He— Ouch!"

I'd been trying to chop a tomato and the dull knife nicked my finger.

"Oh, here—use the tomato knife." Elias reached into a drawer. "So what did Hyde do? I think he and Carspecken have a long history—"

"Did you say this is a tomato knife?" I interrupted, studying the oddly shaped utensil he had placed in my hand. "As in, a knife specifically designed for cutting *tomatoes*?"

"Yep. It's awesome."

"Wow. I don't know many bachelors who can boast of owning their very own tomato knife."

He shrugged. "My mom gave it to me. It's kind of a family inside joke. We exchange crazy kitchen gadgets as stocking stuffers for Christmas."

My eyes lit up. "What else do you have?"

"Let's see . . . a mango pitter . . . a tortilla press . . . Don't think I've ever used that one. Poultry shears, obviously . . ."

"You have poultry shears? I don't even know what that—"

"Doesn't everyone? Did I mention my reversible meat tenderizer?"

I started to giggle.

He opened a drawer and began pulling things out. "There's an egg cuber here, but that was a given. An olive-wood lobster mallet, my personal favorite. A lemon reamer . . . Nah, too pedestrian. Aha. Here we go. The pièce de résistance."

He held up what looked like a deep-sea-diver's mask.

"What's that?"

"Onion goggles, *mais bien sûr*."

I laughed until tears rolled down my cheeks.

"Personally, I still think the spring-loaded ravioli stamp I gave my sister last year wins for sheer usefulness."

I kept laughing and crying until suddenly the tears falling were real tears. I realized I was weeping.

"Alex?"

"Sorry," I sobbed. "I'm—I'm just exhausted. I guess this story is getting to me."

"Oh," he said awkwardly. "I guess having someone attempt to murder you would do that."

"Yeah, there's that. And I keep feeling like there is something . . . terrible going on, and all we've managed to do is nibble around the edges."

"We just have to keep nibbling tomorrow."

I sniffled.

"We'll get there, don't worry. And at least your love life is looking up, right?" he asked.

"What?"

"*'Good morning, luscious legs'?*"

I felt my cheeks flush red. "He's not a boyfriend or anything. Actually, he's . . ." A cackle escaped me. I couldn't help it. "Actually he's more like Petronella's boyfriend."

Elias looked lost. "Petronella? Petronella Black? I thought Thom Carlyle was her boyfriend."

"Things got a little complicated. Make that *very* complicated." I started laughing again through the tears.

Elias stared at me as if I might be unhinged.

I reached for a wad of paper towels. I blew my nose, wiped my eyes, and tried to think of a way to change the subject. "So. A spring-loaded ravioli stamp?"

For the next hour we sat in his little kitchen, eating eggs and burned toast and comparing silly family holiday rituals. Elias's were far more entertaining than mine, although he did seem to enjoy my account of the Christmas when my father ignited his own eyebrows while attempting to make mulled wine.

It was nearly midnight before we slid the dishes into the sink and said good-night. I think Elias was trying to avoid the lumpy futon couch as long as possible. And I . . . I felt happy just to sit with a friend and talk about something trivial. I didn't even mind being sober. Anything to postpone thinking about all the questions rattling around my head. I knew that later I would lie awake, worrying about Thom Carlyle and Nadeem Siddiqui and Lucien Sly. About my daughter. About how to put things right.

45

I had a terrible night.

I tossed and turned and imagined that every creak and whisper of the old house above us was the footfall of someone coming to kill me.

As the hours ticked past, I grew irascible. I lay there and cursed my insomnia. Then I just lay there cursing everyone I could think of.

Hyde, for having agreed to send me to England and for not pulling me off this damn story ten days ago. Edmund Tusk, for not giving me anything on the record. General Carspecken, ditto. Jill, for being a stupid old cow. Thom Carlyle, for dying in the first place. Nadeem, for disappearing and now apparently dying too.

Then there was Lucien, simultaneously so alluring and so utterly unsuitable as a serious romantic prospect. When he'd called to say hi yesterday morning, he sounded odd. Quieter than usual. He had kept telling me to be careful, to move somewhere safe. But he had also taken the time to describe, in detail, everything he planned to do to me under the moonlight on a beach in Bermuda. Despite all the craziness going on, I listened and felt warmth wash through me. How often do you meet a man who can make you weak in the knees with desire, and then not ten minutes later make you fall over laughing? It was true. He was pure pleasure.

I was still turning it all over in my mind when my new cell phone rang.

I looked at the alarm clock: 5:51 a.m. The first fingers of dawn were just creeping across the window.

Hmm. Since Galloni had made me promise, I hadn't used the phone. But caller ID was displaying a UK number. Maybe it was Lucien. Who else would call so early? Curiosity got the better of me.

"Hello?"

"How *dare* you," came the voice on the other end. She didn't bother to identify herself. No need. "How dare you. You little tramp."

"Hello, Petronella." I sat up in bed and squared my shoulders, pulled my stomach muscles tight. I imagined her doing the same thing. Two fighters circling the ring, girding for the first punch.

When she spoke again, she spoke slowly, her plummy voice pitched low and thick with rage. "I'm back in England, you see. I rang Lucien several times yesterday. But no reply. And no one seems to have seen him. Rather strange. And then this morning I bumped into that old dolt Peter. I gather the two of you have met."

Peter? Oh, yes. Pete. Lucien's friend, the one with the glazed eyes, who'd fetched us a round of beers at the pub.

"He told me what a lovely evening you all had at the Eagle the other night," Petronella continued menacingly. "He couldn't quite remember your name, mind you, but he went on in excruciating detail about how Lucien was pawing at some ginger-haired American, positively drooling all over her. And how the two of them left together, and no one's seen Lucien since. Pete seemed to find the whole incident quite hilarious. Quite the jolly tale. So I repeat: How dare you?"

"You have got to be kidding me," I shot back. "You're upset that Lucien and I hit it off? As if you're some loyal girlfriend and you've caught him cheating on you? Do you not see a tiny trace of irony in that position?"

"Please. Spare me the morality lecture. My relationship with Lucien—"

"You didn't have a relationship. You had a *fling*."

She made a sputtering noise, like a deflating tire. Then she asked, "What exactly happened between the two of you?"

"None of your business."

"I rather think it is."

"No. It's not. Not anymore. You just admitted yourself that he's stopped returning your calls."

There was a pause.

"Listen to you," she said then, tauntingly. "Do you actually think you're fit to wipe his boots? Do you have any idea who he is? Who his family is?"

"I gather his father is a duke."

"'I gather his father is a duke,'" she mimicked savagely. "You haven't the faintest clue. He's from one of the oldest families in Britain. His great-grandfather—oh, forget it. Do you really think he's likely to make a go of it with you? With some American, slutty, working-class hack?"

I couldn't think of a comeback for that one. It stung.

Perhaps because she was so insufferable.

Perhaps because she was right.

* * *

AFTER THAT THERE WAS NO point trying to sleep.

I felt like punching a hole in the wall. Instead I dragged myself to the kitchen. Elias had left a note for me on the counter: *Headed to the gym and then straight on to office. See you there?* Yes. First, though, coffee. I couldn't be bothered with the espresso thimbles. I put a proper pot on to brew while I hit the shower.

I stood under the steamy spray for a long time, fantasizing about creative ways to torture Petronella. Then I moved on to trying to come up with a plan for the day. If I didn't think of something before I went into the bureau, I would have to go along with whatever Hyde had dreamed up overnight. Or Jill, God forbid. I was covered in soap and turning various bad ideas over in my mind when the phone began to ring. Not my temporary cell phone. Elias's home phone. I ignored it. Probably a telemarketer.

I dried off, twisted my hair into a knot, and slipped on the wrap dress. The ringing stopped for a few minutes while I hunted for my earrings, then started again. I hesitated. It couldn't be for me. Only Elias and Hyde knew I was here.

When it rang a third time, I gave up and went to the kitchen to answer it.

"Alexandra, is that you?" asked a deep, vaguely familiar voice.

"Yes. Who's this?"

"Lowell Carlyle. I've been trying to reach you."

I stood there trying to process this. It did in fact sound like Lowell Carlyle. But why would the president's lawyer—

"Are you there? Please listen to me carefully. You are in danger."

"But—but how did you get this number?" Not perhaps the most salient point at the moment, but I was still trying to take this in.

"What? From your editor. Hyde Rawlins. I tracked him down and told him it was urgent that I reach you. Are you somewhere safe?"

"I'm at a friend's. Why? What's going on?"

"The situation you wrote about in this morning's paper. It is—more serious than perhaps you may have realized. I can't really say much more. Are you by yourself? Can you drive to somewhere safe, a police station maybe? Or can I send a car over to you?"

My stomach lurched. What did he know that I didn't that made him want to send a driver to come collect me?

"I don't have a car. I can get a taxi. But, Mr. Carlyle, why? I don't understand . . ." I could not seem to collect my thoughts to ask a coherent question.

"Alexandra, you came up by name here this morning. It's a fast-moving situation. We've pulled together a meeting for later today. I can't get into many details. I'm not calling in an official capacity. But as a father—" He cleared his throat. "Please. Get yourself somewhere safe." He hung up.

My heart was racing. I glanced around. Outside the kitchen window the back garden suddenly looked dark and threatening. The lock on the kitchen door was flimsy; a child could break in. I picked up the phone again, considered calling 911. But to tell them what? That I was scared? Who knew how long it might take DC cops to get here, and if I was in as much danger as Mr. Carlyle said . . . No. I didn't want to wait for the police or for a driver or for anyone more sinister who might be coming. I needed to get out of here. Immediately. I raced to the bedroom and found my shoes and wallet. I would sprint to M Street, hail a taxi, head to the news bureau. People would be there by now. The security guard would be at the front desk. It would be safe.

I opened Elias's front door and blinked in the sunlight. The early-morning dew had burned away; thick heat was already beginning to rise off the street. I had turned around to lock the door behind me when I heard a voice.

"How do you do, Miss James. My name is Shaukat Malik. You may know me as Nadeem Siddiqui."

He pushed me back inside, and then the world went dark.

46

When I opened my eyes again, it was to see a small man staring at me. He held a gun in his hands, pointed at my chest.

I blinked and shook my head in an attempt to dispel this awful vision. Pain rolled through me. I lifted my hand to my face and felt warm blood and the raised ridge of a deep cut.

"You shouldn't have tried to run," he scolded. His voice was high and singsongy. "You have been stupid, so stupid, from the beginning."

He was sitting on Elias's futon. I appeared to be sprawled on the floor. Scattered images came back to me. I had tried to leave. . . . I was locking the door. . . . He had said his name. . . .

"Nadeem Siddiqui?" I said, so weakly I wasn't sure he could hear me. "But—I thought you were dead. Your lab said you were dead."

"Nadeem is dead." He nodded. "Now I am Shaukat Malik."

This made no sense. *Malik* . . . That was the name people in Pakistan had kept repeating on the phone. My head throbbed. Would Elias come back to look for me if I didn't show up this morning? *Why hadn't I called the police?*

"I don't understand," I croaked. "What do you want?"

"To kill you."

I decided not to ask the obvious follow-up: *So what are you waiting for?*

Instead I said, "You—you were waiting for me? Outside the door there?"

"Yes. I didn't have a key. But I could see you inside. Getting dressed. I knew you would come out."

I cringed. How long had he watched? What had he seen? I am no prude, but the idea of his seeing me naked was unbearable. Then again, so was the idea of his killing me in the next few minutes. *Think.* I looked desperately around the room for something to use as a weapon. The bike was gone. Elias must have taken it to work. Otherwise there were books, empty CD cases, shoes . . . Nothing.

I studied him. He was short for a man, but muscular. He might out-weigh me by thirty or forty pounds. And there was the small matter that he had a gun.

Think. I kept squinting at him through my right eye—the left one appeared to be swelling shut—and willed the fog in my head to clear. There was no logical next question in this surreal exchange. But surely the longer I kept him talking, the better my chances of finding a way out.

"The bananas—the shipment that arrived this week—that was you?"

An expression of pride passed over his face. "Yes. Brilliant, isn't it? So simple."

"And inside it—is it true? There was a nuclear weapon?"

He pressed his lips together and smiled coldly. "I am the only one who can do that. Do you understand? The others—Atta, Jarrah, al-Shehhi—they were boys. They destroy. They fly their planes. But they do not have my access. My skills. You understand?"

No, I did not. What was he talking about? My head pounded. I tried again. "But—in the banana shipment—is there—"

"Yes!" he snorted impatiently. "Because of my work. My work, you see? Twelve years I train. I get access. I get the codes. It is because of my—my technical *expertise* that we will succeed. So I will not have to die. Not like them. I am too valuable. To the network. But I must disappear now."

"Disappear?"

"Yes, disappear." He lowered his voice to a whisper. "You know why? Because it will be my face they see. My voice, inside the White House. It is already recorded, do you know this? We will spill your blood. And then you will see."

I pressed my hand to my eye. He was completely mad. "I—I'm afraid I don't understand as much as you think I do. What are you talking about? What is already recorded?"

He leaned forward excitedly on the futon. "The video. We will send it to you—all of you journalists—when it is time. And then you will know, this was a Muslim bomb. This is for our brothers in Pakistan. And in Jeddah and Cairo and Palestine.

"Still. It is a shame. You. Thomas Carlyle." He shrugged and gestured with the gun as if he weren't quite sure how it had ended up in his hand. "I am not a killer. I do not kill before. I am a man of science. . . ."

"Of course you are." I tried to sound soothing. I struggled to push myself up a bit higher against the wall. My head felt as if it would split open. "What happened with Thom Carlyle? Were you up in the bell tower that night?"

He frowned. "It was not supposed to happen. He was helpful. Quite helpful. His girlfriend—you saw her?" His eyes clouded briefly with an emotion that I was startled to recognize as lust. "A very beautiful woman."

"You said Thom Carlyle was helpful? He was helping you?" Surely that could not be true.

But Nadeem nodded. "He arranged a White House tour. We had to get in. To make the video. It had to be recorded there, you see? But we did not know how. And then I met Thomas. He was very nice. I told him it was my grandfather's dream."

I tried to follow this. "You mean, Thom helped you get a tour of the White House? Through his dad or something?"

"Yes."

"But—but then why did you kill him?"

Nadeem glared at me. "She invited me to a party. In his rooms, did you know that? She wanted me there. But she was . . . kissing him. Dancing with him." He looked disgusted. His voice turned shrill. "Everyone drunk, everyone smoking. And very loud."

"So what happened?"

"I got a phone call. But the music"—he gestured angrily with his hands—"it was too loud. So I stepped into the back bedroom. It was my contact on the phone. He wanted to go over everything. The shipment, the tracking number. What I would say in the video. We have to do this by phone, you see. Put nothing in writing. And it was a secure line. But when I turned around . . . Thomas was there. Listening. I do not know how much he heard. But enough, I think. Enough."

I closed my eyes against the pain and tried to imagine how it had happened. Nadeem, squat and swarthy and serious, so out of place at a Waspy party in the John Harvard suite. Petronella, probably wearing something indecent, working the crowd, teasing the men buzzing round her. And poor Thom. Why had he wandered into the back bedroom? Had he suspected something? More likely he was just checking on a missing guest. Or maybe he kept supplies back there, maybe the bar had needed replenishing . . . But he had picked the wrong moment.

I opened my eyes. Nadeem was pointing the gun closer now. "I am not a killer. But perhaps it will be easier the second time."

I looked into his black eyes. *Think*. And then it came to me. The lust that had clouded his eyes. He had wanted Petronella, wanted her badly. He was not immune. It was my only chance.

"She was beautiful that night, wasn't she? Nadeem?"

He looked confused.

"So beautiful. And she liked you. She told me." As I spoke I traced my finger down my leg and lifted my dress so that it fell higher on my leg. My voice was hoarse. I felt sick. I kept going. "Did you like it when she danced? Did you watch?" I raised my skirt another inch.

He glanced away, swallowed, looked back.

"She told me she wanted to kiss you. To put her lips . . . her lips . . . on your . . ." I licked my own lips.

He was breathing heavily now.

"She told me she wanted to take your hands and put them . . . here . . ." I swept my fingertips lightly up my thigh. His eyes followed. And then I saw what I was waiting for. His hand slackened on the gun. It tilted down, just a little, away from me. *Wait*. I arched my back and traced a circle over the silk of my dress around my nipple.

"Again. Do that again," he breathed. And then he reached for me.

I waited until his hand brushed against my leg and then I kicked, hard. Both my feet slammed into his groin. The gun skittered across the floor. I bolted up and ran.

I only had a second. *Please, God, please, God, let it be hot*. When he chased me into the kitchen, I was ready. He had the gun—he raised it—but I was faster. The scalding coffee flew from the pot into his eyes. He roared in surprise and pain and rocked backward. His hands reached up to his face—my hands reached up for the gun still in his hand—I found the trigger—I pulled.

There was a deafening noise and then silence. He lay on the floor. I could not bring myself to look at his face. Dark liquid pooled across the tiles. I leaned over the kitchen sink and retched.

My hands trembled as I unlaced his fingers from the gun. From his pocket I pulled a wallet and a phone. The wallet held $300, a receipt from a souvenir vendor on the National Mall, and a Virginia driver's license in the name of Shaukat Malik.

I had to step over him to exit the kitchen. I held my dress down tightly, protectively, around my legs as I did so. I fought the urge to be sick again.

I did not understand what had just happened. I had just shot a man. In Elias's kitchen.

I dropped his phone, his wallet, and his gun into my purse. Then I opened the front door. The heat was dizzying. The sun seemed to have bleached the world white. I felt hollowed out, empty. An old urge swept over me. With my fingernails I scratched at the skin inside my elbows, repeatedly and with force. Droplets of red blood sprang out. I stared at them. I was alive. I needed to get out of here. I walked away, leaving the door wide open behind me.

47

No taxi would stop for me on M Street.

When I caught a glimpse of my reflection in the shop window behind me, I realized why: I looked like a lunatic. White as a ghost, my left eye swollen shut and turning a nasty plum color, blood crusted down my cheek and ear.

I nipped into the nearest café, where the waitress did a double take at my appearance but said nothing. In the ladies' room, I daubed the worst of the blood off my neck. My face was more painful, but I did my best to clean it, then unwound my hair to hang down and hide the gash above my eye. I smoothed and retied my dress. There was blood on that too—whether Nadeem's or mine, I wasn't sure. Nothing I could do about that. With a pair of big sunglasses and lipstick I looked . . . not presentable, but better than before.

I walked back out to the curb, held up my arm, and a taxi stopped.

With relief I slid inside. I had already decided where to go.

Not to the hospital, although I was sure I needed stitches.

Not to the police, although I seemed to be making a habit of fleeing murder scenes.

It would take too long to explain, and I wasn't sure how much time I had. Two things seemed urgent right now: the first was getting somewhere safe, somewhere where Nadeem's associates in the "network," as he'd called it, could not find me. The second was getting his phone and wallet to someone who could figure out what plot he had been involved with, and how to stop it.

This left me only one alternative. I told the driver to take me to the CIA. I would find Edmund Tusk and tell him what had happened. He would know what to do.

The driver crossed the Potomac and turned onto the same pretty, winding parkway I had taken yesterday to meet Tusk. If I remembered correctly, it would take about fifteen minutes to get there. I pressed my shoulder blades back against the vinyl seat and tried to steady myself. I was safe now. Everything would be all right.

Gingerly, as if it might bite, I slipped Nadeem Siddiqui's cell phone out of my bag. This was the second phone of his that I had somehow acquired. What secrets might this one hold? He would have e-mails on here, archived text messages, a contacts list at the very least. I turned it on. Password protected.

NADEEM, I typed. Incorrect password, it flashed.

I tried again.

MALIK.

Incorrect.

I chewed on my fingernail. Of course it wouldn't be his name. What would it be?

NUCLEAR, I typed.

Incorrect.

And now it informed me I had two more tries before the phone was disabled.

It could be anything: the name of his dog, the name of his street, the name of his favorite color . . . Or maybe . . .

BANANAS.

The screen flickered and then a generic picture of a sunset appeared. I clicked on his e-mail in-box. Empty. His address book was too. So much for tracking down his associates. I checked for text messages. Nothing. Then, remembering the phone I'd found in the backpack at Fenner's gym, I opened the call log.

Here there were two phone numbers. Both looked strangely familiar. I stared at them until it hit me. The first one was Elias's home number. Nadeem Siddiqui had called there last night, before we got home. I felt queasy. Had he been outside all night, waiting? I rolled down my window and took great gulps of air. It smelled of gasoline and hot tailpipes and swamp. The river was close. On the side of the road a green sign loomed: GEORGE BUSH CENTER FOR INTELLIGENCE—CIA—NEXT EXIT. Faintly ridiculous, surely, for a secret spy agency to pinpoint its location with a huge road sign.

I rolled the window back up and forced myself to look again at the call log. The second number was an incoming call, received last night, just twelve minutes before Nadeem had called Elias's flat.

The area code was 703. Virginia. I pulled out my reporter's notebook and copied it down. For one wild moment I was tempted just to call it. Who would answer? What would I say? No. I might blow a lead that way. Whoever answered would be expecting to hear the voice of Nadeem Siddiqui, or Shaukat Malik, or whoever he was, the man now dead on the floor of Elias's kitchen.

We turned right into the front gate of Langley. Steel barriers and barbed wire rose up. I knew the drill from yesterday. Ahead lay a visitors' checkpoint where I would need to present identification and let them check my name against a list. It occurred to me that I should have called Tusk to alert him I was coming.

I flicked through my notebook to find the page where I had stapled the scrap of paper he'd handed me as I left. The scrap where he'd scribbled his private phone number. My blood froze. I looked at the paper. I looked at Nadeem's phone in my hand. I looked back and forth between the two, my mind churning.

"Can I help you?" asked a disembodied voice. We had pulled up to a speaker where the guards ask routine security questions before waving cars ahead to the main checkpoint.

I sat still, staring at the phone numbers. They matched. What was this? Was Edmund Tusk already onto Nadeem? Was the CIA way ahead of me? Had they already cracked the plot before I ever got involved? Or had I gotten everything wrong? Was Nadeem somehow a good guy after all? *Had I just shot a CIA agent?*

"Can I help you?" the disembodied voice asked again.

"Lady." The taxi driver had turned around in his seat. "They need your name. You got an appointment, right?"

"I—I—my mistake. Wrong day. I have my dates mixed up. Sorry," I said to the speaker.

I asked the driver to turn around. He sighed and put the car in reverse. "Back to Georgetown? It'll still be full fare, you know."

"Sure. Okay." I couldn't go back to Georgetown. I didn't know where to go. I tried to think. Back on the parkway there was no traffic. Trees whizzed past. Hyde. I should call Hyde. I dug for my own phone in my now crowded handbag. It wasn't there—had I left it on the bed?

Then the phone on my lap vibrated. Nadeem's phone.

The screen glowed with an incoming message:

Is it done?

The message came from Tusk's private number.

In the backseat, I made a strangled sound. There must be some explanation—some other meaning—some subtlety I had not grasped. But I could think of only one thing that Nadeem Siddiqui had been supposed to do this morning. He had been supposed to kill me. And there was no benign reason for Edmund Tusk to know that. *Is it done? . . .* The enormity of evil implicit in that three-word message overwhelmed me.

Then, thankfully, it was as if a part of my brain—the part that held emotion—shut down. A cold impulse for self-preservation took over. I was going to nail these bastards.

Done. All secure now, I typed back.

I waited.

Good. Heading to target now. Inshallah.

I leaned forward and spoke to the driver. "Not back to Georgetown, actually. To the White House, quickly please."

He rolled his eyes and changed lanes. No doubt he suspected I would flake out when we got there, too. But it was all I could think of. The idea of going somewhere "safe" had evaporated; if the clandestine service of the Central Intelligence Agency wanted me dead, I would be in danger even inside the walls of the White House. But I trusted Lowell Carlyle. He had called to warn me. *As a father,* he had said. . . . For an awful split second I considered the possibility that he was also duplicitous. That he had urged me to run, to unlock the door, knowing a murderer was waiting outside . . . No. It didn't feel right. Trust your gut, Hyde says. My gut said to trust Mr. Carlyle.

On my lap the phone vibrated again.

Malik: Why are you moving?

My throat closed and it was several seconds before I could breathe. I stared at the phone. The goddamn phone. Tusk was tracking me by GPS. I had to get rid of it. But as I rolled down the window to throw it from the car, a thought occurred to me. This phone held evidence of Tusk's treachery. Without it I had no proof. It would be his word against mine.

I rolled the window back up. If they could track where the phone was, could they also listen to calls on it? I had no idea how these things worked. I decided not to take a chance.

I leaned forward again.

"I need to borrow your phone."

"You got your own phone. I seen you typing on it."

"I can't use that one. Please. Just one call."

The driver studied me in his rearview mirror. I was sure he saw my swollen eye. He looked as though he was weighing whether I was completely out of my mind. Then he shook his head. "Come on, lady. How I know who you gonna call? I can't be lending my phone out to everybody—"

I pulled $100 out of Nadeem's wallet and shoved it over the seat.

"Please," I begged.

Now he looked sure I was out of my mind. But he pocketed the money and handed over his phone.

I looked up the number in my notebook and dialed.

Lowell Carlyle's secretary answered. She did not sound thrilled to hear from me. "He won't be available at all today. May I take down a message?"

"No. This is an emergency. I am on my way to him right now—"

"That won't be possible. I can take down a—"

"Tell him my name and that I need to see him. I'll be there in ten minutes—"

"Miss James, you're not listening. He's in a meeting with—"

"*RIGHT NOW*," I roared. "Find him. Tell him I have Nadeem Siddiqui's phone. Tell him he was right. They came after me. Tell him I am on my way."

I hung up. I tried to catch the driver's eye in the rearview mirror. He avoided looking at me. "Just one more call," I said, and punched in Hyde's cell number. Maybe he could meet me there.

The taxi was crawling along Constitution Avenue. We passed the

State Department. Twenty-first Street. Just a few blocks to go, but traffic was bumper-to-bumper. Hyde's phone rang and rang. Was it my imagination, or was the black SUV several cars behind us weaving strangely?

"I need you to go faster, please. Right now."

"Yeah, I'd like that too," the driver replied. "But welcome to DC traffic. Nothing you can do." He fiddled with the radio.

I looked back. The SUV had disappeared. Something wasn't right.

"Could you lock the car doors?" The gash on my forehead prickled. A matted stickiness in my hair suggested that it had begun to bleed again.

I craned around, trying to spot the SUV. Then—*oh, Jesus*. It was mounting the curb. Two tires were fully up on the sidewalk, the other two in the bike lane, and it was surging ahead of the lines of the idling cars.

"*GO!*" I yelled. "You need to go! That car is coming after us!"

To my utter disbelief, the driver did the opposite. He stuck out his lip and slammed the gear into Park. "You better get out, lady. You got yourself some serious problems."

I was near to panic. My heart crashed against my rib cage. The SUV was close now. Could I somehow climb over the seat, elbow the driver over, and step on the gas myself?

Then I remembered. I fished in my bag one more time and drew out the gun. I pointed it squarely at his head. When I spoke my voice was steady.

"Put on your hazard lights. Pull across the yellow line, drive down the wrong side of the road if you have to, and get me to the White House. Now. *NOW!*"

He didn't argue. The taxi shot into oncoming traffic. Horns blared. I heard a siren start up. I couldn't see the black SUV. I held the gun in one hand, the car-door handle in the other, and I prayed.

The taxi careened up Seventeenth Street, honking wildly and scattering pedestrians. At the corner of Seventeenth and Pennsylvania he screeched to a stop. Concrete blast barriers prevented us from actually driving right up to 1600 Pennsylvania Avenue. The three blocks in front of the White House were always shut to traffic, to try to stop car bombers and sharpshooters and nuts like me from getting close. I would have to run.

I dropped the rest of Nadeem's money on the backseat.

"I'm sorry," I shouted. "I'm so sorry!"

And then I was sprinting, my dress hiked up around my thighs, my lungs burning. I could hear noises behind me—more cars slamming on their brakes—footsteps pounding—were they behind me?

I didn't look back. Would Mr. Carlyle's secretary have warned the guards at the gate?

"Move! Move!" I pushed at a tourist who stepped in front of me.

I was close. I could see a flag rippling on the green lawn behind the fence. Then the gate, and two Secret Service agents standing in front of it, wearing white uniforms and armed with enormous assault rifles.

"Help! Help me!" I screamed.

"Name?" called the closer one.

"Alex James!"

The guards parted and pushed me roughly behind them. The gate clanged shut. I sank to my knees, gasping for air, amazed that I was still alive.

48

What can you buy for $25 million?

The answer is, not as much as you might think.

Edmund Tusk had spent much of the past two years pondering this precise question, and he had concluded that for a man of his age, $25 million represented a tidy sum but not a vast fortune.

On the plus side, he would not be paying taxes.

On the negative side, he had to factor in the cost of constantly moving, of plastic surgeries and disguises and new identities, of covering his tracks. When you actually ran the numbers, it was clear he would not be living out his retirement on a giant yacht, or amassing a private collection of Ferraris. But that was fine. Better to keep a low profile. And there would be enough. Enough in the bank to pay for good hotels and business-class flights and cases of Barolo, not Budweiser. And, hell— anything beat retiring to a condo in McLean.

On a purely symbolic level, he had been pleased to negotiate a salary that put him on par with Osama bin Laden. Twenty-five million dollars. That was the bounty the FBI had offered for bin Laden all those years. And that was apparently what Tusk's services were worth as well. Tusk found it fascinating that two such different skill sets commanded the same amount in the global market. Bin Laden, of course, had sought fame. He had wanted to change history, to have his face—his voice— recognized around the world. Such pursuits did not interest Edmund Tusk. His ideology, in the end, boiled down to this: if an event was inevitable, he might as well walk away from it well compensated.

And this is exactly how he had come to view the situation he had now put in motion. When the men had first invited him to meet in Abu Dhabi, he had declined. Sure, he was cynical and disillusioned. But he was no terrorist.

For months, though, they had continued to work on him. To flatter him. The network was compact, and two made the pitch: the money guy (as Tusk thought of him), a Saudi banker claiming to represent a number of wealthy donors; and the religion guy, a pious Pakistani physicist who was both feared and revered by his country's military and intelligence chiefs. Together they had the funding. They had the bomb. They had a man, whom they called Malik, who had the technical expertise to arrange transfer of the weapon to Washington. All they needed was someone with the right access, at the right levels, inside the US government apparatus. They were willing to pay.

When they came to him, Tusk was serving as CIA station chief in Islamabad, watching the country collapse from the inside. Pakistan's politicians were rotten, its business leaders corrupt, its middle class decaying, even the military now scared of its own shadow. It didn't take a wild imagination to put two and two together. Rising extremism plus rising instability equaled the possibility—no, the probability—that the nuclear arsenal would one day fall into the wrong hands.

Most frustrating was that there were no good guys in this game. US policy toward Pakistan was whacked. Tusk's job as CIA station chief could be described as an elaborate dance: lying to the Pakistanis, letting them lie to him, then returning to the embassy to lie to his own staff. Every so often, in the case of a coup (Pakistan) or an election (Washington), he changed partners. And then the dance carried on. Tusk was not naive. He had run the Agency stations in Kabul and Amman; he knew how this part of the world worked. But in Pakistan he simply could not see the point. An Army general he'd once worked with was fond of asking, *Tell me how this ends?*

Surprisingly, the money guy and the religion guy had supplied the answer. When they approached him a third time about a meeting in Abu Dhabi, Tusk accepted. Their pitch was blunt: It's going to happen. We are going to steal a bomb from Pakistan's arsenal and detonate it inside the United States. Why not help us? Why not get rich and retire to South America, when it's going to happen anyway?

Slowly he had been drawn in. He was canny enough to ask for the money in installments. A third up front, right after they agreed the terms in Abu Dhabi. A third just this week, when he had been able to confirm the bomb had arrived on US soil. And the final $8.33 million would be wired to a Swiss account today, as soon as detonation was confirmed.

Today. It had been a long time coming. He had encountered and dispensed with numerous bumps and setbacks along the way. People always surprised you. Some proved quite easy to manage. Jake Pearson in London, for example: a capable lackey, and so helpfully disinclined to ask questions. Pearson's little undercover mission to Claridge's had been rather useful.

Shaukat Malik, on the other hand, had proved an unexpected challenge. Such a quiet, queer man. Fastidious in some ways, but then so careless in others: always losing his phone, and worse, blabbing within earshot of Thomas Carlyle. Malik's unilateral decision to take out Carlyle had proved the riskiest in the entire trajectory of the project. Tusk's mouth twisted in fury just thinking about it. So unnecessary. It had brought publicity. It had brought the girl. The reporter. Almost despite herself, Alexandra James had seemed to stumble along in the right direction, asking inconvenient questions so insistently that he had been left with no choice but to eliminate her as well.

He was still not sure what had happened this morning. He had given Malik a gun, for Christ's sake; surely the man was not so inept as to screw up yet again. The texted confirmation seemed in order. But why had Malik not responded to his last message? Why had his phone GPS shown him moving toward downtown Washington? Those were not his instructions. Tusk didn't understand and this worried him.

Now he had been waiting an annoyingly long time to be cleared inside the building. It was hot, even with the car air-conditioning at full tilt. Sweat dampened his shirt under the armpits. He needed to piss. Soon he would have been in the car a full hour. Tusk adjusted his protruding gut to a more comfortable position against the steering wheel. He brushed a cat hair off his pants.

At last it was his turn. He rolled down his window.

"Hi, Bill."

"Hi, Ed. Sorry about the wait. Crazy day, huh?"

"You're telling me. I gotta get up to this meeting, though. Any chance of speeding things up?"

The security guard nodded. "Just be a sec." Almost apologetically, he passed the long-handled mirror along the underside of Tusk's car. Both sides, and around the tires. Routine bomb check.

"You're all set. Have a good one."

"Thanks, you too, Bill."

The black metal gates swung open. If Tusk hurried, he could still make it inside for the start of the meeting.

49

This time I did not have to wait to see Lowell Carlyle.

The two Secret Service officers who had met me at the gate rushed me across the lawn, into the West Wing door, through the wide waiting room. Doors swung open ahead of us. The staffers clogging the hallways were made to stand back.

Mr. Carlyle's secretary was standing up at her desk outside his office, looking grim. When she saw me, she let out a little gasp. Then she reached for the phone on her desk, hit a button, and said, "She's here. . . . Yes. Mr. Carlyle asked to be notified."

She stepped out from behind the desk.

"Thank you," I said to her, gesturing at the guards still flanking me. "Thank you for having them ready."

She nodded, and I watched her eyes widen as she took in the full state of my appearance. She picked up the phone again and spoke quickly. "Dr. Patterson? It's Tess. Could you step in here for a minute? . . . No, no, he's fine. But bring your bag."

A minute later Lowell Carlyle appeared. He looked even wearier than when I had met him two days ago, as if he had not slept in years. His dark suit was creased and his eyes were red and pouchy. Their expression was kind, though, as he motioned me into his office and toward a chair.

He sat down in another chair opposite me and put his hand on my wrist. "Are you all right?"

"Yes. I'm fine. But you were right. After you called—just after you called—he was there."

"Who was there?"

"Nadeem Siddiqui. When I opened the front door—"

"Nadeem Siddiqui? I don't understand."

"I don't either, entirely. He is"—I took a breath—"he's dead now."

Carlyle looked carefully at me. "Siddiqui died sometime last week, Alexandra. In Pakistan. His name was highlighted this morning in the PDB—the daily intel brief. There must be some mistake."

"Yeah, I heard that too," I said, suddenly angry. "But someone who seemed to know an awful lot about him showed up at my door this morning and gave me this." I lifted my hair.

Carlyle blanched. Then he reached over to a phone on a side table and hit a button. "Tess. Could you get Dr. Patterson— Oh, he's here?"

The office door swung open to admit a middle-aged man who I assumed must be the White House physician. He bustled in, inspected my face, and started pulling wipes and bandages out of a leather bag. "You'll need stitches. Quite a few, by the look of it. That's a whopper. Why don't you come with me—"

"No," said Lowell Carlyle abruptly. "I'm sorry, we'll get to that, but I need her first. Can you just clean her up a bit?"

The doctor raised his eyebrows but got to work.

Carlyle spoke again. "You said—in the message that was passed to me, it said you had his phone?"

I nodded and clutched my bag closer to me. "And his wallet. I had his gun, too, but I had to leave it at security."

I saw the doctor and Carlyle exchange looks. He held up his hand to stop me talking.

"I'm not sure I'm the best person for you to be telling this to. But as it happens, those guys are here. We've got a deputies meeting about to get under way downstairs. I'm going to pull the CIA and FBI officers out and let you speak directly to them. In the interest of not wasting time—"

"No," I interrupted. "That's the problem. That's why I came to you. You don't understand. I think the CIA is involved."

"Involved? With what?"

"They were talking with Nadeem Siddiqui. I think they sent him to kill me."

Mr. Carlyle sat back in his chair and studied me for a long moment. For the second time in less than hour, I watched a man weighing whether I might be completely mad.

When he spoke, his voice was gentle. "Alexandra. You know that can't be true. I think—I know you've had a traumatic morning. It's going to be all right. I need you to tell us what happened, all the details, and then Dr. Patterson here is going to take care of you. "

"I know what you're thinking. You're thinking that I'm deranged," I said hotly. "But I have proof that the CIA—"

"Let's just set that aside for the moment, shall we?" Carlyle cut in, sounding less kindly now and more like the president's lawyer. "Here is what is going to happen. You are going to tell us exactly what you saw this morning. Just what you saw, nothing else. And then you're free to go. Wait here." His tone made it clear there was no point arguing.

Carlyle and the doctor left the office and shut the door behind them. God knows what they were saying about me outside. I half-expected the doctor to sneak back in with a giant sedative shot to knock me out and cart me away. I wouldn't have blamed him.

But the door stayed shut, and I let my eyes wander around the room. They fell on the phone Carlyle had used, sitting on the end table. I wondered if it had an outside line. I wondered how long I had.

I picked it up, dialed 9, and heard an ordinary dial tone. I had to try.

"Elias Thottrup," he answered.

"Elias!"

"Alex. Where are you?"

"At the White House," I whispered. "In Lowell Carlyle's office. Listen. I've got to talk fast. Nadeem Siddiqui—he was alive. He came to the house this morning—"

"He WHAT?"

"With a gun. He tried to kill me, and I—I shot him. Shh, be quiet and listen to me, okay? I took his phone, and he was talking to Edmund Tusk. The CIA guy. They were sending messages. Do you understand? So I came here. I brought the phone here. I told Carlyle and now he wants to question me—"

"Alex, slow down—"

"I can't. There's a big meeting here. Carlyle said it was a . . . What did he call it? A deputies meeting."

"Uh-huh. That's all the number two guys. The deputy secretary of state, the NSC deputy, the deputy SecDef . . . It's when they're worried about something but not quite worried enough to call a cabinet meeting."

"I think they're meeting about our story," I said. "I mean, not our story specifically, but the banana shipment and Nadeem and . . . whether there's a bomb. I think it's real, Elias."

Silence.

"Elias?"

"Did you say you *shot* him?"

"Tell Hyde. Tell him exactly what I just told you. Can you write something and get it up on the website? That the national security team is meeting, at least? I'm about to go down there—"

At that moment the office door swung open. I slammed the phone down and turned beet red.

A tall, powerfully built man walked in. He wore a boxy, dark blue suit, his hair was shaved close to his skull, and the coil of an earpiece hung down. He looked from the phone to my burning cheeks. "Looks like you're going to keep me busy." Then he stuck out his hand. "Captain McNamara, US Secret Service."

I took his hand. "I'm Alex. But you must know that. You said McNamara, as in Ralph McNamara? Marco Galloni's friend?"

The smallest of smiles played across his lips. "He said to keep an eye on you. Also said you were a lot of trouble." He took in the bandage over my eye and the bloodstains splattered down my dress. "I hear you made quite the entrance this morning."

"At the guard station, you mean? Yeah. It wasn't the most . . . subtle approach I've ever made."

The smile flickered again and then he turned serious. "From now on, you don't move without me. Got it? I am officially your shadow. Now, we're headed downstairs. Let's go."

We walked in silence along a corridor and down a set of stairs into the West Wing basement. McNamara stopped in front of a desk manned by a uniformed guard.

"We wait here," he said.

"Where are we?"

He nodded across the hall at a polished mahogany door. THE SITUATION ROOM, read a brass plaque. After a minute the door opened. My view was partly blocked, but I could see a room full of people. Some were sitting at a conference table; others formed an outer ring, chairs pushed back against the walls. The deputies to the deputies, I assumed.

Carlyle was standing, leaning over one end of the table and whispering urgently. I scanned the other faces. And then I froze.

Edmund Tusk. He was sitting right there, in the outer ring of chairs. He was studying a stack of papers on his lap. He looked bored.

"That's him," I hissed, yanking on McNamara's sleeve.

He caught my hand and held it down firmly. "What? Who?"

"That man." I pointed. "That's Edmund Tusk. He's CIA. You need to question him."

"What?" McNamara looked confused. "No. I think you're supposed to meet with someone else. Our instructions are to wait here for Lowell Carlyle."

"I know, but—" I wanted to scream with frustration. Actually, maybe that wasn't a bad idea.

"Mr. Carlyle!" I called loudly into the room. "Mr. Carlyle—"

The whole room fell momentarily silent at this appalling lapse of etiquette. Tusk looked up. For one moment our eyes met. Then Lowell Carlyle was barreling toward me, looking supremely annoyed, two other men in tow.

The door to the Situation Room slammed shut behind them. I felt myself being dragged down the hall by the elbow after Carlyle and the other men.

I shut my eyes and heard Tusk's whisper from yesterday echo in my head:

If you were a terrorist and you had just one—you're not going to waste it, are you?

ACROSS THE TABLE OF A small conference room three men sat glaring at me.

I glared back.

I felt mutinous. My eye throbbed. I had nearly been murdered twice this week. And now Lowell Carlyle was scolding me for causing a scene.

"I will remind you, Alexandra," he was saying grimly, "that you are here only as a courtesy, and that any further behavior like that will mean I have to remove you from—"

"Yes. Thank you," I cut in. "I grasp the point. But I assume these gentlemen have more pressing things to worry about than my lack of decorum. I need you all just to listen to me."

We were down the hall from the Situation Room, crammed into a windowless cell with powder-blue walls and mauve carpeting. It evoked the lobby decor of an Embassy Suites in Des Moines. Captain McNamara was standing guard outside the door. The other two men inside had been introduced as C.J. from the CIA and Bruce from the FBI. They were both now looking at me aghast. I ought to have been intimidated, but I was too damn mad.

"The reason I yelled back there is because I saw Edmund Tusk. He was sitting in there, right behind you," I said, turning to C.J. "We need to go get him and pull him out because he knows—"

"Ed Tusk? What the hell is she talking about?" growled C.J., shifting in his chair. "She is right about one thing, and that's that I've got better things to worry about than some loose-cannon reporter—"

"Alexandra, we agreed not to get into this," Mr. Carlyle warned.

"But he's involved," I insisted. "What I'm trying to tell you is, Tusk's involved in this whole situation—"

"Of course he's involved!" shouted C.J. "He's the fucking deputy head of the National Clandestine Service, you idiot!"

The door opened then, and the woman I recognized as head of the White House press office stuck her head into the room. She looked murderously at me, then handed a piece of paper to Mr. Carlyle. "You need to see this."

He read for a moment. "Oh my. But when—? Ah. In my office. Of course."

The other two men leaned over to read. Finally they passed it to me.

The short news item had been printed minutes ago from the *Chronicle* website:

WASHINGTON—Top administration officials were huddled in an emergency session at the White House this morning, meeting to address what appear to be rapidly mounting concerns about the possible smuggling of a hostile nuclear weapon into the United States.

The meeting in the White House Situation Room included senior officials from the Pentagon, the CIA, the FBI and other agencies.

While details of the fast-moving situation remain murky . . .

Most damning for me was this line, at the bottom:

This article was reported by Alexandra James at the White House and written by Elias Thottrup.

For a moment all you could hear was the sound of five people breathing. I smoothed an imaginary wrinkle in my dress. It occurred to me to wonder just how far my Secret Service protection would extend. Was Ralph McNamara honor-bound to protect me if senior officials from the White House, CIA, and FBI all decided to launch themselves across the table and wring my neck?

It almost made me smile. Instead I forced myself to look up and meet their eyes. There was no point backing down now.

Bruce from the FBI spoke first. "Do you have any idea," he began slowly, "any idea the damage that story will do—"

"Is anything in that story wrong?"

"That's not the point!" Bruce exploded.

"Is there a single fact in that story that's wrong?" I persisted.

"Bruce is right," interrupted Mr. Carlyle. "Alexandra, how could you?"

"It's my job. Now, listen. The name Edmund Tusk is not in that story. But it will be in the next one—"

"Oh, for Christ's sake. I've had enough." C.J. pushed back from the table.

I raised my voice: "What I am trying to tell you is Tusk is collaborating with Nadeem Siddiqui. Or Shaukat Malik, if you want to use that name instead. Tusk was messaging him all morning—"

"*What* did you just say?" the CIA man said sharply.

"I said Tusk was messaging—"

"No. You just said Shaukat Malik. How do you know that name?"

"Well, he introduced himself that way. Right before he gave me this." I pointed at my bandaged eye.

C.J. sank heavily into his chair. I appeared to have his full attention now. "But that's classified. I haven't even briefed the deputies meeting yet. . . . How do you . . ." He looked utterly disoriented.

I hesitated a split second. I had no idea where his loyalties lay, or what the CIA was up to, or whether Tusk was acting alone. But what choice did I have? I pulled the wallet with the Virginia ID from my handbag and held it up.

"Here he is. Mr. Shaukat Malik. Apparently a driver in good standing in the fine state of Virginia."

C.J.'s eyes widened and he reached out to snatch it from me.

I pulled back. "I'll be glad to hand it over. Just as soon as you go find Tusk."

"Now you listen here," C.J. hissed. "You have no idea what you're playing at. Finding Shaukat Malik is a matter of national security, do you understand? We need to get that photo out. Give me the—"

"*WILL YOU LISTEN?*" I bellowed. "I *know* where Shaukat Malik is. He is lying dead on the kitchen floor of number 3027 Dumbarton Street. Okay? I know because I shot him. With his own gun. This morning."

Four faces gaped at me. C.J. had gone very white. The press secretary gripped the back of a chair as if her knees were about to buckle.

"C.J., who is this Shaukat Malik?" asked Mr. Carlyle quietly.

C.J. sat staring at the wall, blinking rapidly.

Carlyle turned to me. "Alex? I thought you said it was Nadeem Siddiqui who came to your door this morning? And who hit you? I don't understand."

"Please," I was begging now. "I'll tell you everything I know. I have been *trying* to tell you this whole time. But first, please: find Edmund Tusk. Is he still in there?"

Carlyle frowned, then gave a barely perceptible nod.

He banged open the door and began barking orders at Ralph McNamara. Everyone else rushed out of the room. More guards appeared. The door closed again. Outside I could hear people running, doors slamming, voices shouting.

Several long minutes passed. I paced up and down the narrow space between the wall and table. I rattled the door handle. Locked from the outside.

"McNamara? You out there?" I called.

"I'm here. Sit tight."

Finally the door swung open. The first face I saw was McNamara's. Next to him, to my surprise, stood the erect figure of General Carspecken.

He peered down at me. At first the only thought my frazzled mind could muster was that the national security adviser was wearing his red Marine Corps tie again. Or perhaps he had several of them. I imagined the interior of his closet, stuffed with row after row of dark suits and Semper Fi ties. I was tempted to lift his jacket sleeve and check whether he was wearing the cuff links too.

Stop it, Alex. Pull yourself together. He was saying something now.

". . . need you to step back into the Situation Room with me. And you will tell us exactly what happened this morning. We're ready now, please."

I nodded. My mouth felt dry. He stepped aside to let me out of the little conference room into the hall.

"Edmund Tusk?" I whispered.

The general shook his head. "He's gone."

50

Over the next two hours, one of the many remarkable things that happened was I got a phone call from Lucien Sly.

When the call came, I was sitting in the Situation Room, an arrangement that did not come about without controversy. Bruce, the FBI deputy, had thrown a full-blown tantrum. He pointed out that not only did I lack the appropriate security clearances to enter, but I had also been—as he put it—"broadcasting every goddamn move to the enemy."

General Carspecken overruled him. "She's also the only one here who's actually met and talked to Siddiqui—or Malik rather. Can we get some clarity on the name, please?" Carspecken turned impatiently to an aide. "What are we calling this guy?"

"Mike!" Bruce interjected. "Can I remind you it's actually a *crime* to have a reporter in here when we're talking classified information? As in, leaking sensitive national-security information to the press? I don't want to be the one hauled up to testify under oath at some Senate hearing, on why we leaked sources and methods—"

"And I don't want to be the one hauled up to testify on why we failed to stop a nuclear weapon detonating on US soil! You want to be the one to explain why we banished from the room someone who might be able to help us? While you're at it, you want to tell me why, when we've got a fifty-*billion*-dollar US intelligence budget, it took a girl reporter from Boston to find him and hand me this?" Carspecken brandished the Virginia driver's license. "Christ sake, what do you guys do all day?"

Bruce glowered but said nothing.

"I want her here," the general went on more calmly. "And I'm pretty sure it's legal if the president says it is. Lowell"—he turned to Mr. Carlyle—"can you get your office to draft something granting temporary authority?"

With that the room returned to a general hum of frantic activity.

I wasn't clear on what exactly I was supposed to be doing, now that I'd won the right to sit there. I tucked myself into a corner chair, only a few seats away from where Tusk had sat. I was listening uneasily, trying to make myself invisible, when an aide approached and beckoned for me to follow him. After all the ruckus over my presence, no one paid attention when I stood up to leave. The door slid open. Captain McNamara, true to his word, was waiting outside along with several other guards. Silently the aide led me back to the tiny conference room where I'd sat before. This time the aide pointed toward a black phone on the center of the table.

"Line four," he said, and left.

I could not imagine who would be calling. Elias? Hyde? Surely neither of them had the clout to get a call patched into the Situation Room of the White House in the middle of a nuclear crisis.

"Hello?"

"Alex! Are you all right? Where are you? Where exactly, I mean?"

I nearly fell over when I heard his voice. "*Lucien?* How on earth— how did you know I was here?"

"Actually, anyone on the planet with access to an Internet connection can see that you're at the White House this morning. Cheeky little article, I must say."

"No, but—I mean, how did you reach me here? They just pulled me out of a secure communications room to take this call."

"A secure—you don't mean the Situation Room? How in God's name did you talk your way in there? Never mind, doesn't matter. Here's what you've got to—"

"How do you know what the Situation Room is? No, wait, back up. You didn't answer how you got through on this number. Not because of your dad, is it? Does he have that kind of pull?"

"Alex. Listen to me." Lucien's voice sounded strained and urgent, nothing like the Lucien I knew. "There are some things I need to explain, and which I will explain. Later. Right now trust me when I say I am risking my job to get this call routed through Langley to you. You need to get out of there, right now. Will you do that for me?"

His call was routed through Langley? What was he talking about? Had he gone completely mad? My mind raced.

"No. I can't leave now," I said haltingly. "Lucien, I don't understand."

"I know. I'm sorry. I shouldn't have . . . Here's the thing. I know a bit more about Nadeem Siddiqui than I've let on. I searched his room too. The room he was renting in Cambridge, from the barmy old lady near the train station? I got there before you."

"You . . . searched . . . Nadeem's room . . . ," I trailed off. "But why? You mean, before I even told you about him? But what about that morning when we woke up—and I wanted you to call Pakistan—"

"Alex," he cut in sharply. "This isn't a clean line. People may be listening on both ends."

I snorted. He *was* crazy.

And then, all of a sudden, I understood. "You just said you were risking your job? What job? I thought you were a graduate student."

"It doesn't matter. I need to tell you what—"

"What job, Lucien? Where do you work?"

Silence.

"You've got three seconds or I hang up."

"I—I work for British intelligence," he said finally. "That's all I can say. I'm sorry. And I can only tell you this next bit off the record—although I suppose it hardly matters now." He sighed. "I can only tell you this next bit because it is being conveyed as we speak through official government channels. They searched his desk. Back in Pakistan. They found files, loads of them, stuffed with maps and diagrams. Not the kind of stuff that's publicly available. He had—oh, hell, he had the Eiffel Tower, and Buckingham Palace here in London. But mostly he had plans of the White House. Floor plans and detailed calculations of which walls are weight-bearing, where the ventilation shafts go, that type thing. Do you understand? Alex?"

It was too much. I was still trying to process the first half of what he'd said. "You're telling me that you're a *spy*?"

"Yes."

"And you—does that mean—have you been spying on *me*?"

"No! Well, rather—yes. But only after we had already—"

"How dare you! You bastard!"

"Fine. I'm a bastard. But you knew that already."

"You lying, miserable, wretched . . ." I was spitting with rage. "I am going to come and strangle you, you son of a bitch!"

"Right. I'll look forward to your strangling me at your earliest convenience. But can we focus, please? Alex? You were right about the banana shipments. You were right about Nadeem. You were right about everything. And maybe you've already figured this out, too, but what I am trying to tell you is that it appears the target is the White House."

I was silent.

"And just because you killed him—nice work, by the way—that doesn't mean the operation won't go ahead. There's a whole cell behind this. We believe Nadeem was working with someone inside the US intelligence apparatus, someone with quite senior clearances—"

"Edmund Tusk," I said dully.

"What?"

"He's the number two—"

"I know who he is." Now it was Lucien's turn to sound shocked.

A moment passed.

Then he said, "I need to go. I'm so sorry, about everything. We can talk later. Please get out of there. Just go, will you? I don't know how long before the bomb . . . how long you have."

He hung up on the other end, and I sat very still. There is something soul-destroying about learning that a man who has made love to you has also been lying to you. I could feel tears rolling down my cheeks. I batted them away. It did not matter what his motivations had been, why he had wanted me in bed. And I had worse problems to grapple with today. The specter of nuclear annihilation does tend to focus the mind.

But salty tears kept running down my face. I ripped the bandage off my eye. It was bleeding again, swollen firmly shut, and now I was having trouble breathing through my left nostril. I wondered whether Nadeem had broken my nose as well. That horrible, evil little man.

And Lucien. It was hard to say which of them I hated more at that moment. Lucien did deserve to be strangled. I was looking forward to it. I forced myself to stand up, and blood and anger sluiced so forcefully through my veins I had to put my hands on the table to steady myself. I felt capable of anything.

* * *

WHEN I REAPPEARED IN THE Situation Room, I stopped conversation for the second time that day.

I gathered from the horrified looks around the conference table that I must look ghastly.

I ignored them. I walked over to General Carspecken and leaned in close. "Forgive me if you already know this, but I just spoke to . . . to a well-placed source. They said an attack could be imminent. And that the target is the White House."

The general raised his eyebrows. "We're already operating under the assumption that time is short. Who's your source? And where are they getting information on potential targets?"

I hesitated. "It's a source in British intelligence."

"British intelligence?" he repeated skeptically.

"Well, you know they were monitoring him. Nadeem, I mean. Apparently he had drawings stashed in his desk. White House floor plans, and diagrams of ventilation shafts, that type thing. It makes sense, doesn't it? I told you what Tusk said—that he was headed to the target. And about how you wouldn't waste a bomb, if you had just one."

"I'm not sure I buy this business about Tusk. He's been an outstanding CIA officer for thirty years. But you're telling me Nadeem Siddiqui had White House *floor plans*? And the Brits know about it? And they didn't think this was worth mentioning?" Carspecken looked outraged.

Several people started to speak at once, and then the door to the room opened and C.J. careened in.

"We just got off the horn with London," he panted. "They're making a pretty compelling case that *this* is the target. The White House. The Paks went through his desk at Kahuta and turns out—"

"That he had White House floor plans in there?" Carspecken interrupted wryly. "Yeah, so I'm told. Alexandra here has just been briefing us."

C.J. whipped around and glared at me.

I shrugged.

"You knew about the floor plans?" he asked accusingly.

"No. I just found out when you did. I got a call."

"Who from?"

"Sounds like the same people who called you."

"You know, I doubt that, seeing as I just got off a secure comm between Langley and Britain's Secret Intelligence Service."

I said nothing.

C.J. raised his eyebrows challengingly. "Really not the time to be coy, Ms. James."

"I told you. I talked to the same people you did."

"Riiiight," he dragged the word out sarcastically. "You're telling me MI6 is phoning in to the Situation Room with hot news tips for you?"

I picked at my hemline. "Something like that."

He cracked his knuckles and regarded me with an expression somewhere between disbelief and wonder.

"Whatever," he said finally. "Completely ludicrous and impossible, but whatever. It is true that it would have been nice for the bastard Brits to have shared what they knew a little earlier. At any rate—"

But the door swung open again and a tall man rushed in with a stapled stack of papers. He whispered to General Carspecken, flipped through the stack, then pointed momentously to something on one of the last pages.

Carspecken scanned it and went rigid. "I believe most of you know Dick. Our director of the Secret Service. Please share this with everyone," the general commanded hoarsely.

Dick held up the papers. "It's our visitors' record. Everyone who's been cleared in and out over the last week. Shaukat Malik was here. Two days ago. His photo's in the system and everything. Same guy as on that Virginia driver's license."

I gasped and clamped my hand over my mouth. "He said that. This morning. He said he was in the White House." I struggled to remember the exact words. "He said . . . something about a video. About making a video, so everyone would know it was a Muslim bomb."

"What, like a martyrdom video?" said Bruce. "That would make sense. All the jihadi groups do them. If he actually got inside the White House to film one . . ." Bruce puffed the air out of his cheeks. "Holy shit. That would be one hell of a terrorist recruitment tool."

The general held up his hand for quiet. "Let's get back to the facts. How did he get cleared in?"

Dick scanned his records again. "He was on a VIP guest list. Special access, along with another guy, for an after-hours tour. Says here he was sponsored by"—Dick bit his lip—"by Lowell Carlyle's office."

I glanced around. Mr. Carlyle was not in the room to defend himself.

"I know about that too," I said softly. "It was Thom Carlyle who set it up. He didn't know about—"

But the general held his hand up again to stop me. "We can sort out who did what and why later on," he ordered. "Right now we need to understand who we're dealing with. What do we know about Shaukat Malik? Where did he come from? And is he dead, or not?"

"Oh, he's dead, all right," I muttered.

"If our journalist friend could control herself for a moment, I'll be glad to brief everyone on the professional assessment of the US intelligence community," C.J. spat.

I rolled my eyes. "Sure. All yours."

C.J. started holding forth on how Shaukat Malik and Nadeem Siddiqui were believed to be one and the same person. The consensus view at the CIA and the National Counterterrorism Center was that he had used the name Nadeem for his daily life in Pakistan and England, and the Shaukat Malik moniker for everything to do with the clandestine nuclear plot.

"Yeah, fine, but is he dead?" Carspecken interrupted after a minute.

"Well"—C.J. shot me a look—"we just picked up a body in northwest DC. At the Dumbarton Street address she gave us. Positive identification will take some time. But it looks like it could be him. Meanwhile, we're working with MI6 to paint a picture of his movements over the last several weeks. . . ."

I sat half-listening and trying to put my finger on why all this seemed irrelevant. It wasn't just that I already knew most of what C.J. was saying. It was that whatever Nadeem's precise role had been, it was over. Yes, that was it. Nadeem or Shaukat or whatever we were supposed to call him was now irrelevant. What was urgent at this moment was to figure out where the bomb was.

C.J. was droning on about the exact nature of Nadeem Siddiqui's work at the nuclear facility back in Pakistan when Dick, the Secret Service chief, popped his head around the door and said, "One more thing. You asked us to find Ed Tusk. He's not picking up his phone. So I just put a dog team on it. K9 unit. They'll find him."

General Carspecken looked pained. "Is he still on White House grounds?"

"His badge hasn't scanned out. He's around."

"Good. When you find him, bring him here. We'll get this nonsense straightened out." Carspecken looked severely at me.

Dick turned to go.

Suddenly I stiffened. "You said he hasn't scanned out? That's the wrong question."

"Why?" Carspecken asked testily, as though he was regretting having argued for me to stay.

"Forget whether he badged out." I looked at Dick. "Where did he badge *in*? Where and when? Did he drive here?"

Carspecken looked confused. "Does it matter?"

"Well, I don't know, Mike. I guess only if you care about trying to track down the bomb," I snapped. Then I took a deep breath and tried to adopt a more polite tone. "You can build a nuclear weapon with less than forty pounds of weapons-grade uranium. Tusk told me that. That's not much. The whole thing would fit in the trunk of a car."

Bruce, the FBI man, cut in. "No. It's not that simple. . . . The Soviets used to get everybody pissing their pants over this stuff. You guys remember that old crackpot KGB general—General Lebed, was it? He used to talk about suitcase nukes. How they'd lost dozens from the stockpile. And how they lacked the standard safety devices to prevent unauthorized detonation. Turns out it was a total fantasy. They never existed."

"Just because the Soviets didn't have them doesn't mean they don't exist now," somebody piped up from the back of the room.

"Okay, fine. But you can't just slap one together. This banana shipment hit US soil on Tuesday. That's three days ago, people. You're telling me that's enough time to assemble and deliver a precision, self-contained nuclear device?"

"That's the point! It doesn't have to be precision." I whipped my notebook out of my bag and flipped through until I found the right page.

"'It doesn't have to be reliable,'" I read out. "'Even if it fizzles and doesn't work that well, you've still succeeded at producing a complete fucking catastrophe.'" I paused. "That's Edmund Tusk. His exact words from yesterday. Direct quote."

Everyone turned to look at General Carspecken. He was rocking back and forth in his chair, his lazy eye cocked crazily at the ceiling, his good one twitching with anger.

"Goddamn it." He slammed his fists down onto the table. He turned to Dick. "Find out, will you? Where he badged in. We need that right now. And I need you to get POTUS and FLOTUS to a safe location. Actually, I need you boys to get this whole damn complex evacuated. The West Wing, the Residence, the Executive Office Building, everything. We gotta get people out of here. Immediately."

The Secret Service director nodded and scurried from the room.

"Not us," added Carspecken. "We stay here and see this through. Everybody, get your superiors up and on the line. I want the highest-ranking person at every relevant agency in Washington, either here in person or on secure video where I can see them. Fast as you can."

Staffers started grabbing papers and screaming on telephones. A bank of video monitors began lighting up, illuminating tense faces at the State Department, at the Pentagon, at Treasury, all over the city. The door to the Situation Room banged open and shut. Outside I could see the evacuation order being carried out. Uniformed Secret Service guards were hustling people down the hallway, yelling at the men to drop their briefcases, yelling at the women to kick off their high heels, yelling at everyone to run.

A FEW MINUTES LATER I joined the swarm.

Whatever temporary authorization Lowell Carlyle had secured for me was deemed to have been overtaken by events. Captain McNamara was ordered to get me off White House grounds, along with everyone else. The corridors were thronged with people. McNamara bustled me along, one hand on my back, the other clamped over his earpiece, listening.

At the bottom of the stairs back up to the main level, he stopped and held his finger to his lips. His face screwed up in concentration. "Gotta turn around. Other way." He spun me back into the hallway.

"Why?"

"They found the car."

"Tusk's car?"

He nodded, still listening.

"And? Where is it?"

"Here. In the staff garage under the Old Executive Office Building. He badged in this morning at the Seventeenth Street gate. So we're being diverted from that side. This way, let's move."

"But have they looked inside? Is there—" I was starting to panic.

"Shh," he barked. "They've got a NEST squad on it."

I stared at him blankly.

"Nuclear Emergency Support Team. Now come on, keep moving."

"But don't you all check?" I asked, clammy now with fear. "I mean, can somebody just drive a car packed with nuclear explosives right into the White House complex, without someone noticing?"

"If you've got his level of security clearance? And you're in an official Agency vehicle? Yeah, you can."

He was dragging me along by the elbow.

"They would have swept underneath the vehicle with mirrors," McNamara mumbled. "But they wouldn't have suspected . . . You know what? Wait a second." He stopped in his tracks. "I'm thinking down that hall might be fastest. Yeah. This way."

And he led me down another corridor, twisting beneath the White House.

51

The Nuclear Emergency Support Team had found Tusk's car easily, once they knew what they were looking for.

He had hidden in plain sight.

A VIP parking space right in the front row. The white, unmarked SUV was riding low on its chassis due to the freight packed behind its tinted windows. A complete nuclear bomb. Explosives nestled around a core of highly enriched uranium, the whole package tucked neatly behind the backseat.

The team's most senior engineer stared at it. The whole thing could be booby-trapped, wired to blow at the slightest vibration. There might be proximity sensors, registering when someone moved too close. You couldn't just start unscrewing bolts.

Eyeballing it he could see that the design was sophisticated. He had trained on similar models. But who knew what lay under the casing? The engineer signaled for X-ray and infrared-imaging tools. He needed to know what they were dealing with.

EDMUND TUSK HURRIED UP FIFTEENTH Street, his mind working fast.

He could not quite comprehend how the day had managed to go so spectacularly wrong.

He was trained to turn on a dime when events did not go to plan. They rarely did in the clandestine world, and no one made it to the senior ranks of the CIA without learning how to fix a situation gone bad. Or at least how to cover it up, how to bury it so deep that it would take generations of congressional investigators and Agency Inspector General reports to unravel all the threads.

But what *were* all the threads at this point? How much had Alex James figured out? And what exactly might Siddiqui have divulged to her, before she somehow managed to waste him with his own gun? Tusk shuddered. He had understood he was in extreme danger when she appeared this morning and locked eyes with him across the Situation Room. He had felt his bowels turn liquid. So he had bolted.

But now he was not sure. Perhaps—perhaps—the plan could still proceed. Why not? He would just have to move more quickly. The bomb was still in place, after all. They might not be able to find and disarm it in time.

And he had planned his escape quite carefully. At the private airstrip out in Prince Georges County, his plane stood fueled and ready. A Cessna 172, single-engine, four-seater. He had registered it months ago under one of his cover names, Anthony Blunt. Early this morning Tusk had driven out and dropped his duffel bag. And into the front passenger seat he had strapped Philby, mewing inside his cat carrier. Tusk had stroked his fur and left the window cracked for air.

Once he was airborne and at a safe distance, he would dial the cell phone connected to the arming switch he had left in the SUV. It could all still work. He could execute within ninety minutes, depending on traffic out to the airstrip.

It was not ideal. It was a goddamn million miles away from ideal. But there might still be time.

MCNAMARA AND I RUSHED DOWN the hallway, weaving our way through the tide of people evacuating. He paused for a moment to help a man struggling with crutches, then took my elbow again. "Almost there. Just around this corner and then we can—"

And then the corridor went black.

My heart slammed against my throat. *What was happening?* I could see nothing.

McNamara's grip tightened, hard enough to break my arm. Then his training must have kicked in. "Get down!" he yelled. "Everybody down!" He threw himself on top of me.

All around us people were hitting the floor.

For a moment we lay there in complete darkness. His weight crushing me, his chest heaving against mine, pressing me down. I fought to breathe.

On the carpet beside me I could hear a woman crying, jagged little gasps. I reached out. Found her hand and wrapped it in mine. Squeezed until she squeezed back.

What had she been told about why we were evacuating? I wondered how many of these people had any idea what was happening. Did they understand this was no ordinary bomb threat?

* * *

THE NEST ENGINEER STRAINED AND twisted, but it was no use. His face shield was fogged again. And no matter how he wrenched his arm, he could get no purchase on the seam.

It had been deemed too risky to move the bomb. It remained inside the SUV, illuminated by floodlights they'd wheeled in. He was now attempting to cut into the casing, to get at the core. The vehicle's back door had been removed to give him room to work. But the angle was still wrong, and the bulk of his hazmat suit was slowing him down.

The engineer cursed. Yanked off his helmet and gloves. Sweat poured down his face.

The team commander shook his head, hard. *Can't let you do it.*

"I can't see. If I fail, we're all dead anyway."

The commander hesitated, then nodded. He wasn't sure if solidarity required him to do the same. The rest of the team decided for him. Off came the helmets.

The engineer turned back to work.

TUSK STEPPED OUT OF THE metro on the eastern edge of the city. He had a rental car parked nearby, the keys hidden in a metal sleeve above the rear left tire. It would get him to the airstrip.

He glanced around. Checked his watch. Just over an hour now since he had slipped out of the White House. Everything here seemed eerily . . . normal. At a sidewalk café, a wilted-looking waitress fanned herself, ignoring a table of teenagers agitating for refills. A man at the curb banged on a parking meter, chasing a lost coin. Traffic flowed smoothly; there was no police presence. It felt like any other stiflingly hot and airless afternoon in July.

Tusk struggled with himself.

On the one hand, the plan depended on no one locating him, no one knowing he'd ever left the White House.

On the other, he needed to know what was happening.

He pulled out his phone and eyed it. He would have to play this carefully.

IT COULD ONLY HAVE BEEN a few seconds, but it felt like a long time, lying there with McNamara pressing down on me, before a generator began to hum and weak lights flickered back on.

McNamara rolled onto the carpet. He raised his hand to his earpiece, listening. I could see a vein in his neck throbbing, purplish blue against the taut muscles. Then he slumped over.

"It's okay," he murmured to me, relief in his voice. He listened another moment. Then he called out, louder, "It's okay, people. They've switched to backup power. Don't know why. But everything's okay. Let's keep moving, up you go."

People pulled themselves to their hands and knees, and then onto their feet, wordlessly, as in a dream. We stumbled toward the nearest stairwell and the exit. No one spoke. The lights cast a ghostly glow.

DEEPER UNDERGROUND, IN THE CATACOMBS of the parking garage, the NEST commander held his breath.

This was it.

One shot. No room for error.

They had trained their lives for this moment, earned PhDs from elite universities, but in the end it was steady hands that mattered. Nimble fingers standing between them and the abyss.

The engineer cocked his eyebrows. *Ready?*

The commander nodded his assent. Closed his eyes, thought of his wife, his sons. If he lived he would kiss them, never stop kissing them.

The engineer took aim.

Now.

MCNAMARA FROZE. HIS EARPIECE WAS crackling, a sudden explosion of noise. He cupped his hand around it. A stunned look spread over his face.

"What is it? What are they saying?" I tugged on his arm.

He smacked me away.

"What?"

He walked away a few feet, hunched over to listen. When he turned around, he had a stupid grin on his face.

"They did it. I can't—I can't quite tell, everyone's yelling at once. But it sounds like the bomb team just radioed out word of successful resolution."

I stared at him.

He kept grinning at me.

And then I let out a whoop loud enough to shatter glass.

TUSK SAT SPRAWLED ON THE sidewalk, his legs bent beneath him at unnatural angles.

Charley Foster had delivered the news.

One of his oldest friends. One of his only friends. They had come up through the ranks together, serving side by side in various hellholes across the Middle East. Now Charley had a desk on the seventh floor at Langley.

Charley had picked up on the first ring, already crowing.

Tusk had not at first been able to take it in.

"We're gonna get these assholes!" Charley was shouting. "Whatever assholes were planning this little party, they are going to rot in hell. The gloves will really come off this time, and when they do—"

"But what happened, Charley? Are you telling me the NEST team managed—"

"Christ, where the hell are you that you don't know this?"

"Long story. But the nuke—did they—"

"Buddy, I gotta run. All I know is we got a confirm four minutes ago that the nuke was disabled."

Charley kept talking, but Tusk no longer trusted his voice to respond.

He ended the call. Felt a wave of nausea wrench through him. Swayed, sank to his knees, then plunked all the way down, hard. His legs seemed to have stopped working.

The waitress eyed him. An overweight, overheated man sprawled on her sidewalk. She wondered if she should rouse herself to call an ambulance.

The blue-and-white umbrellas of the sidewalk café fluttered above Tusk's head. God, he felt tired. So tired. The concrete was rough and warm. It was tempting just to lie all the way down and let them come for him. It was over. What did it matter?

He closed his eyes. He had come awfully close to pulling it off. Down to the plane, still waiting for him, Philby in his little cage inside. The thought of the cat jerked his head up. Poor Philby. What would happen to him? Tusk couldn't do it. Couldn't just leave him to starve. He loved that damn cat.

Slowly, painfully, his mind began to crank through a different series of calculations. The plane, the cat, the money in the Swiss account—it was all still there. He could think of only one person who posed a threat. Tusk felt the stab of a new emotion now, overriding his tiredness. Anger.

With great effort he hauled himself to his feet. Raised his middle finger to the waitress, not thirty feet away, who hadn't even offered him a glass of water. He began hobbling toward the rental car. With each step, he felt his anger harden.

52

Outside the White House I blinked in the heat and the quiet.

It was not what I was expecting. I was expecting—I don't know—more chaos.

But guards had been ordered to assume a perimeter several hundred yards outside the fence. They had cordoned off streets and set up machine guns. Tourists and television news crews were being kept well back. The White House lawn was deserted.

McNamara walked me to the main front gate where I had entered this morning and then hesitated. "I'm not actually sure whether you're allowed to leave or not."

"Well, unless you're planning on arresting me, I'm leaving. Anyway, based on the experience of the last hour, I'm thinking I'll feel a whole lot safer outside this fence than inside it."

He frowned. "Fair point, but my orders are to protect you and—"

"And so you have. But it's over, right?" I gestured toward the West Wing entrance behind him. "And we're all still here. I think you've done your duty."

He frowned again. "There should be ambulance crews over there." He waved in the direction of a cluster of blue and red lights flashing at the edge of the security perimeter. "I'll just take you over to those guys, get them to drive you to the ER, get that eye stitched up."

"It's feeling better, actually," I insisted. McNamara ignored me. But it was. Perhaps I was in shock; perhaps it was the relief of knowing we were out of danger.

We walked toward the flashing lights. To our left, Lafayette Square was empty, the grass singed short and brown. It was late afternoon by now, but the heat was still stupefying. It had to be close to a hundred degrees. I was suddenly unspeakably thirsty. Water. I was going to drink a huge, icy mug of water, then another, and then a large gin had my name on it. Yes. Make that two large gins. Then, maybe, the world might begin to make sense again.

We passed the Treasury building on the right and finally reached the security perimeter that had been set up at Fifteenth Street. I turned to McNamara, smiled, and touched his arm in thanks.

He handed me off to two guards wearing black jumpsuits, emblazoned with the logo US SECRET SERVICE K9 UNIT. Their dogs sniffed me.

I rubbed their noses.

The guards marked my name down on a list. They asked for a contact number and address. Then they stepped back, lifted a strip of police tape, and let me pass.

Cameras clicked. A journalist ran up and tried to stick a microphone in my face. I shoved it aside and gave him such a dirty look that he did not persist. A tourist snapped my photo with his cell phone. I yanked it out of his hand.

"Do you mind?" I asked. "I'm really not in the mood."

"Sorry. Just—that's a pretty gnarly cut. Did you get it in there? Were you inside?"

I glared at him. Then I remembered his phone, still in my hand.

"Actually, if I could make just one quick call," I said, punching in the number before he could object. "There's someone I should let know I'm still alive. It'll just take a sec."

The line took ages to connect. The cellular networks had to be over-loaded. Everyone around us seemed to be holding a phone to his ear. It was amazing the system hadn't crashed altogether.

Finally he answered. "Hello?"

"Hyde," I said, so happy to hear his voice I almost cried.

"James? Ms. James! Is that you?"

"It's me."

"It's her!" he yelled. "I've got Alex on the line!"

Behind him I heard a cheer go up in the newsroom. People were whooping. I thought I could make out Elias's voice above the din. And now the tears did come.

"Are you all right? Where are you?" Hyde demanded.

"I'm okay," I sniffled. "Yeah, in the big-picture sense, I'm just fine." I caught my breath and tried to pull it together. "I just exited White House grounds. They've got everything locked down tight. Tell me what you know and I'll feed you what info I can."

"We don't know anything. Nora said the building was being evacuated—she came sprinting over here to the bureau when they ordered everybody out—but they wouldn't tell her why. And you never came. But—but you're all right?"

I started filling in the pieces as best as I could. I dictated an account of what had happened in the moments before and after I'd been rushed out of the Situation Room. I told him about Tusk's car.

Hyde kept interrupting. No doubt my story was hard to follow. He pressed me to clarify how I knew certain things and in what order events had unfolded. I tried, but there were too many details, too many names to keep straight, and too many gaps in what I myself knew at that point. Behind me ambulance and police sirens were blaring. From farther away I could hear drivers leaning on their car horns, infuriated at the road-blocks.

"So do we have a last name on this C.J. guy from CIA? Can we quote his stuff on the record?" Hyde was asking.

"I have no idea at this point what's on the record and what's not. There hasn't exactly been a lot of spare time today to ponder journalism ethics, Hyde."

"Well, quite, but—"

"Also, I think I need to see a doctor at some point. And first, I need a drink."

"Sure. Grab yourself a bottle of water and then—"

"No. I mean a *drink*."

"Oh, no, young lady. What you need is to get yourself back to the bureau and write this story. Elias and I will take a first whack based on what you've just given me, but this is your baby. Don't worry. We'll sort you out with some guava brandy in good time."

But I was no longer listening. "I'll be there in thirty minutes."

"Ms. James!" he yelled, his voice turning sharp. "I insist. In fact, I am ordering you—"

"Hyde, we can't get scooped, don't worry. No one knows the stuff I know. And I can barely think straight. I think I've earned a quick one en route."

I was already walking, the tourist whose phone I'd purloined trotting anxiously alongside.

"No. What you've earned is a chance to get your butt back here and write the story of your life. Also, the police want to speak with you. Something about the minor matter of your having shot and killed a man in Elias's flat this morning. And I know you. You don't stop at one drink. I need you sober."

I grinned, despite myself. "Actually, I have to tell you I'm leaning pretty heavily in favor of the pursuit of nonsobriety."

"Alex!"

"Half an hour, Hyde."

I handed the tourist back his phone. "Thanks for that. Any chance you could point me toward the nearest bar?"

53

Fifty yards away, Tusk stood watching her.

He had a baseball cap pulled low over his eyes, but this was a largely unnecessary precaution: Tusk had a gift for not standing out in a crowd. His colorless hair clung damply to his head, and a ring of sweat was widening above his waistband. Every few minutes he reached up to wipe away the humidity condensing on his glasses. But the main thing anyone looking at him would have noticed was that he was shaking, literally vibrating with rage.

She had ruined everything. *She*, that woman, Alexandra James.

His shot at the final $8.33 million installment was gone. Nothing he could do about that. But the clinching blow was that he would now face a life on the run. Had things gone to plan, no one would have looked for him. He would have been presumed dead in the nuclear explosion. That was why he'd made a point of shoving his electronic ID down a potted plant in the West Wing. So there would be no record of his leaving. So he would be able to vanish without a trace. He would always have had to be careful, sure, but now . . . Christ. Once those bozos at FBI put two and two together, they would be racing to paste his picture onto their Most Wanted list. Not to mention the UTN network, looking for a refund on their $16.66 million down payment. Not to mention US military intelligence. The National Security Agency. The CIA itself. They would all be chasing him. It would make the manhunt for bin Laden look like a Boy Scout treasure hunt.

Tusk's brain churned. Wasn't there still a way to contain the damage? At this point, really, wasn't it his word against hers? Nadeem Siddiqui was helpfully dead, the only positive development of this appalling day. The car . . . well, the car was a problem. But plenty of people had access to those Agency SUVs. Lots of people signed them out; other people's prints would be all over it. No one could prove he'd *known* there was a bomb in the backseat. As for other inconvenient details, he could handle them. He had already remotely wiped the phones: the phone Alex had taken off Nadeem this morning, the temporary mobile she had apparently borrowed from her office, Tusk's own devices. He had erased his last mobile just minutes ago. Crushed the chip and then dropped it and the actual phone into two separate trash cans.

The only serious obstacle now was the girl. That notebook she scribbled in was a liability. Her word against his.

He watched as she strode down the block, a cell phone pressed against her ear. Who was she talking to? And where had she gotten yet another phone? He could just keep her in sight as she ducked left and disappeared inside a hotel. Tusk surveyed the building. The number of floors, the location of doors leading in and out. Old habit from the field.

Alexandra James must be eliminated.

This time he would take care of it himself.

54

The nearest bar turned out to be a swanky joint on the roof of the Hotel Washington.

The bouncer did not initially look inclined to let me in. My usual tactic when faced with a surly bouncer is to smile and bat my eyelashes, but this is harder to pull off when your eye is swollen shut. Instead I slipped him a few folded bills. He lifted the velvet rope and let me pass.

The place was packed. We were on an open-air terrace that ran the full length of the hotel. With the nuclear doomsday rumors that must be flying, you would think people would be stampeding to get out of Washington. But, no, several hundred people were jammed in here. Some looked like tourists, some as if they'd walked over from nearby law firms and think tanks. The place was oddly quiet. No music, no Friday happy-hour vibe. Aside from a small knot around the bar, most people were piled four- and five-deep at the railing, clicking pictures on their cell phones and ogling the action below. The view was gorgeous, out across the Potomac River and the city's stately monuments. And the White House. We were close, so close it was surprising the terrace hadn't been evacuated. But then, we were a block outside the security perimeter, and the police presumably had enough to keep them busy today without forcing tipsy customers from hotel bars out onto the streets.

I got my bearings and headed first for the ladies' room. Inside I opened the tap at the sink and used my hands to scoop up great gulps of cool water. I drank and drank. Water trickled down my arms and stung when it reached my elbows, the red scratch marks where I had clawed myself. I stared down. Had that really been just this morning? I splashed more water on my face, rinsing off layers of dried sweat and blood. It was agony. In the mirror I inspected myself. Better, though still not a pretty sight.

On my way back to the bar I swiped a pair of sunglasses off a table. They were too big—probably a man's—but I hoped they would hide the worst of my wound.

Apparently not.

"Honey, you all right?" The lady bartender let out a low whistle. "You look like you seen the wrong end of a hockey stick."

"I'm fine. Two large G and T's, please. Hendrick's, if you've got it."

"We got it. And no bar brawls on my shift, okay, hon? We got enough going on down there as it is." She motioned toward the White House.

I smiled to be polite, paid, and picked up the drinks.

At the far end of the terrace, I elbowed my way in to claim a space at the railing. People pressed against me on both sides. The first drink went down in one long swallow. The bartender had made it strong, and the gin froze my throat. I felt better almost instantly. Hyde was right.

I don't generally stop at one, or at two for that matter. But today I would. I would savor the second one, maybe even order something to eat, then go to the bureau to write my story. Everything would be all right.

I sipped the second drink and looked out. The river sparkled, a silver ribbon under the setting sun. A few blocks away the Washington Monument stretched skyward. And below me, just past the Treasury building, there was the White House. A giant American flag billowed on the roof. Was it my imagination, or were there people up there? I thought I could make out the dark silhouettes of figures scurrying around the edges.

I squinted and craned forward, trying to see.

"It's Secret Service. The ERT, I would imagine—Emergency Response Team. Useless little gits."

The voice in my ear was flat, accentless. And yet I knew it. My breath caught.

Behind me, leaning down so close his tongue flicked against my ear, stood Edmund Tusk.

He had positioned himself so that I was pinned between him and the metal railing. His flaccid belly pushed against my back. I felt bile rise up my throat.

"You followed me?"

"Why, yes. I think we have some unfinished business, don't you agree?"

I arched my neck and twisted around to look at him. His eyes were cloaked behind the enormous spectacles. His face was expressionless. Bizarrely, he was wearing what appeared to be a brand-new, ill-fitting Nationals baseball cap.

"Nice disguise. Suits you," I said, frantically scanning the crowd over his shoulder, searching for some way out.

"Thank you. I thought so. You'll notice as you look around that we're packed in quite tight. You won't be able to run. Also, that is a gun you feel. Pointed at you."

Something round and hard was in fact digging into my side. Tusk had his suit jacket thrown over his arm, and he pushed it aside slightly, allowing me to glimpse the steel in his hand.

"A pity it's come to this, my dear. You. Thom Carlyle. That poor Irish woman—what was her name? Polly Murphy." His lips curled up. "So much youthful beauty gone to waste."

"Was that you?" I whispered. "The woman next to me on the plane?"

"Well, not me personally. I would have gotten it right."

I shrank away from him. "And Thom Carlyle? Nadeem talked about it this morning. Did you—did you order him to kill Thom?"

"God, no. That was Mr. Malik's unfortunate initiative. Quite stupid." Tusk paused. "I presume you have figured out who Nadeem Siddiqui is? That he and Shaukat Malik are one and the same?"

I nodded.

"If I may ask, how did you survive your little tête-à-tête with him this morning?"

I closed my eyes and pictured Nadeem, his mouth slack with lust, pawing at my thigh. My stomach lurched with disgust.

"I seduced him," I mumbled.

"You *seduced* him? Really?" Tusk looked impressed. "I wouldn't have thought he was the type. Resourceful of you, though. Shame we didn't recruit you for ourselves."

"What about the bomb? How did you—"

But he shook his head. "No. As pleasant as this little debriefing has been, we're done. I'd like for you to hand me your notebook, please. And then we're going to take a walk."

I swallowed. Perhaps it was the gin that spoke next.

"No."

"I beg your pardon?"

"No. Just shoot me, if that's what you're going to do anyway. But I'm not going with you."

There was a silence. Then Tusk lost his temper. "You don't have to make this difficult, you know," he hissed. "You didn't have to make any of this so difficult. This is all . . . so . . . unnecessary. You are such a *bitch*."

He blinked rapidly several times behind the thick lenses. I sensed his effort to steady himself.

After a moment he spoke again, his voice more controlled. "I have been curious to meet you, though. I have wondered: what kind of a mother wants her own child dead?"

I froze. The world went quite still and white. "*What* did you just say?"

He looked smug. "She didn't even live a day, did she? Your daughter? Very strange. A perfectly healthy baby dying like that."

The gin glass slipped from my fingers and smashed against the tile floor. It felt as though I had been punched; my breath came in sharp little pants.

"How—how did you . . ."

"Oh, it always pays to know your enemy. Find out something they don't know. Or something they do know and would prefer you didn't. Tends to come in handy. In your case, I thought it might prove difficult to dig up some dirt. But it wasn't. Everyone has their secrets, I suppose." Tusk smiled triumphantly. "It wasn't hard. I mean, when your day job is tracking down international terrorists and weapons traffickers, digging up a birth certificate in Maine doesn't present much of a challenge."

My mind was reeling. "But that was all sealed. I was a minor. And it wasn't my fault—"

"Wasn't it? You didn't exactly fatigue yourself trying to save her, did you?"

I stared at him.

He continued, "You know, as a general rule, I find that when one wishes to keep something secret, it's best not to write it down. Even in one's own diary."

And now I could not breathe at all. I pictured my apartment in Harvard Square, my journals lined up on the bedroom bookcase. I live alone, no need to hide them. Had Tusk come personally or would he have sent someone? Surely the latter. They would not have had to read back far to discover my deepest fear. That her death had been my fault, all my fault. The memory of that day—the blood, her little body—crashed over me. The gin bubbled back up, a hot stream searing my throat. I doubled over and retched.

He leaned in close, his breath moist and rancid in my ear. "What kind of a person are you, Alex? But, no. Let me put this a different way. Would you like to live to have another? Would you like to live to be a mother?"

Then he pushed the gun hard into my rib cage, bruising me.

"Shall we take our walk, then? Straight ahead. Slowly. I'll tell you where to go."

I knew that leaving a crowded place was the worst thing I could do. He would kill me for sure. My eyes darted around the bar. Perhaps I could cause a scene. Would he shoot me on the spot if I just started screaming?

I was so busy scanning for escape routes that I did not notice the matter was now out of my hands.

I did not notice the crowd had parted, didn't notice it had gone quiet, didn't notice the three new guns trained on us, didn't notice anything at all until the voice of Ralph McNamara rang out.

"Mr. Tusk. It's over."

"AND YOU ARE?" TUSK ANSWERED coldly.

"Captain Ralph McNamara, US Secret Service. Drop your weapon, please, sir."

"Oh, I don't think that would be a good idea, Captain. If you'll step aside, Miss James and I were just leaving."

"Your weapon, sir," repeated McNamara.

"I know it hasn't been a banner day for you boys," Tusk replied.

"What with a nuclear *bomb* turning up in the White House and everything. But do you think it's wise to compound the error by threatening a senior officer of the Central Intelligence Agency?"

McNamara stood his ground. "Last chance."

"I think perhaps you're misreading the situation." Tusk lowered his voice. "At the Agency we work in more . . . shall we say *nuanced* ways than you law-enforcement types. We run double agents, for example." Here he cocked his head in my direction. "And when the situation requires, we clean up our mistakes. Which is precisely what I am doing now. What I have been *ordered* to do, by someone well above your pay grade, Captain. Regrettably, national security considerations prevent me from going into greater detail. But I think you'll find it very much in your interest, from a career-advancement point of view, not to screw up my operation."

McNamara hesitated. "You're saying—you're saying that she is a double agent?"

Tusk inclined his head in confirmation.

I still felt shell-shocked, but this was too much. "You're out of your mind," I told Tusk. "Completely out of your mind. A double agent? What two sides am I supposed to be working?"

I turned to McNamara. "Look, you know who I am. Galloni vouched for me. I'm a journalist for the *New England Chronicle*. That's it. Anyway, it doesn't matter. Do whatever you need to do to me. Just please, don't let him go."

We all stared at each other.

"I think we're finished here. Back up, gentlemen," warned Tusk.

But McNamara squared his pistol. "Sorry, I don't take orders from you."

For a long moment we stood there, the air hot and heavy, the crowded bar hushed.

Then Tusk shook his jacket off his arm to fully expose his gun. He held it tight against my ribs. "Too bad. It would have been easier to do this my way. One move—from any of you—and I will shoot her." He glanced around and I could see him weighing his options.

Then he was pushing me away from the entrance, back to the railing.

I stopped, not sure what was happening.

"Let's go. Over it," he ordered, raising the gun to my temple and hoisting his own plump leg over the edge. What, did he want me to jump? I shook my head. I'd rather be shot.

But when I ventured a look, I saw that it was not a sheer drop, as I had imagined. On the other side of the railing was a slim stone ledge, maybe a foot wide. It appeared to circle the top floor of the building. It was invisible from the roof terrace unless you leaned right out over the rail. Tusk pushed the gun harder into my head. I climbed over.

Now we stood side by side on the ledge, our backs pressed against the solid brick of the building. Our heads were level with the ankles of people on the terrace. They were so close, only a few feet away. But if I tried to twist away and clamber back up, Tusk would surely shoot me. And there was no margin for error here. Just a foot of ledge between us and the dizzying drop. I recalled the elevator ride up. The bar was on the eleventh floor. That meant a free fall of a hundred feet, at least. You wouldn't survive.

"We go this way," Tusk said, nodding toward the front of the building. Nervousness had crept into his voice. We began to inch along.

Above us I could see the Secret Service guards holding the crowd back from the railing. McNamara had a walkie-talkie to his mouth and was speaking fast. I concentrated on squeezing my shoulder blades against the wall and stepping as slowly as I dared.

"What happens now?" I asked. "Do you have a plan?"

Tusk didn't answer. I was about to take that for a no when he spoke.

"There are advantages to a life in the clandestine service. Such as acquiring the habit of noting every entrance and exit to a building before you walk in. Every fire escape. You don't even realize you're doing it, after a while. You just keep the map in your head. So. In this case, if I'm not mistaken, this ledge is going to wrap around. At the corner up there. And then your friends will no longer be able to see us. For a few seconds at least. It shouldn't be too difficult to find our way into a window and to a service elevator from there."

"And then what?"

"And then we shall see for how much longer you remain useful to me."

I shivered. We inched along another few steps. A bird swooped past, quite close, floating lazily on the evening breeze. My heart pounded. We were getting close to the end of the building. I glanced up at the rooftop again.

Strange. Captain McNamara was looking right at me.

Duck, he mouthed.

What? I stiffened.

"Keep moving," ordered Tusk.

I looked back at McNamara.

Duck! he mouthed again, his face twisting with urgency.

So I did.

A bullet tore through the air. Tusk cried out and clutched his arm, the arm holding the gun. A scarlet stain erupted on his shirt. He spun around and staggered, and before I could run, before I could think anything at all, he had grabbed my wrist. He was teetering, pulling me backward, toward the edge. I dug in my heels and closed my eyes.

And then another bullet ripped across the sky. It took me a split second to understand we were being fired on from the White House roof. This time the Secret Service sniper found his mark. The shot hit Tusk between the shoulder blades. There was a crack, lead against bone. Then a moment of perfect silence, before Tusk crumpled. I quickly wrenched my hand free. He swung his good arm, clawing behind him, grabbing for a gutter, a loose tile, anything.

There was nothing and he fell, wide-eyed, into the gathering twilight below.

55

I t was hours before they let me go.

Hours of questioning by investigators representing God knows how many federal agencies. Captain McNamara stayed by my side, and he insisted that the interrogations unfold mostly in the emergency room of George Washington University Hospital, where doctors x-rayed me, sewed a long row of stitches above my left eye, and wrapped my scalp under a turban of antiseptic bandages. I was resting, propped up against a pile of pillows, when Hyde showed up. He kissed me softly on the cheek. Then he announced that unless I was under arrest, I was leaving with him.

"Do I have to?" I moaned. They had given me painkillers that made me woozy. I was naked under the hospital gown.

"No rest for the weary, Ms. James. You would hate me forever if I let you get a good night's sleep instead of getting your byline up on tomorrow's front page. Besides, they tell me you'll live."

I moaned again, but nodded.

"I think the first priority is going to be your firsthand account of what happened up on that roof terrace. I want to get that written and up on the website immediately. And then we can start working backward, stitching together everything that led to that moment. I've got the graphics team in, I'm thinking a time line—"

But I had leaned forward and gripped his arm. "He knew about my daughter, Hyde."

"What? Who?"

"Ed Tusk."

Hyde looked doubtfully at me. "Are you sure?"

"He said he found her birth certificate."

"But—how would he know about that? Or be discussing it with you today, of all days? That doesn't make any sense." Hyde's eyes flicked to the chart above my bed, as though he suspected they might have dosed me with too much morphine.

"He dug up dirt on me. To have something to threaten me with, I guess. To try to stop me."

Hyde furrowed his brow. He seemed unsure what to say. Finally he managed, "Let's talk about this later. When we've all had some rest. I've called your parents, by the way. Told them you're okay. You can phone them on the way to the bureau if you like."

"Sure."

At the door he hesitated. "I'm sorry you got so mixed up in this. But you're safe now. It's over."

"Yes. I think it finally is."

* * *

HYDE STEPPED OUT INTO THE hall while I changed.

It didn't take long.

My filthy dress had been removed from the room, surely headed for the garbage chute. Or perhaps for police evidence. I could think of at least three people's blood that might be spattered on it. That was counting my own. I might be the first woman since Monica Lewinsky to have my dress confiscated as evidence in a national crisis. Blech.

When I appeared, I was wearing the now dusty Tod's flats, a baggy set of blue nurse scrubs, and the bandages turban.

Hyde looked guiltily at me. He slid off his suit jacket and wrapped it around my shoulders.

"Not much longer now," he whispered. "Then you can rest."

"I gather it's not my best look."

"Nonsense. You look smashing. Surgical scrubs are all the rage this season, everyone knows that. Now, let's go."

He steered me into the corridor. McNamara was waiting.

"You'll want to go this way," he said protectively. "There's a pack of reporters down that hall."

"Why?" I asked.

"Waiting for you."

"For *me?*"

"A guy caught that whole scene on the hotel ledge on his cell phone. The video's been playing over and over on TV. You're the story now, I imagine."

I shot an alarmed look at Hyde.

"Well, you did manage to kill off most of the other protagonists." He shrugged. "There's no one else left to interview."

I sighed. We headed down the hallway, McNamara steering us toward a back elevator.

Hyde had his phone out, scrawling through messages. "They've found his plane. Tusk had a Cessna gassed up and waiting for him at Freeway Airport out in Bowie." Hyde kept reading, snorted. "Elias has it from a good source that all they found in the plane was a duffel bag stuffed with fake passports, and a half-starved cat."

"Philby," I said.

"You know his *cat?*"

"It was jumping all over him. When I interviewed Tusk, out at Langley. He said it lived in his office. Said Philby was—how did he put it? 'One of the milder eccentricities' out there."

Hyde had stopped walking and stared at me. "Philby. You're telling me that Tusk had a cat . . . named *Philby?*"

I looked at him, puzzled. "Yes, that's what I said."

Hyde whistled. "Well, the man might have been a complete psychopath, but he had a sense of humor."

"I'm not following."

"Kim Philby. British spy? Turned double agent and sold secrets to Moscow? Maybe the most famous spy ring ever? Come on, those guys all met at Cambridge University. You of all people should know them."

The name was starting to sound familiar. But I hadn't made the connection before. Apparently no one at the CIA had either. Or more likely, they had, and it was an inside joke.

"Christ, it's frightfully clever," said Hyde, on a roll now. "We ought to be able to do something with that. . . ." He snapped his fingers. "I've got it! I'll wake up Charlie Swift in London and get him to whip up a sidebar feature. About how Tusk was parading around CIA headquarters with a cat named for the most notorious double agent in MI6 history. Then again . . . no. No, it's too good to waste on Charlie. I'll write it myself." He started tapping away on his phone.

I yawned. An exit sign glowed ahead. The fluorescent hospital lights hurt my brain. How many days since I had slept? It required all my concentration to stay upright.

Hyde glanced at me and stuffed his phone back in his pocket. "Come on, you've got a scoop to write. You dictate. I'll type. Elias will help. And we'll make Jill go out and buy us doughnuts."

We grinned at each other.

When we stepped outside, the heat had broken. It was raining, a steady downpour coating the sidewalk. I pulled Hyde's jacket up over my head to keep the bandages dry. McNamara waved down a taxi. It splashed through a puddle as it pulled up, soaking us. Water sloshed between my toes.

Hyde reached out a damp arm to open the car door.

He caught my eye.

I might be wrong, but I'm pretty sure I knew what he was thinking. It was just the right weather for a Burberry coat.

56

I am not fearless anymore.

That was one of the consequences of last summer, and of the strange chain of events that began—for me at least—with the death of Thomas Carlyle.

I miss it sometimes. Not the nights on my kitchen floor, or the grief that drove me to scratch myself and rip out fistfuls of my own hair. They haven't gone away, not entirely. Some sorrow is unending.

But I do miss the fearlessness that comes from believing you have nothing to lose. Because now I do. That's a story for another day. Suffice to say that Lucien and I were not quite finished with each other. I have yet to strangle him, although he tempts me daily. Most mornings now he wakes up beside me. Given the number of expensively tailored suits he has shifted to my hall closet, he seems to consider this a permanent arrangement.

The answer to Tusk's question, meanwhile, is yes. I would like to live to be a mother someday. I had never admitted that to myself. Strange, the truths that come to you, dangling off a ledge one hundred feet up. I imagine giving birth again will be the most terrifying thing I've ever done. Given everything that has happened, that's saying something.

Now, do not get the impression that last summer left me an entirely changed woman.

I still drink too much.

I still spend too much money on ludicrously impractical shoes. I adore them. So sue me.

But now a thin, white scar snakes above my left eye. Elias says that combined with my fiery hair, it makes me look like a pirate. I tell him he's just jealous. He retaliates by launching into an impression of Captain Jack Sparrow. Life goes on.

I did find it hard, after my brush with covering nuclear terrorism, to summon enthusiasm for the ivory-tower beat. So I switched beats and moved cities. I live in Washington now. I've started over. I've had to pay my dues again, covering the mundane, bread-and-butter stories that fill the inside pages of the *Chronicle*.

But I've been digging. Hustling. And do you know what? Just this week, there it was. The old itchy feeling. The itchy feeling I get when I'm onto a story, but I don't quite know yet what it is.

What do you want to bet I have a good time figuring it out?

Acknowledgments

Writing a novel is a solitary endeavor, so it's remarkable to contemplate how many people played a role in making this one a reality.

My thanks have to start with my colleagues at NPR. Barbara Rehm and Loren Jenkins created the intelligence beat for me and then supported me in every possible way. My editors Bruce Auster, Ted Clark, and Steve Drummond have talents bordering on the magical; every script they touch emerges better. Chris Turpin and Madhulika Sikka made room on their shows for my spy stories (nearly) every time I asked. Steve Inskeep believed in me and in this book at moments when I wanted to quit.

Dick Clarke, Simon Conway, Bill Harlow, David Ignatius, and Allison Leotta shared insights from the trenches on how the heck to get a first novel published these days. I owe a debt to Steve Coll, for incisive reporting on all kinds of subjects, and from whom I learned that bananas get waved past radiation detectors. Matthew Bunn and Jeffrey Richelson patiently explained how nuclear devices and NEST teams work. Gordon Corera set me straight on MI6 lingo. Any mistakes are mine.

I am indebted to everyone at Gallery/Simon & Schuster, including Louise Burke, Jen Bergstrom, and most especially my editor Kathy Sagan. Thank you for taking a chance on me.

It is no exaggeration to say this book would not exist without my amazing agent, Victoria Skurnick. She made me rewrite it twice, and that was before she agreed to take me on as a client. (Sample comment on an early draft: "This is pretty bad. Actually, it's awful.") That it got better is testament to Victoria's talent. My sincere gratitude to her, to Jim Levine, and to the entire team at the Levine-Greenberg Literary Agency.

I smile just thinking about Becca and Jim Zug, who between them boast both the most infectious laugh ever, and an inspirational collection of kitchen gadgets. Anne Mitchell volunteered her guest room and her wise counsel at critical points along this journey. Susie King has been by my side in Washington and at the bottom of icy slopes in Wyoming. To Sasha, Kate, Kat, Paula, Christina, Kerry, Kathy, Tracy, Meg, and Jess, aka the Forces of Nature: It was twenty years ago that we threw the party to end all parties at the top of the Eliot House bell tower. I didn't know then that I might use the setting in a novel one day. But I did know those women would stick with me. And so they have. Together we have survived bad haircuts and broken hearts and hurricanes, not to mention some truly hideous bridesmaids' dresses (I plead guilty). My circle of Harvard friends ranks among my greatest blessings. Thank you for embracing this latest project with your usual gusto!

I had the enormous good fortune to marry into a huge, loud, crazy, and wonderful Scottish family. When combined, the Boyle, Farquhar, and McNamara clans make up roughly half the population of Scotland, and if they each follow through on their promise to buy a copy, this book will do just fine.

On this side of the Atlantic, my brother, C.J., provided probably the most helpful (and definitely the most entertaining) comments of my early readers. There really aren't words adequate to thank my parents, Jim and Carol Kelly. They have championed my writing since the fourth grade, when I founded the *Lemons Ridge Bugle* and enlisted Mom to write the Recipe of the Month column, and Dad to pick up the photocopying bill. I never quite grasped how much they've done for me, until Nick and I produced two miscreants of our own.

Anonymous Sources was mostly written in a sunny room in Italy, with my husband delivering a steady stream of espresso throughout the day. At a certain point each afternoon he would switch me from coffee to Chianti, and that's usually when the writing got good. We worked out the plot together, on long, looping runs through olive groves, with me agonizing over the latest way I'd managed to paint a character into a corner, and Nick coming up with a brilliant way to fix it. If there is a heaven on earth, it is racing your husband down a hill in Tuscany, swapping ideas for how to kill off your villain. (Peach, I am saving the death by silver-tipped cane for the sequel.)

Our sons are the reason I wrote this book. I wanted to find a way to do what I love, and still be there every day when they came home from school. Alexander and James, you are too young to read this story. But you already know that I named Alexandra James for you. When you're old enough to read it, I hope you like her, and I hope you know that your mother loves you, so much.